SHE COULDN'T MEET HIS GAZE

The shirt hung to the middle of her thighs and would have easily wrapped around her twice. With incredible gentleness, he smoothed it into place. "Better?"

"Yes." And it really, really was.

Silence, then, "You okay?"

Head down, she nodded. "Yes."

Clint hesitated before touching her chin and lifting her face until she had to look into his eyes. "Those are an awful lot of yeses you're giving me, Julie Rose."

Mesmerized, Julie got caught in his gaze again. His eyes were . . . well, there was nothing ordinary about them, though she couldn't really say the green was anything special. There was just so much intensity, so much emotion there. They'd looked cold earlier, but now they burned with heat.

The bonfire behind her reflected in his face and made pronounced shadows beneath his high cheekbones, his sculpted jaw, his square chin. He wasn't what she would have termed a classically attractive man, but he was a hero. A bona fide, kick-ass, more than capable hero who offered her safety, and to Julie, that made him the most beautiful man she'd ever seen.

Lori Foster's Books

Too Much Temptation
Never Too Much
Unexpected
Say No to Joe?
The Secret Life of Bryan
When Bruce Met Cyn
Just a Hint—Clint
Jamie
Murphy's Law
Jude's Law

Anthologies
All Through the Night
I Brake for Bad Boys
Bad Boys on Board
I Love Bad Boys
Jingle Bell Rock
Bad Boys to Go
I'm Your Santa
A Very Merry Christmas
Bad Boys of Summer
When Good Things Happen to Bad Boys
The Night Before Christmas
Star Quality
Perfect for the Beach
Bad Boys in Black Tie
Truth or Dare
The Watson Brothers

Just a Hint—Clint

LORI FOSTER

ZEBRA BOOKS
KENSINGTON PUBLISHING CORP.
http://www.kensingtonbooks.com

ZEBRA BOOKS are published by

Kensington Publishing Corp.
119 West 40th Street
New York, NY 10018

All Kensington titles, imprints, and distributed lines are available at special quantity discounts for bulk purchases for sales promotion, premiums, fund-raising, educational, or institutional use.

Special book excerpts or customized printings can also be created to fit specific needs. For details, write or phone the office of the Kensington Special Sales Manager: Attn. Special Sales Department. Kensington Publishing Corp., 119 West 40th Street, New York, NY 10018. Phone: 1-800-221-2647.

Zebra and the Z logo Reg. U.S. Pat. & TM Off.

ISBN-13: 978-1-4201-1245-0
ISBN-10: 1-4201-1245-7

First Brava Books Trade Paperback Printing: October 2004
First Zebra Books Mass-Market Paperback Printing: June 2010

10 9 8 7 6 5 4 3 2 1

Printed in the United States of America

Chapter One

"Why would he take her?"

Those rough, rumbled words carried a dose of suspicion—and accusation. Equal parts nervous and concerned, Robert Burns swallowed hard. He was a man of influence, damn it, a man of wealth and standing with his own source of power.

This man-for-hire, a grunt that now worked for him, would not intimidate him.

It didn't matter that Clint Evans wore an aura of danger as thick and suffocating as an electrical storm, or that his eyes were so . . . Jesus, his eyes were so sharp they seemed to cut right through Robert.

Forcing himself to lounge back in his chair, Robert feigned an insouciance that eluded him.

Evans's reputation hadn't been exaggerated. This man was more than capable of killing. Robert could see that just by looking at him, and it suited his purposes even as it set his nerves jangling.

"I can't think of anyone else it could be." That much was true, because as far as Robert knew, Julie had no enemies.

But *he* did, and now he'd been reduced to a man he didn't recognize, a man he couldn't respect. That thought made him ill, but it was still possible that he'd get Julie back unharmed and be rid of some trouble at the same time.

Robert lowered his head in what he hoped looked like hesitation, when in fact he teemed with frustration. The ransom note, now somewhat crumpled and smudged, rested on his desktop as an ugly, grim reminder of what his life had become. He detested himself for what he planned to do, but damn it, he had no alternative.

"I hate to admit it," Robert murmured low, "but Julie's something of a . . . tease." He sighed and raised his face. "Her father did his best with her, but she'd do things, see . . . certain men, just to enrage him, just to prove he had no real authority over her. After his death, well, she seems to enjoy dishing the same provocation onto Drew."

"Drew?"

"Drew Johnson, her uncle, the executor of her trust fund and the man now forced to monitor her behavior." When Clint said nothing, Robert felt compelled to explain further. "Drew and her father were close, as family and as business partners. He loves Julie, never doubt that. But she's always done just as she pleased regardless of how it damaged the family name." He shrugged. "Sometimes it pleased her to flirt with danger."

"You're saying she got snatched because she flirted with the wrong man?"

"It's possible. She's done it before. Once she even had a liaison with a stable hand."

A funny expression, almost like satisfaction, passed over Clint's hard face. "Do tell."

Robert shook his head. "It was a huge scandal, and Julie wouldn't even bother to deny it to anyone, not even the press. She almost seemed to enjoy the untoward attention."

Amusement brought a crooked smile to one side of Clint's unhandsome face.

Robert scowled at the awful ransom note. "It's possible she's been up to her old tricks, and now she's gotten herself into trouble. That's all I can come up with."

"You think she flirted with Asa Ragon?"

Swallowing down his uneasiness, Robert began his fabrication of the facts. "After the note, there was . . . one phone call."

A new alertness entered Clint's already intimidating expression. "What was said?"

Robert wanted to back up a step. He wanted to stop now, to call it quits. But he couldn't. "Only that I should wait to hear from the kidnapper. He said he'd call and give me a time and place to take the money."

"That was in the note. Why make a call if there wasn't anything new to add?"

"He wanted to reiterate that if I involved the

cops, or anyone else, they'd kill her." Robert gulped, and tried to appear convincing. "The voice . . . It sounded like Asa."

"You've met him?"

"Yes, and once you do," Robert said, finally able to give the unadulterated truth, "you don't forget him. You definitely don't forget his voice. It's rough, sort of gravelly. Maybe even damaged."

"I'm curious." Clint crossed his arms over his chest and sized Robert up with a look. "What kind of relationship does an up-and-coming social type like you have with a thug?"

"We're certainly not friends!" His confidence ruffled, Robert made a show of straightening his tie, tugging on his cuffs. "I'm a well-respected financial advisor. One of the corporations I work for wanted to buy waterfront property from Asa. He was . . . was there during the discussion."

"What was your recommendation on it?"

"That area is rife with development, but the city had no plans to extend public water and roadways onto that property. It would have cost more to develop it than it was worth, so naturally I advised against it." A chill skated down Robert's spine. At the time, he hadn't realized the level of Asa's influence. When he'd talked the corporation out of the property, convincing them to buy a property he represented instead, he'd talked himself into more trouble than he could handle.

"I'll bet Asa wasn't too thrilled with your interference."

"He's a lowlife scum of no importance to me." Except that Asa had been enraged, and he'd demanded that Robert reimburse him for the money he'd lost on the deal—or else.

"You think Asa took your fiancée to get even with you?"

"Of course not." Frazzled, Robert rearranged a gold pen on his desk just to hide his loss of composure. He couldn't let Evans know of his own involvement or everything would crumble around him. That meant there had to be another reason for Asa to take Julie, one of her own making.

"Julie happened to be with me during that meeting. We were leaving straight from there to a play. I hate to say this, but you must have facts." The lies burned like acid in his throat, but Robert told them anyway. "She . . . well, for lack of a better word, she seemed impressed with Asa."

Clint turned his back on Robert. He picked up a small photo of Julie from the bookshelf. "You think she got involved with him?"

"I don't know." Jesus, Robert just wanted this over with. He didn't want to talk it to death. "But I do know that Asa has a lot of connections. If he didn't take her, he knows who did." Robert stared at Clint's back, thankful that those piercing eyes weren't on him. "It was definitely him on the phone."

With careful precision, Clint replaced the photo. "You say she's a reckless flirt, that she got herself in this predicament by playing dangerous games." He didn't look away from Julie's image as he spoke, and there was a raw edge to his tone. "Yet you still planned to marry her."

Despite the pep talk he'd just given himself, Robert shivered. His smile felt sickly, and the sound of his heartbeat drummed in his ears.

"Understand, Evans, I love Julie, and love is often blind. Besides, I don't really blame her for how she is. Her father could be overbearing in his efforts to protect her. He always tried to control Julie by controlling her money, gifting it out in small doses as he saw fit."

And in the process, he'd made sure that Robert couldn't skim from the funds. The bastard.

Clint turned his head to stare at Robert. "I take it she didn't like that."

"Julie hated it, and sometimes she hated him. I see her behavior as rebellion." Robert raised his gaze cautiously to lock with Clint's. "After we're married, she'll settle down."

Evans said nothing to that. The silence dragged on until Robert felt stretched taut, until his skin prickled and his nerves twitched. Damn it, he would not cower. This was too important.

He stood and rounded the desk. "When you find her—" And he had no doubts Evans would do just that, one way or another. He cleared his throat and forced the words out. "You should be aware that Asa is very dangerous. Don't underestimate him, don't go after him unarmed."

That eerie green gaze, unblinking and ice cold, pinned Robert. "You want me to shoot him?"

Instinct told Robert to deny it, but he couldn't.

"Despite her brazenness, Julie doesn't deserve to be ransomed by a lawless ruffian. She doesn't deserve to be frightened, mauled, and . . ."

Evans's eyes narrowed.

Robert shook, his voice, his hands, even his heart. He tried to hide his revulsion, to swallow his awful guilt. "God only knows what else they've done to her." A shudder ran through his body, brought on by worry, by hope and fear.

Important, this was *so* goddamned important.

"I want him out of her life." *I want him out of my life.*

"You want him dead?"

Oh, God. "If she's been touched," Robert stressed, knowing she surely had been and hating his part in it, "if she's been hurt at all, yes, I want him dead."

The words fell like a sledgehammer between the two men. Evans didn't blink, didn't change expressions at all, so Robert continued. "Either way, Julie definitely doesn't deserve the bad publicity that'll result if you bring a kidnapper in to the police. She's had enough of that already."

"By being a flirt?"

"Yes. The only way to protect her now is to make sure this is never known. That's why I hired you specifically, rather than someone . . . better known."

A cynical half smile touched Clint's hard mouth. "Rather than someone more legitimate, you mean."

Robert tightened his jaw. Was the bastard taunting him? If society ever found out that he'd hired a borderline criminal to save his fiancée, he'd never live it down.

Drew would certainly be outraged.

He'd given Robert the funds to ransom Julie, never suspecting that Robert would try a different tact to get her back. If Drew knew, he'd cut Robert out—financially and socially. He'd be ruined.

But Robert wouldn't change his mind now. He honestly didn't want Julie harmed, but he had no choices left.

"Julie's an heiress. I can pay the money if it comes to that." Or rather, he'd pay half. The other half would hopefully go toward buying him some time. But Evans didn't need to know that. "I was afraid if I paid the ransom, they'd kill her."

Evans nodded his agreement to that.

"And I was afraid someone else would feel honor bound to go by the book, to drag in a bunch of animals for prosecution."

"Probably."

"Julie's reputation has already suffered several blows. I'm afraid she couldn't weather another scandal."

Lifting one eyebrow, Evans said, "Sounds to me like you're afraid of a lot of things."

Robert's male pride quailed under the verbal blow. "I'm afraid *for Julie.*"

Evans reached for the photo again. "Uh huh. It's touching, all this love and devotion you have for a woman who sounds like a royal pain in the ass." He gave a careless shrug. "So I'm to be judge, jury, and executioner for this Asa Ragon, assuming he's the only guy involved. I suppose there could be more."

"Would more be a problem?"

"No."

Did the bastard have to sound so cocksure of himself? Robert locked his knees. "Good." He hoped he looked more enthusiastic than he felt. "I'll be her husband. I want to protect her, even if I have to protect her from herself."

Turning the framed photo over, Evans pried off the backing, cracking the expensive hand-carved frame in the process. With a gentleness that belied the iron strength in his massive hands, he laid the broken pieces aside.

Alarmed, Robert took a step closer. "What are you doing?"

Those steely eyes were impassive when they looked at Robert. "I'm keeping this." Evans slid the photo into the back pocket of his disreputable jeans.

For a man who commanded such an exorbitant fee, Clint Evans didn't dress very well. His black T-shirt had faded to a dull gray, his Levis had to be ten years old, and his black lace-up boots had scuffed toes.

In fact, if it weren't for the large, lethally honed body beneath those clothes and those dead eyes, Evans wouldn't seem so imposing at all. He was an older man, probably nearing forty. His unkempt black hair had grayed at his temples and a timeworn weariness etched his unhandsome face.

But those eyes . . .

When Clint turned toward him, Robert shrank back, then shrank some more when he kept coming until Robert was forced to lean back awkwardly over his desk. Chest to chest, hands flat on the desktop and thick arms rippling with muscle, Clint Evans caged him in. He was bigger, harder, stronger, and Robert smelled his own fear.

This man would kill for money.

Robert wondered if he'd kill for pleasure, too.

That awful thought pinned him to the spot, making his lungs burn and his stomach clench.

Clint's small smile held such a look of malice, Robert felt faint.

"Yeah, I'm capable of killing." The hushed whisper of his words only made them more menacing.

"I . . . I see." Robert hated him in that moment, and he hated himself. He'd be so glad when this was all over. "That's . . . good."

"I also know a liar when I see one." Clint's eyes narrowed more, pinpoints of green fire. "Call it a sixth sense, intuition, but I always know when someone is bullshitting me."

A warning? *No.* He couldn't know, Robert tried to convince himself. But the tension built and Robert thought he'd made a horrible mistake, that Evans would kill him on the spot and no one would know who had done it, because no one knew he'd hired him. No one.

Sick defeat washed over him.

Then Evans leaned back, his smile crooked, smug. "That's something you might want to remember, Bobby-boy." He turned and walked toward the door, saying at last, "I've got everything I need. I'll check your lead right now."

"Now?" Just the thought of Clint Evans getting near Asa filled Robert with anxiety. If Asa found out that Robert had hired Clint, he'd be dead before nightfall. "You can't mention my name, Evans. You can't let him know I sent you there—"

Clint either ignored his panic, or just didn't care. "You have my number, but only use it in an emergency."

"Damn you, Evans." Clint Evans's business card listed a phone number, but no name, no address. Robert didn't like it. Things were too out of control, too unstable. "Listen to me!"

"Sit tight and don't do a damn thing until you hear from me." Clint disappeared through the door, his gait relaxed, his attitude more so.

Robert slumped. His heart beat too fast and his knees felt like gelatin. Sweat dampened his brow.

Was Evans really that good? It'd be too perfect if both he and Julie survived this mess.

Robert hadn't chosen Clint Evans lightly. In rapid order, he'd read the reports, and he knew about Evans's major fuck-up two years ago. Only the most elite circles were privy to that information, but Robert had influential friends who were good at snooping. Evans walked a very fine line these days.

Since the awful fiasco, Evans hadn't done much work-for-hire at all. He'd been too busy struggling to keep himself afloat and to pay his heavy legal bills. He'd sunk so low, he worked as a repo man, and by all accounts he was damn good at that job. Just as he used to snatch people back, he now reclaimed planes, yachts, and RVs, with little fanfare or fuss.

But the past was still there, still tainting him.

Clint Evans lived close enough, only a few hours away, so he was expedient. Given his tarnished reputation, he was capable of anything. And best of all, he was desperate. Those traits combined to make him the right man for this particular job.

Robert rubbed the bridge of his nose. He was doing the right thing, for himself and for Julie, he was sure of it. Second guessing himself now would be pointless.

If anyone could bring Julie back safe and sound, and at the same time get the better of Asa, Robert would put his money on Clint. Hell, he *had* put his money on him. But what Evans would get was a paltry amount in comparison to what Robert would gain—the love of his life, his freedom, a new start.

Dropping into his chair with an enormous sigh, Robert tried to believe his own reassurances.

But he kept seeing those eyes, and he knew stark fear.

The early evening June sun was high in the sky, broiling hot on such a cloudless day. Clint Evans slipped on mirrored sunglasses as he strode away from the enormous, ritzy house in an expensive Cincinnati suburb. He was very aware of that small photo in his back pocket, and very aware of the woman who needed him. He wanted to pull it out and look at her again, but he didn't. Studying her further wouldn't help. It'd just make him nuts, and his stomach was already unsettled.

Rage always cramped his guts, made him literally sick, and Robert Burns enraged him.

Clint drew a deep breath and considered what needed to be done in order to save Julie Rose. She wasn't a beautiful woman. Hell, she wasn't even all that pretty. But she had looked delicate and very proud.

Burns told him she was a schoolteacher. She fit the stereotype physically: mousy brown, medium-length hair, intelligent brown eyes. That serene, yet taunting half smile that meant she'd have the patience and the wit to deal well with kids—and men.

She was twenty-nine and looked it. Maybe she even looked a bit older.

According to Burns, Julie was a hellion and a sexual tease. Clint smiled. Yeah, it was that more than anything else that intrigued him. A mousy, intelligent schoolteacher—who liked to screw around. He shook his head, indulging in a private chuckle.

Even while distracted with thoughts of Julie Rose, Clint scanned the area. An inbred caution had kept him alive and kicking through a hell of a lot. He lived with a heightened awareness of his surroundings that few people ever experienced for a single moment, much less an eternity.

Appearing casual and relaxed, Clint rounded

the block of the old, ostentatious homes. A green minivan, out of place in the upscale neighborhood of luxury cars, pulled alongside him and stopped. Clint opened the door and slid in. There was no one around to pay him any mind. He supposed rich folk didn't sit on the front porch and wave at neighbors the way they did in his neighborhood.

"So?" Red Carter quirked a blond brow in curiosity, while gently accelerating the vehicle forward.

"I don't trust him."

Red nodded. "Me either."

"No? Why not?" So it wouldn't get bent, Clint pulled the photo out of his pocket and held it in his hand. He studied Julie Rose once more. Her big brown eyes, glinting with mischief, smiled back at him. Damn. "You haven't even met him yet."

"You don't trust him, so I don't trust him." Then with a frown at the photo, "S'that her?"

"Yeah." Clint held it up so Red could see.

"What a shame," Red lamented. "She looks awful sweet and sassy."

His tone squeezed around Clint's lungs, pissing him off, making him edgier. "She's not dead yet."

"No, but probably wishing she was."

Clint didn't like that probability at all. Maybe his insight was influenced by his disdain of the wealthy. Who the hell knew? But whatever the reason, he didn't believe a word of Robert Burns's story, and that meant Julie Rose was in more trouble than first assumed. "I don't think Asa Ragon has her."

The ransom note had been of a typical sort. Disguised lettering in a hodgepodge style, simple and straightforward. They'd be in touch soon on where and when to deliver the money. A quarter of a million dollars in exchange for Julie Rose's life. If the cops were called, she'd die. No signature.

The note was plain enough. Why would there have been a follow-up phone call? Especially when no additional info was given.

Luckily the ransom amount, twenty times over, was held in a trust for her. Robert Burns claimed he had the money if it was needed to keep Julie alive. But Clint agreed with him on at least that much.

Paying would more likely ensure her death, rather than prevent it. Clint intended to have her safe and sound long before they could realize that no money was forthcoming.

"I thought Asa was the only possibility." As Red drove, the landscape changed. The houses gradually grew smaller in scale and closer together.

"There are always other possibilities. It's just that when Robert mentioned Asa . . . I dunno. It didn't feel right." As a small-time crook with big-time ambitions, Asa was a suspect. The man had a record a mile long and was certainly capable of real cruelty. One of the first things Clint had done was run a check on Asa. He was a scumbag, with prior connections to theft, possession of illegal arms, drug trafficking, assault and battery, extortion, and organized gambling. The list was long but had nothing on the scale of kidnapping. Asa ran his slum-area neighborhood like a warlord, but he'd never served maximum time.

It just didn't set right with Clint. He didn't want to waste time making false assumptions that could end up fatal—to Julie Rose.

Red drove and stole peeking glances at Clint at the same time. "So if he doesn't have her, who does?"

"Not sure yet. But I want to talk to this Asa character. Julie's been missing for twelve hours now. If I'm wrong and he does have her, maybe he'll give something away."

Red nodded. "I've got his address in here somewhere." One-handed, Red began riffling through the printouts he'd collected on Asa Ragon the moment they'd accepted the case.

Clint had every confidence in Red. They'd known each other for a lifetime, along with Mojo Dray, and between the three of them, there wasn't much they couldn't accomplish. Though they hadn't worked together in this capacity recently, not since . . .

Clint shook his head. He wouldn't go there, not now. It'd only distract him when the last thing he needed was distractions. He'd missed the fieldwork, truth be known, and he sensed that Red and Mojo felt the same.

They were all more than able to dominate in a physical confrontation, but Red usually worked as the inside man, able to dredge up information from seemingly nowhere. What he didn't know he could always find out through an intricate web of associations in and out of the police force.

He was six years Clint's junior, taller, leaner, and according to Daisy, his new, deliriously happy wife, better looking.

With blond hair and blue eyes, Red had a misleading nickname. He'd been dubbed Red years ago after a fistfight, because his fair skin had turned florid and stayed that way for hours. Red was a mean son-of-a-bitch, except when it came to women. Then he was a complete and total pushover.

When it came to Daisy, he was a lamb.

Clint and Mojo both considered it a blessing to have their friend happily and safely married to a very nice girl. It had been far too common for women to take advantage of Red, and more common still for Red not to mind in the least. Daisy kept all other women away from him.

Mojo was quiet, the supply guy with barbaric tendencies. He never said much, but when he did, Clint listened. And whenever Clint needed something, anything, Mojo got it. Though Mojo wasn't married, he was involved in a long-term relationship, and Clint suspected marriage would be next on the list.

Clint provided leadership, organization, and muscle. Though at thirty-eight, he considered retiring that last accolade. He also considered himself too old and far too settled in his ways to ever inflict his life on a woman. He had good old-fashioned brief affairs when he craved them, and that suited him just fine.

Clint tipped his head, looking at the photo of Julie Rose. Judging by what he could see of the upper-body shot, she was a very slender woman, to the point of being skinny. The idea of her being abused made his stomach lurch.

But then, the idea of her marrying that ass, Robert Burns, didn't sit much better.

"Got it." Red interrupted Clint's thoughts by fanning a single sheet of paper. "I knew I had it in there somewhere. Asa lives downtown, in a not-so-nice area. Judging by the map, we're about half an hour away. His house should be easy enough to spot. It's on a cul-de-sac and has a black door, so we can't miss it. You wanna visit?"

"Don't sound so eager, Red. I just want to check around, see if I think he actually has Julie before we go tearing the place down."

"Meaning you want to walk in alone, huh?"

Clint settled back in his seat and laid the photo, facedown, on his thigh. He stared out the window at the passing scenery. "I'll be careful."

Red pulled the minivan into traffic and headed for the highway ramp. "Why would Burns lie about it? You said he's sure Asa has her, right?"

Robert had said that and more. When Clint had loomed over him, it wasn't just to intimidate the worm. He'd used the moment to place a special bug against the phone on Robert's desk. The high-tech listening device was voice activated, so any conversation, either in the room or on the telephone, would be recorded and saved until Clint retrieved it by the simple means of a cell phone call that worked like the message retrieval on a regular answering machine. The device could hold up to ninety hours' worth of chitchat, but he'd check it long before then.

"I have no idea why he'd lie—yet. But I'll find out."

"So you're sure he *is* lying?"

Clint rubbed his tired eyes. He'd gotten the call from Robert early that morning, and he'd been running ever since. It was crucial that they act quickly, so there'd been no time to slow down, to eat, or to indulge in quiet introspection.

The usual rush of adrenaline and anticipation had bombarded Clint. But the moment he'd seen Julie Rose's soft eyes and sly smile in that small photograph, other more confusing emotions had invaded. They were starting to make him edgy.

"By nature, Robert Burns is an insincere, cowardly creep. Is he lying about this? Hell, I'm not sure. But I don't like him, and I don't like this whole setup." Clint twisted in his seat to face Red. "If someone took Daisy—"

"The motherfucker would be dead already."

Clint rolled his eyes. Red was so sick in love with his wife, he couldn't bear for her to yawn. "Yeah, right, that much I assumed. But if you were Robert Burns, with his money and influence, and someone took your fiancée, would you be worried about sparing her reputation?"

Red snorted. "I already answered this. Severed heads would roll."

Because he couldn't help himself, Clint turned the photo over and examined it yet again. He wasn't sure what he looked for, but he'd know it if he saw it. "He claims she's a runaround, that she's wild at heart and gave her father nothing but grief."

"Uh huh. The same father who endowed her with riches at his death?" Red's tone dripped with sarcasm.

"Riches that are in a trust and inaccessible to her, or so Robert claims. But I believe him about that. Why else would a rich, young, pampered society babe choose to be a teacher, unless she couldn't get to her own money?"

"You're asking the wrong person. Remember that I'm more than capable of providing for my wife, yet she insists on working in a damn dirty factory."

Clint grinned despite his gnawing uncertainties. Daisy Carter did like to keep her husband on his toes. "Daisy works because she knows if she let you, you'd completely take her over."

Red stared straight ahead, but his hands tightened on the steering wheel in telling agitation. "I love her. I want what's best for her."

"Yeah? And who would know what that might be more than Daisy herself?"

Red growled, "If you're suggesting I'm too—"

"She married you, right?" Clint barely restrained his grin. "She must think you're what's best."

Predictably enough, Red flushed hotly, making Clint chuckle. Clint spent the rest of the drive annoying his pal, but his humor died a quick death when they turned onto Buxton Street.

"There it is, that big brick building." Red pulled

up to the curb several houses away. They didn't want to look too obvious by getting any closer. Already, the green van was as conspicuous here as it had been in the ritzy neighborhood.

But for opposite reasons.

The rundown houses, some of them no more than shacks, were mostly abandoned. What vehicles cluttered the road were either rusted with age or sleek and black and parked in front of Asa Ragon's home.

A family-type minivan didn't fit in.

Clint opened the door and stepped out. Elderly people on a sloped porch across the street stared at him, then got up and ambled inside.

"You got your piece?" Red asked through the open door.

"I don't answer stupid questions." His gun and his knife were a part of him. He'd go without underwear before he'd leave either one behind. But it was a rare occasion indeed when Clint used them. More often than not, his hands and feet served well enough as weapons. "I'll be back in twenty minutes."

He started to slam the door, but Red stopped him. "If you're not, I'm driving right through the front picture window."

Clint grinned, knowing Red would do exactly that.

The cracked sidewalk had weeds poking through it, mixed with pieces of broken glass and cigarette butts. The pavement around Asa Ragon's house, however, had been swept clean. At the end of the cul-de-sac, it towered over the other houses, an impressive brick two story with sturdy shutters and a tall chain-link fence. As Clint neared that fence, a man appeared in the front door.

Clint never slowed. He went through the un-locked gate and up the path to the porch steps. The man stepped out and glared. "Who are you and whatdya want?"

"I'm here to see Asa."

"He ain't home."

"Liar."

Outraged color flooded the man's face two seconds before he attacked. Clint caught the raised gun hand and pulled him forward, at the same time driving an elbow into his jaw. The man went down hard and fast, and Clint was barely able to keep him from toppling down the steps. He didn't want any broken necks on his con-science—his stomach wouldn't survive.

He propped the poor fellow against the porch rail and entered through the front door.

Voices trailed from down a long hall. As Clint neared, he realized he'd busted in on a party. He passed a modern kitchen where several people milled about. Two men turned to stare at him in disbelief. A woman eyed him up and down with a *hello* smile.

Clint ignored them all.

Through an open doorway, he saw the family room. Walls had been removed in an obvious ren-ovation so that the family room was extra long, filled with a billiard table, wet bar, and sliding doors that opened to a patio and built-in pool.

Over twenty people crowded the room, men and women, all chatting and drinking. More couples lingered outside on lounge chairs and in the water. The sickening sweet scent of pot clouded the air, mingling with tobacco smoke and the drone of drunken conversation. Everyone was so busy laughing and drinking, no one noticed him.

Amazing.

Clint lounged in the doorway. "Where's Asa?"

At the intrusion of his voice, heads turned his way. The sudden silence left only loud rap music vibrating in the air.

A middle-aged man, stylish but overweight, with graying hair and a noticeable scar on his nose, laughed in amazement. "I have an uninvited guest?"

Even if Clint hadn't recognized the air of importance, he'd have noticed the sandpaper voice. This was Asa Ragon. Deference got thrown his way, and protection was silently offered by the swarming of other men. "I need a minute of your time; then you can get back to your party."

Incredulous, Asa looked around and when he laughed, everyone else followed suit.

Clint kept his arms loose at his sides, his posture relaxed, his expression bored. He stared at Asa with his most intimidating expression, and the laughter died.

The women in the room—most of them young, some of them beautiful—all moved nervously, getting out of the way as if expecting an explosion. The men edged closer to Asa, displaying loyalty and the willingness to serve.

With a lazy look, Clint said, "That's not necessary, you know. Right now, all I want to do is talk."

Disbelief hung heavy in the air.

A few of the men made an aggressive move toward Clint, but Asa held them back with a lift of his hand. "I'm curious," he rasped with a rough laugh. "And intrigued. You have balls, friend, to come in here like this."

Clint glanced around at the men stiffened with hostility, and he smiled, too. He looked back at Asa. "I'm not your friend. But I would prefer to do this the easy way, so less questions get asked. I'm guessing you don't like questions any more than I do."

"But you still intend to ask a few?"

"Yeah."

Asa hauled himself off the couch, pausing to whisper to the woman at his right, then pat the woman's butt to his left. "Through here." He gestured to Clint, indicating a door located behind the pool table.

Clint strolled forward. Though he looked unconcerned, he had a heightened awareness of every breath around him, every nuance of anticipation. He stayed loose limbed, prepared to move in any direction if necessary. He preceded Asa into the room and was followed by three hulks before Asa entered. The door shut behind them.

Clint turned to face Asa and the others, waiting to see what would happen now, ready for whatever it might be.

Asa tilted his head in a curious fashion. "Give

me one good reason why I shouldn't have my men beat you senseless."

Clint shrugged. "They're of more use to you alive than dead."

"Meaning?"

"Meaning I can't guarantee they'll survive if they attack me." Clint looked at the livid man closest to him and shook his head. He was large, muscle bound, and in his late twenties. He would pose no challenge at all. "I know you want to, son, but the humiliation might be more than you can bear."

Asa again chose to be amused. His scratchy laugh filled the air until tears ran down his pudgy cheeks. The other men saw no humor. Finally, Asa gestured toward a table. "Sit, sit. I can tell you won't bore me."

This room wasn't as nice as the game room. A round wooden table and four chairs were in the middle of the floor. A bare bulb hung overhead. The room was small and crowded and as he sat, Clint planned a number of moves in case things turned ugly.

Asa seated himself across from him, and the other men stationed themselves around the room. "Who are you?"

"You can call me Clint."

"No last names, eh? A wise man. So tell me, Clint, who do you work for?"

"Myself."

"Ah, no, I don't think so. Someone has paid you to come here."

"Actually, someone likely wants you dead."
Clint thought of Robert's expression whenever
Asa was mentioned, and then the panic when
he feared Clint might give away his name. Was
Julie's reputation really what motivated him, or
was it something else? "That's not why I'm here,
though. I'm looking for a woman."

Asa nodded, and his own smile turned pa-
tronizing, sarcastic. "I can see why you'd seek my
help. You wouldn't exactly be a prize to the ladies,
would you? Not with that face."

Clint knew what he looked like: His nose had
been broken more than once. A small scar cut
through his left eyebrow, another across his chin
and one over his upper lip. Too many fights had
left his face craggy from abuse.

He also knew that despite his appearance,
women gravitated toward him because they liked
the sense of danger. They were silly bitches, but
when he only wanted to fuck, the reasons for
their interest didn't matter all that much.

Cutting to the point, Clint said, "I want to return a certain woman to someone else, someone
you supposedly stole her from. And I want to return her unharmed."

For the first time, the humor, the indulgent
amusement, was gone. Asa turned livid. "I should
kill you for that accusation."

Well, well, well. What a telling reaction. Clint
leaned back in his chair and stretched out his legs
in a deceptive pose, making it easier for him to
roll away from the man closest to him, and to use
the table for a shield if necessary. "Here's the

thing," he muttered. "I don't know you, so I have no idea what you're capable of."

For a fat man, Asa shot to his feet with surprising speed. He flattened his beringed hands on the table and leaned toward Clint. "I'm *capable* of anything." The hatred in his eyes, coupled with his growl, gave credence to that claim. "But I'm not a cowardly monster who would abuse a woman, any woman."

Clint contemplated him for a long time before coming to his own conclusions. Damn it, he believed him.

Why had Robert been so sure Asa had her? "Here, in your element, you're powerful."

Asa held up a large fist, squeezed tight. "Yes. I use my power to crush men who oppose me. I use my power to make a better life for my family." The fist relaxed. "I have no need of hurting women, and any man who does is an animal who should be permanently removed from this earth. Point him out to me and I'll gladly have him killed."

Clint narrowed his eyes. "I was hoping you could point him out to me."

Asa snarled, and Clint hurried to say, "It's not that I don't believe you. But seeing as you don't have her as I was told, I hoped that given your influence and connections, you might have heard something else that'd give me a clue how to get her back."

"Who told you I had her?"

"That I can't say." He didn't want Robert's death on his conscience.

Asa straightened in thought. "But you want my help?"

"I want information."

"What do I get in return?"

Turning his own words back on him, Clint said, "The satisfaction of knowing I'll take care of the man who took her in the first place."

Asa was thoughtful for long moments. "When was she taken?"

"Twelve, maybe thirteen hours ago."

In question, Asa looked around at his men. They nodded, shrugged. A small, very private conversation took place, ending when Asa belted one man across the face. The man staggered, nearly fell, then straightened as if awaiting more punishment.

Asa paced back to Clint, his expression livid. "I have information, though I didn't realize until just now that it involved a woman."

Clint's blood surged; his heartbeat quickened. "Go on."

"Unfortunately, it's anonymous information. I fucking hate anonymity. It's cowardly."

Thinking of Robert's preferences, Clint said, "I agree."

Asa slashed a hand through the air. "Everyone knows I keep track of what happens in my neighborhood. Keeping information from me can prove . . . deadly." He smiled and shrugged, as if such a penalty was to be expected. "I knew there was a kidnapping, but my man just told me that it was a woman taken. When I first heard of it, I made the mistake of assuming it was a local job, and that it was a man."

"She's not local."

"Not if she's still alive." Asa worked his jaw. "No one around here can pay a ransom, so if anyone's taken, it's to be punished."

"She's being ransomed."

"Which makes her not local."

Impatience thrummed inside Clint, so it was a good thing he didn't have long to wait.

Wearing an air of satisfaction, Asa faced him. "Normally such information would cost you dearly. But considering it's a woman . . ." He held out his arms, a king filled with benevolence. "It would be my honor to retrieve her for you."

Clint declined that offer with a shake of his head. "Tell me where she is. I can take care of it."

"There's more than one man."

Clint shrugged.

"Yes." Asa chuckled anew. "I believe you can handle yourself. But you see, I have a personal dislike of those who mistreat women."

Clint crossed his arms and frowned, ready to have an end to the meeting. "Yeah? Me, too."

There was no time for small talk. At this very moment, Julie Rose could be hurt, suffering abuse. Awareness of her, of her situation, flowed through Clint's blood with every beat of his heart.

Asa gave up with a good-natured shake of his graying head. "Fine. I'll tell you what I know, which is the direction they were headed, and the area where they're likely hidden."

It was too easy. The whole scenario seemed far too pat to allow Clint to relax.

As if reading his thoughts, Asa said, "Yes, it smells like a trap, doesn't it? I wish I knew the man who shared the details, but I don't."

"Do you at least have a description?"

Asa gestured to the man who still wore a handprint on his left cheek.

Military style, the man stepped forward. "A small guy. Wiry, and like a punk."

"A punk?"

"Long, dark hair, earring. Maybe in his midtwenties."

Asa dismissed the man. "If there was a trap, it was probably against me, not you."

Clint couldn't argue that.

"Likely, the informant assumed I'd go after her. And I would have, if I'd realized it was a woman. But understand, too, around here, anyone who finds out anything reports back to me. It's not surprising that I've heard about it."

"Just tell me what you know and I'll take care of the rest." And if it was a trap, Clint would handle that, too.

"Fine. But the information comes with a friendly warning—you punish the bastards or I will."

Clint nodded agreement. "I'll hurt them." And if they'd hurt Julie Rose, he might even kill them, as Robert probably wanted him to.

Five minutes later, with descriptions and directions and a lot of haste, Clint reached for the door. His reasons were twofold—he felt pushed to get to Julie fast now that he knew where to find her and knew the caliber of the men who'd taken her. They were scum, without the slanted moral code to which Asa subscribed.

Also, the likelihood existed that Red, having counted out the requisite twenty minutes, would be parked in the living room at any moment.

Asa bid him farewell. "Trent will show you out. Next time you visit, it will be with a modicum of courtesy."

Clint didn't intend to be back, so he shrugged. "I'll do my best."

Trent kept pace with Clint's hurried stride. When they stepped onto the porch, he looked down at his fallen buddy, still out cold. "What did you do to him?"

"Nothing he won't recover from." Clint went halfway down the steps, then paused. It was unusual, but curiosity got the better of him. "Tell me why Asa is such a champion of women."

Trent grunted. "It's not a secret. His mother was killed trying to fight off three men who beat and raped his sister."

Clint went still in surprise. "His sister?"

"She was in her early teens when it happened, and now she's all the family he has left."

Chapter Two

A bead of sweat took a slow path down his throat and into the neckline of his dark T-shirt. Pushed by a hot, insubstantial breeze, a weed brushed his cheek.

Clint never moved.

Through the shifting shadows of the pulled blinds, he could detect activity in the small cabin. The low drone of voices filtered out the screen door, but Clint couldn't make out any of the slurred conversation.

Next to him, Red stirred. In little more than a breath of sound, he said, "Fuck, I hate waiting."

Wary of a trap, Clint wanted the entire area checked. Mojo chose that moment to slip silently into the grass beside them. He'd done a surveillance of the cabin, the surrounding grounds, and probably gotten a good peek in the back window. Mojo could be invisible and eerily silent when he chose.

"All's clear."

Something tightened inside Clint. "She's in there?"

"Alive but pissed off and real scared." Mojo's obsidian eyes narrowed. "Four men. They've got her tied up."

Clint silently worked his jaw, fighting for his famed icy control. The entire situation was bizarre. How was it Asa knew exactly where in northern Kentucky to find the men, yet they didn't appear to expect an interruption? He didn't doubt Asa's power, but this was just a bit too pat for Clint. Had Robert deliberately fed the info to Asa, to embroil him in a trap, so Clint would kill him? And why would Robert want Asa dead?

Somehow, both he and Julie Rose were pawns. But for what purpose?

Clint's rage grew, clawing to be freed, making his stomach pitch with the violent need to act. "They're armed?"

Mojo nodded with evil delight. "And on their way out."

Given that a small bonfire lit the clearing in front of the cabin, Clint wasn't surprised that they would venture outside. The hunting cabin was deep in the hills, mostly surrounded by thick woods. Obviously, the kidnappers felt confident in their seclusion.

He'd have found them eventually, Clint thought,

but Asa's tip had proved invaluable. And a bit too fucking convenient.

So far, nothing added up, and that made him more cautious than anything else could have.

He'd work it out as they went along. The drive had cost them an hour and a half, with another half hour crawling through the woods. It was a little after ten at night. They'd had Julie for almost sixteen hours.

But now Clint had them.

The cabin door opened and two men stumbled out under the glare of a yellow bug light. One wore jeans and an unbuttoned shirt; the other was shirtless, showing off a variety of tattoos on his skinny chest. They looked youngish and drunk and stupid. They looked cruel.

Raucous laughter echoed around the small clearing, disturbed only by a feminine voice, shrill with fear and anger, as two other men dragged Julie Rose outside.

She wasn't crying.

No, sir. Julie Rose was too busy complaining to cry.

Her torn nightgown hung off her right shoulder nearly to her waist, exposing one small pale breast. She struggled against hard hands and deliberate roughness until she was shoved, landing on her right hip in the barren area in front of the house. With her hands tied behind her back, she had no way to brace herself. She fell flat, but quickly struggled into a sitting position.

The glow of the bonfire reflected on her bruised,

dirty face—and in her furious eyes. She was frightened, she had to be, but she hid it beneath bravado.

"I think we should finish stripping her," one of the men said.

Julie's bare feet pedaled against the uneven ground as she tried to move farther away.

The men laughed some more, and the one who'd spoken went onto his haunches in front of her. He caught her bare ankle, immobilizing her.

"Not too much longer, bitch. I'll be making that call in just a few minutes. They'll send the money for you in the morning." He stroked her leg, up to her knee, higher. "After that, who cares what I do with you, huh?" He laughed. "You getting anxious?"

Her chest heaved; her lips quivered.

She spit on him.

Clint was on his feet in an instant, striding through the tall grass and into the clearing before Mojo's or Red's hissed curses could register. The four men, standing in a cluster, turned to look at him with various expressions of astonishment, confusion, and horror. They were slow to react, and Clint realized they were not only young and foolish, but more than a little drunk, too. Idiots.

One of the young fools reached behind his back.

"You." Clint stabbed him with a fast lethal look while keeping his long, ground-eating pace to Julie. "Touch that weapon and I'll break your leg."

The guy blanched—and promptly dropped his hands.

Clint didn't think of anything other than his need to get between Julie and the most immediate threat. But without giving it conscious thought, he knew that Mojo and Red would back him up. If any guns were drawn, theirs would fire first.

The man who'd been abusing Julie snorted in disdain at the interference. He took a step forward, saying, "Just who the hell do you think you—"

Reflexes on automatic, driven by a blinding rage, Clint pivoted to the side and kicked out hard and fast. The force of his boot heel caught the man on the chin with satisfying impact. He sprawled flat with a raw groan that dwindled into blackness. He didn't move.

That galvanized another man into action. He leapt forward. Clint stepped to the side and, like clockwork, kicked out a knee, following with a punch to the throat. The obscene sounds of breaking bone and cartilage and the accompanying gurgle of pain split the night, sending nocturnal creatures to scurry through the leaves.

Clint glanced at Julie's white face, saw she was frozen in shock, and headed toward the two remaining men. Eyes wide, they started to back up, and Clint curled his mouth into the semblance of a smile. "I don't think so."

A gun was finally drawn, but not in time to be fired. Clint grabbed the man's wrist and, with a sharp movement, twisted up and back.

"I think you broke my arm," the man yelped.

Clint said, "No," and twisted once more. *"Now* it's broke."

Still holding him, Clint pulled him forward and into a solid punch to the stomach. Without breath, the painful shouts ended real quick.

Robert Burns had said not to bring anyone in. Clint couldn't see committing random murder, and that's what it'd be if he started breaking heads now. But in an effort to protect Julie Rose and her apparently already tattered reputation, he wouldn't turn them over to the law either.

That didn't mean he'd let them go. He had a plan, one that would give retribution without involving Julie Rose. For now . . . Clint, fed up and ready to end it, turned to the fourth man. He threw a punch at the man's nose and another at his ribs and finally one to his kidneys. He watched the guy crumble to his knees, then to his face, wheezing for breath.

They wouldn't be up and running anytime soon.

Behind Clint, Red's dry tone intruded. "Well, that was efficient."

Clint struggled with himself for only an instant before realizing he had no one else to fight. He jerked around, saw Julie Rose held in wide-eyed terror, and his stomach tumbled. Mojo stepped out of the way as Clint lurched to the bushes.

Anger turned to acid in his gut.

Typically, at least for Clint Evans and his weak-ass stomach, he puked.

* * *

Julie could hardly believe her eyes. One minute she'd known she would be raped and probably killed, and the fear had been all consuming, a live, clawing dread inside her that made rational thought impossible.

Now . . . now she didn't know what had happened. Three men, looking like angelic convicts, had burst into the clearing. Well no, that wasn't right. The first man hadn't burst anywhere. He'd strode in, casual as you please, and then proceeded to make mincemeat out of her abductors.

He'd taken on four men as if they were no more than gnats.

She'd never seen that type of brawling. His blows hadn't been designed to slow down an opponent, or to bruise or hurt. One strike—and the men had dropped like dead weights. Even the sight of the gun hadn't fazed him. He moved so fast, so smoothly, the weapon hadn't mattered at all.

When he'd delivered those awesome strikes, his expression, hard and cold, hadn't changed. A kick here, a punch there, and the men who'd held her, taunted her, the men who had seemed terrifyingly invincible to her, were no longer a threat.

He was amazing, awesome. He was . . . *throwing up*.

Her heart pounded in slow, deep thumps that hurt her breastbone and made it difficult to draw an even breath. The relief flooding over her in drowning force didn't feel much different than her fear had.

Her awareness of that man was almost worse.

Like spotting Superman, or a wild animal or a combination of both, she felt awed and amazed and disbelieving.

She was safe now, but was she really?

One of the saviors approached her. He was fair, with blond hair and light eyes, though she couldn't see the exact color in the dark night with only the fire for illumination. Trying to make himself look less like a convict, he gave her a slight smile.

A wasted effort.

He moved real slow, watchful and gentle. "Don't pay any mind to Clint." He spoke in a low, melodic croon. "He always pukes afterward."

Her savior's name was Clint.

Julie blinked several times, trying to gather her wits and calm the spinning in her head. "He does?"

Another man approached, equally cautious, just as gentle. But he had black hair and blacker eyes. He didn't say anything, just stood next to the other man and surveyed her bruised face with an awful frown that should have been alarming, but wasn't.

The blond nodded. "Yeah. Hurtin' people— even people who deserve it like these bastards did—always upsets Clint's stomach. He'll be all right in a minute."

Julie ached, her body, her heart, her mind. She'd long ago lost the feeling in her arms, but every place else pulsed with relentless prickling pain. She looked over at Clint. He had his hands on his knees, his head hanging. The poor man. "He was saving me, wasn't he?"

"Oh. Yes, ma'am. We're here to take you home. Everything will be okay now." His glance darted to her chest and quickly away.

Julie realized she wasn't decently covered, but with her hands tied tightly behind her back, she couldn't do anything about it. She felt conspicuous and vulnerable and ready to cry. In an effort to better conceal herself, she did her best to hunch her aching shoulders before looking back at Clint.

Just the sight of him, big, powerful, brave, gave her a measure of reassurance. He straightened slowly, drew several deep breaths.

He was an enormous man, layered in sleek muscle with wide shoulders and a tapered waist and long, thick thighs. His biceps were as large as her legs, his hands easily twice the size of her own.

Eyes closed, he tipped his head back and swallowed several times, drinking in the cooler, humid night air. At that moment, he looked very weak.

He hadn't looked weak while pulverizing those men. Julie licked her dry lips and fought off another wave of the strange dizziness.

Clint flicked a glance toward her, and their gazes locked together with a sharp snap, shocking Julie down to the soles of her bare dirty feet.

He looked annoyed by the near tactile contact.

Julie felt electrified. Her pains faded away into oblivion.

It took a few moments, but his forced smile, meant to be reassuring, was a tad sickly. Still watching her, he reached into his front pocket and pulled out a small silver flask. He tipped it up, swished his mouth out, and spit.

All the while, he held her with that implacable burning gaze.

When he replaced the flask in his pocket and started toward her, every nerve ending in Julie's body came alive with expectation. Fear, alarm, relief—she wasn't at all certain what she felt, she just knew she felt it in spades. Her breath rose to choke her, her body quaked, and strangely enough, tears filled her eyes.

I will not cry, I will not cry . . .

She rubbed her eye on her shoulder and spoke to the two men, just to help pull herself together. "Should he be drinking?"

Blondie said, "Oh, no. It's mouthwash." And with a smile, "He always carries it with him, cuz of his stomach and the way he usually—"

The dark man nudged the blonde, and they both fell silent.

Mouthwash. She hadn't figured on that.

She wanted to ignore him, but her gaze was drawn to him like a lodestone. Fascinated, she watched as Clint drew nearer. During his approach, he peeled his shirt off over his head, then stopped in front of her, blocking her from the others. They took the hint and gave her their backs.

Julie stared at that broad, dark, hairy chest. He

was more man than any man she'd ever seen, and the dizziness assailed her again.

With a surprisingly gentle touch, Clint went to one knee and laid the shirt over her chest. It was warm and damp from his body. His voice was low, a little rough when he spoke. "I'm going to cut your hands free. Just hold still a second, okay?"

Julie didn't answer. She *couldn't* answer. She'd been scared for so long now, what seemed like weeks but hadn't even been a full day. And now she was rescued.

She was safe.

A large, lethal blade appeared in Clint's capable hands, but Julie felt no fear. Not now. Not with him so close.

He didn't go behind her to free her hands. He reached around her while looking over her shoulder and blocking her body with his own. Absurdly, she became aware of his hot scent, rich with the odor of sweat and anger and man. After smelling her own fear for hours on end, it was a delicious treat for her senses. She closed her eyes and concentrated on the smell of him, on his warmth and obvious strength and stunning ability.

He enveloped her with his size, and with the promise of safety.

She felt a small tug, and the ropes fell away. But as Julie tried to move, red-hot fire rushed through her arms, into her shoulders and wrists, forcing a groan of sharp-edged agony from her tight lips.

"Shhh, easy now." As if he'd known exactly what she'd feel, Clint sat in front of her. His long legs opened around her, and he braced her against his bare upper body. His flesh was hot, smooth beneath her cheek.

Slowly, carefully, he brought her arms around and allowed her to muffle her moans against his shoulder. He massaged her, kneading and rubbing from her upper back, her shoulders to her elbows to her wrists, and still crooning to her in that low voice. His hard fingers dug deep into her soft flesh, working out the cramps with merciless determination and loosening her stiff joints that seemed frozen in place.

As the pain eased, tiredness sank in, and Julie slumped against him. She'd been living off adrenaline for hours, and now being safe left her utterly drained, unable to stay upright.

It was like propping herself against a warm, vibrant brick wall. There was no give to Clint's hard shoulder, and that comforted Julie.

One thought kept reverberating through her weary brain: *He really saved me.*

For a single moment, he seemed wary at her limp acceptance of him. Then, as if handling an infant, his arms came around her. Large, rough hands opened on her back, cradling, soothing.

"Mojo," he said quietly, "how bad's the damage?"

The man who was darker than sin lifted one massive shoulder. "Same as usual."

The blonde filled in with a grin in his tone.

"No one's dead, Clint, but you broke a jaw, busted a knee, broke at least one wrist . . ."

Clint leaned slightly away from Julie and looked around at the scattered, moaning bodies with a scowl. "Shit." Julie felt his tension, though his voice and his touch didn't change. "They can still talk?"

"Yeah." Grim relish imbued Mojo's tone. "I'll make 'em talk."

"I'd like to kill them," Clint said in that same moderate tone, "but I suppose I've done enough."

Mojo looked down at Julie, his devil's gaze filled with tenderness. "They had it coming."

"Yeah." Clint's big hand cradled the side of her face. "Can you stand?"

As in use her legs? "Of course." But Julie wasn't sure. Humiliated by her own weakness, she clung to Clint as he lifted them both to their feet. The second she was upright, she burrowed close again. He stood so much taller than her, her face came even with his bare chest. Crisp hair tickled her nose, her chin.

Facing the world was more than she could handle just yet. She was . . . ashamed. Embarrassed. Still shaken. And she felt very needy—something that didn't sit right with her—but she'd used up all her reserves and couldn't find the gumption to fight off the feeling.

This man seemed willing to hold her, and for the moment, she was more than willing to let him. God knew, there was no one else.

A strange stillness hummed in the air as all

three men went silent. Someone cleared his throat. Someone shifted. The evening breeze swirled around them, mingling the male scents and dispersing the sense of danger with fresh air.

Clint spoke close to her ear, and she detected the minty mouthwash on his breath. "Why don't you let me get this shirt on you, okay?"

More humiliation swamped her senses. She'd completely forgotten that her nightgown was torn. Remembering how her abductors had gotten increasingly mean as they drank, she shivered. She didn't want to let Clint go—so she didn't.

With her nose pressed to his chest, she whispered, "Petie tried to touch me, but I couldn't . . . couldn't let him but he held onto my gown and then it ripped and they . . ." Her voice dwindled to an embarrassing croak.

"Shhh. I know." Clint did some more rubbing, then offered as a balm, "I broke his jaw."

Fierce satisfaction filled her. "Good."

His whiskered jaw teased her temple when he smiled. "C'mere. Let's turn you around." Still holding her close, he rotated them both so that her back was to the other men. To her relief, he didn't force any space between them. "Your arms feel better now?"

"Yes." They did, but not much. Petie had tied her hands as soon as he'd taken her, and then kept them tied. Her limbs had first gone to sleep, then gone numb. She ached. Not just her muscles, but deep down inside herself.

Keeping her against him as much as possible, Clint carefully removed his shirt from where it had been draped over her front. He shook it out onc-handed, not looking at where her exposed breast flattened against his wide, naked chest.

Julie didn't need to look. She felt the mingling of their heartbeats, hers too fast, his slow and easy and, given her circumstances, very reassuring.

Using infinite care, he lifted her right arm and began dressing her.

Julie let him, aware of the caution in his touch, his breath on her shoulder, the softness of the worn cotton as it pulled over her head, down her arms. He eased her an inch away, and the material slid over her breast, over her nipple.

She couldn't meet his gaze.

The shirt hung to the middle of her thighs and would have easily wrapped around her twice. With incredible gentleness, he smoothed it into place. "Better?"

"Yes." And it really, really was.

Silence, then, "You okay?"

Head down, she nodded. "Yes."

Clint hesitated before touching her chin and lifting her face until she had to look into his eyes. "Those are an awful lot of yeses you're giving me, Julie Rose."

Mesmerized, Julie got caught in his gaze again. His eyes were . . . well, there was nothing ordinary about them, though she couldn't really say the green was anything special. There was just so much intensity, so much emotion there. They'd looked cold earlier, but now they burned with heat.

The bonfire behind her reflected in his face and made pronounced shadows beneath his high cheekbones, his sculpted jaw, his square chin. He wasn't what she would have termed a classically attractive man, but he was a hero. A bona fide, kick-ass, more than capable hero who offered her safety, and to Julie, that made him the most beautiful man she'd ever seen.

When she continued to stare up at him, he tried another smile. This one looked better than the one he'd given her right after throwing up. It was a smile of encouragement, of understanding. A little arrogant, a lot sweet.

He smoothed her tangled hair, lifted it out of the neckline of the shirt. "Did I scare you?"

He'd spoken in a whisper, so Julie did the same. "When?"

"A little bit ago. When I was . . ." His mouth flattened as he searched for the right word.

"When you were beating them up for me?"

Surprise shone in his face at the way she'd worded that, but he didn't correct her. "Yeah."

"I wasn't afraid." She turned her cheek into his big hand, wanting him to understand that she wasn't a coward. "I was relieved."

"Good."

Julie almost smiled, too, but then Petie groaned, a broken sound of horrible pain. She turned her head.

"It's okay, Julie Rose," Clint told her. "He can't hurt you now."

Wondering at the way he'd used her full name, Julie turned away from the man who'd taken her, abused her. She curled into her rescuer's side. "I know."

"We should go."

She was a schoolteacher, a woman used to taking control of unruly classes and dealing with difficult, often exasperating parents. She held her own in all situations, even standing up to Drew whenever necessary. She wouldn't keep acting like a fool now. It was over. She was safe.

Julie nodded. "Go where?"

Clint stalled. His heavy arm rested over her shoulders. His body was alongside hers, powerful and comforting. He didn't look at her for the longest time.

"Back to your fiancé," he finally said.

Julie blinked up at him and then leaned away. She didn't know if it was the relief of finally being safe or the lack of food and water, but she suddenly felt dizzy.

She swayed, and Clint caught her close. "Hey."

The other two men moved in, crowding around her, hands reaching out. "What's wrong with her?" and "Damn, she looks like she's going to faint," got said at about the same time that her vision narrowed, closing in.

The bruising male voices were tainted with alarm, and the idea that these big, rough men could be distressed over something so silly struck her.

Julie tried to shake her head and wasn't sure if she succeeded or not. She'd never fainted in her life, and she didn't want to faint on them now. She wasn't a person who had fits of nerves.

She was willful and headstrong and stubborn. Her father had always said so.

The world tilted, and she realized someone had scooped her up. Strange, how she felt so boneless, so empty.

"I've got you." Clint's voice seemed to come from far away, a hollow echo that swirled around her. "We'll have you home safe and sound in no time."

Home sounded wonderful—as long as he didn't leave her yet. That thought brought a measure of panic that shocked her, but couldn't be suppressed. She tried to grip him, knowing she had to tell him, that she had to explain.

"Easy. Just relax, Julie Rose."

Clint's mouth brushed her temple in what might have been a kiss, but was probably just an accident.

She sighed. "Okay." Everything dimmed, darker and darker. She had to tell him now, before it was too late. "Clint?"

He bent to her. "Yes?"

It wasn't easy, but she got the words out. "I . . ."

He started moving, carrying her along in his arms. "What is it, Julie Rose?"

His hold was lax, as if she weighed nothing at all. Her world tilted. "I'm not . . . engaged."

Julie felt Clint pause, his arms tighten, and she faded into oblivion.

Clint sat on the floor of the minivan, her slim body partially held in his arms, her head resting on the crook of his knee. The unpaved back road was rough and rutted. She got jostled as Red drove, but she slept on.

He was starting to worry, and damn it, he didn't want to worry. Worry was for old women and spineless men.

But she was such a small woman. Not short, but fine boned and delicate and, as he'd suspected, skinny. She had a long, elegant throat—though he'd never noticed a woman's throat before. Now that he had noticed, he could only think of it as elegant.

Her arms were smooth, her thighs long, her rib cage narrow. His shirt hung on her, the neckline falling over her shoulder until it nearly exposed her breast again.

Sweat dampened Clint's back. Using just his fingertips, he eased the shirt back up to her chin. He could take a lot, but he couldn't take Julie Rose's partial nudity. Seeing her breast once was enough. Not that he'd stared, because he wasn't an animal. She'd been through enough without that.

But he hadn't needed to stare. The impression of that soft, pale flesh, the small pink nipple, was burned into his brain, annoying him, stirring him on some dark, carnal level when all he should have felt was sympathy and the urge to protect.

And he *did* feel those things, damn it.

But he was also aware of her as a woman.

Earlier, when she'd hugged him, trusting him, he'd absorbed her femininity, the feel of her slender body in his arms, her breast, her stiffened nipple against his flesh, the way a dying man would absorb life.

She wouldn't act so secure with him if she knew the path his mind had taken. Not that she ever would know, because no way in hell would he tell her, and he sure as certain wouldn't act on it.

Clint cupped her cheeks, determined to keep his thoughts on the straight and narrow. His thumb brushed her jaw, hoping to revive her.

Mumbling a swear word and swatting at him, Julie Rose stirred.

Mojo turned in his seat and frowned in inquiry.

"She's coming around." Relieved, Clint poured a little more water on the towel and stroked her face. She'd been out too long, and he sensed it was her reluctance to face what had happened as much as any possible injury that kept her asleep. "C'mon, Julie Rose. Enough is enough, woman. Quit hiding."

Her long, golden brown lashes fluttered, and her eyes blinked open. She stared up at him in blank confusion. Her eyes nearly crossed for a long moment before a flash of alarm made her gasp.

"It's all right." Clint held her still. "You're safe, remember? I'm not about to let anyone hurt you."

Her lips parted; her shoulders relaxed.

In the next heartbeat, she was holding him again, her arms raised so that she clasped his neck. For a woman coming out of a dead faint, she had surprising strength. Her hands slid up and locked around him, forcing him to lean closer to her.

It was the position of lovers, and Clint tried to ease away from her tenacious grip.

She didn't allow it.

"What did you do to me?"

Giving up, Clint cuddled her closer, making her comfortable. "I saved you." She needed to remember that.

"Yes, but afterward . . . What happened?" She looked at him, realized how they were embracing, and apparently decided to sit up.

"Easy." Clint helped her, propping her against his leg. "I didn't do anything to you, you just keeled over. Are you hurt?"

She scooted real close, so close he could smell her subtle scent. Her nails stung as she gripped his arm like a lifeline, and served a stark counterpoint to the forced calm in her expression.

"Hurt as in sore? Yes. Hurt as in damaged, no." She looked around, jittery, uncertain, and trying real hard to hide it. "Where are we?"

Red spoke up. "In my van, heading home."

"Where are . . ." She swallowed hard, squeezed closer. Her voice dropped. "Where are those men?"

Deliberately, the light inside the van was dim. Clint had wanted to give her the security of shadows to conceal her fear. He already knew that she didn't like showing fear or upset. But earlier it had been bright, and he had seen the bruises on her pale flesh, the raw scrapes on her knees and elbows.

He pried her fingers loose and put his arm around her, hauling her into his side. She seemed to need his touch, so no one needed to know that he *liked* holding her.

"We had to leave them behind."

Her eyes flared wide. "You just let them go?"

Clint didn't want to bring up her fiancé again, or the possibility of a scandal, so he shrugged. "Sort of. I left them to crawl into their car, which they've probably already done."

Her face fell. "So they're just getting away with . . . with taking me?"

"I punished them." He stared at her steadily, making sure she understood. "I don't normally maim people when I make a rescue. Not if I can help it."

She bit her lips, then nodded. "And I appreciate it, I really do."

She appreciated it? Clint didn't know what the hell to make of that.

"But once they heal, they might . . ."

Cupping her cheek, Clint said, "No way would I let that happen. Mojo dicked with their engine just enough to make sure it'd only make it a few miles before it breaks down."

"What good will that do?"

"It'll make it easier for the cops to find them."

"The cops are looking for them?"

Red looked at her through the rearview mirror. "They are now that I called and made an anonymous report that I saw rifles and drugs in their trunk."

"Oh."

"We didn't plant them there," Red explained. "The bust will be legit."

Clint smoothed away a smudge of dirt on the side of her jaw. "They'll do some time, but you won't have to be involved."

Of course, Red had gathered up plenty of info first, including the registration that had been left in the car. If they managed to escape the cops, Clint knew who they were, and he'd know how to find them.

What he didn't know was who had hired them, because they hadn't known. They were given money and instructions by another street thug who worked for an anonymous man. Robert? Asa? Clint had no idea. And he had no way to find the one responsible. Yet.

Julie didn't look quite convinced, so Clint added, "I didn't think you'd want them in the van with us."

Defeat took the tension out of her spine, and she slumped against him. "You're right."

He'd expected hysterics, shock. She was too composed and he didn't like it. He wanted to keep her talking. "Do you know any of their names?"

"Just Petie." She shivered again from saying his name. "He was the worst."

Clint gave her a reassuring hug.

"Did you really break his jaw?"

"Yeah. I'd have done more than that if you hadn't gone and fainted on me."

Her eyes searched his, looking for answers. "You were worried about me?"

"Let's just say I prioritized." Clint had had his hands full of soft, limp woman, so he'd left the questioning to his friends. "One of them never came to."

"Do you think he was dead?"

"No. He had a steady pulse." She hadn't sounded particularly upset by the prospect of death, just curious. But there was still a small frown on her brow, a look of discomfort, confusion. Clint leaned down to see her averted face. "Julie Rose, are you—"

"I'm fine."

Her rushed reply came a little too fast to suit him. "You don't have to tell me any of the details if you don't want to, but—"

"Us."

"What?"

She glanced at him, at the front seat of the van where Mojo and Red sat, then down at her lap. She curled her legs under the skirt of her tattered gown. "There are three of you," she emphasized in a low tone, "and they're certainly close enough to hear, so anything I say would be to all of you. The proper pronoun would be us, plural."

He supposed that was the teacher in her coming out.

After that small lecture, she avoided his gaze.

"Do you want to introduce me to your friends? I don't even know some of their names yet."

To Clint's speculative eye, she looked a little woozy, in pain, and God knew she was babbling. But she'd awakened as easily as she'd passed out.

And he was still worried.

Clint propped his back against the side of the van and nodded. "Yeah, sure. Why not? It's not like we've got more important stuff to talk about."

She glared at him, pleasing him with her gumption.

"The driver is Red, and the man staring at you is Mojo."

As if they'd known each other a long time, Julie cuddled comfortably into his side. Her tangled, shoulder-length hair tickled Clint's skin as she nestled her head against his chest. He noticed she had a couple of broken fingernails when she rested one slim hand across his bare abdomen. When she turned her body toward him, her thigh half covered his.

Damn. She was crawling onto him, getting under his skin so fast that it made his head swim.

To distract himself, Clint stared down at her exposed ankles and bare dirty feet.

"Red and Mojo? But what are your real names?"

Red chuckled while maneuvering through the dark night. Clint knew he hadn't missed a thing, that he was aware of little Julie Rose holding on to him for dear life. But Red would never make her uncomfortable by mentioning it.

"Oh, no." Red shook his head. "Forget it. You don't need to know my real name."

Mojo muttered, "Hell, I don't even remember mine anymore."

Julie smiled. It was an amazing sight, that small, sweet smile.

Her fingertips absently curled against Clint's skin in a discreet caress that about made him nuts. "So Mojo and Red, I suppose I owe you my thanks also. Your timing was a little off—I mean, a few hours earlier would have been better—but still, you did get me away before they could do what they really wanted to do, and I'm eternally grateful."

"What did they really want to do?"

She frowned at Clint. "Don't growl at me."

"Answer me, Julie Rose."

Rolling her eyes, then quickly turning her face down so that her false bravado couldn't be unmasked, she said, "They wanted to . . . rape me."

"Is that right?"

She nodded. "They said so enough."

"They told you they were going to rape you?"

"Yes, after they got the money. Then they'd have killed me. They told me that, too." She drew a breath and deliberately lightened her tone. "But thanks to all of you, their plans were routed."

The men shared a look of understanding. Red spoke first. "We're glad we could help."

Julie held silent for a long moment. "Do you do this for a living, then? Run around rescuing people, I mean."

Clint felt aggrieved. There were things they needed to ask her, things they needed to know.

She was dirty, bruised. She'd fainted. And she wanted to indulge in chitchat. "Julie Rose—"

Without lifting her head from his shoulder, she tipped her face up to him. "Why do you keep calling me by my first and last name? Just Julie will do. I mean, you're my champion, right?" She gave a nervous little laugh. "We should be on a first name basis."

He liked her name, and he liked her. However, keeping an emotional distance was necessary, and he could help accomplish that by *not* getting too friendly.

When he didn't answer, she sighed. "Where did you learn to fight like that?"

Clint dropped his head back against the side of the van and closed his eyes. Why the hell was she so chatty?

Julie nudged him. "Did any of you get hurt?"

Clint squeezed her to let her know that was something of an insulting question. He decided to get things back on track. "Are you hungry?"

"Famished."

Red again spied her in the rearview mirror, and he smiled. "We'll be on the main road in another ten minutes. I'll pull into a fast-food place and get you something. Anything in particular sound good?"

"Yes. Whatever you see first. That sounds perfect." She smiled at Clint. "Do you see how I'm actually answering questions, not just ignoring them? It's easy enough to do. I'm sure you could manage if you try."

Clint's eyes widened. She'd just chastised him, and her efforts at subtlety were absurd. *"I* have questions," he told her, and though he didn't mean to, he frowned.

Julie nodded. "Okay, but we'll take turns." She peeked up at him. "I suppose you'll insist on going first?"

Mojo snickered.

Because it was important, Clint tipped her face up. He could read the truth of her words in her dark, expressive eyes. "Are you hurt?"

"I already told you no." Again, that answer came too fast.

He opened his hand on the side of her face, tunneling his fingers into her baby-fine hair. He wanted to spare her as much as possible, so he leaned down until his forehead touched hers and spoke very softly, for her ears only. "You have a lot of scrapes and bruises, Julie Rose. If you need a doctor, we can take you—"

Her doe eyes darkened even more, and her breath came low and fast. "You still think they raped me."

The question had to be forced out of Clint's tight throat. "Did they?"

She shook her head hard. *"No."*

"Julie . . ."

"No, they didn't," she insisted. "They would have, but they hadn't yet. They . . ." She looked around, saw that Mojo and Red were pretending to pay no attention. "They touched me," she whispered. "And hurt me. Just to be mean, just to scare me . . ."

The rage was unbearable, but Clint kept his hold on her light and easy. Without conscious decision, he pressed a kiss to her forehead. "I should have killed them."

She bit her lip, nodded. "You could have. I mean, you're capable of killing, right?"

Lying to her would be pointless. "Yes."

"You've killed before?"

In the military, he had. But he didn't want to frighten her, so he said nothing.

"We agreed," she reminded him with a nudge. "I answered questions, and now it's your turn."

He shook his head at her.

"Is that a no, you haven't killed, or no, you won't answer?"

"That was a sign of exasperation, actually."

"Oh." She looked thoughtful. "Do you always throw up after you've hurt someone?"

Christ. Clint heard Mojo muttering, Red chuckling. The woman had been kidnapped, held captive, abused and bruised, and all she wanted to do was ask questions.

If he'd measured his words more carefully before he spoke, then maybe he wouldn't have sounded so defensive. "It has nothing to do with guilt, if that's what you're thinking."

Her arched brows lifted. "Oh? Then why do you get sick?"

Assuming she needed to talk, that she needed the distraction of mundane conversation, Clint explained. But he felt stupid doing it. "I have a bad stomach."

Her expression softened. "And a big heart."

That was too absurd to deserve a response. More often than not, the descriptions given him included "heartless" at the very top of the list.

Her hand trembled when she touched his jaw. "I might have died if it wasn't for you."

Clint tended to agree. What they needed to find out now was who the hell wanted her dead, and why.

Mojo cleared his throat. "Want me to check her now?"

Alarm stiffened Julie's fragile body. Clint soothed her, stroked her. "Mojo has medical training. The way you fainted has us all concerned. If you say there's no need for a doctor, well, that's up to you. But we've got a long night ahead of us and we'll all feel better if you let him check you over, just to make sure."

She tucked her face into his neck. Her breath was hot, her words muffled against his flesh. "No offense, Mr. Mojo, but I don't think so."

Clint met Mojo's questioning gaze and nodded. Mojo wasn't much of a conversationalist, but he needed to talk to her, to reassure her.

Mojo gave in with a frown so black, it would've scared grown men. His tone, however, was soft and gentle and coaxing.

"Just Mojo, no mister to it. I'll be painless. I need to see if you have a concussion, if you have any breaks."

"No one hit my head, and you already saw me walk."

Red said, "No, ma'am. You stood up, but then you fainted without taking a single step."

Her head lifted with a startled expression. "That's right." And then to Clint, "How did I get to this van?"

"I carried you."

Her brow puckered. "I don't remember it."

"That's because you *fainted*, which is why Mojo needs to look you over."

"How far?"

"What?"

"How far did you have to carry me?"

Clint huffed. "You have more damn questions than—"

"And you *never* answer me."

Red laughed outright, while Mojo struggled to hide his smile.

Clint worked his jaw. "Not far, all right?"

At about the same time, Mojo said, "Close to two miles."

Julie's plain face looked adorable in her astonishment. "Two miles! You're kidding."

For a closed-mouthed bastard, Mojo was suddenly full of confidences. "A rough two miles. Woods, weeds, roots. Not much moon, so the path was hard to see—"

Clint thought about slugging Mojo. He silenced him with a look, then turned his attention to Julie Rose. "You don't weigh a thing. It was no big deal."

Even in the dim light of the van, Clint could see her blush. She fidgeted and then nodded to Mojo. "All right, you may check me." Her body pressed closer to Clint's. "But be quick about it."

Clint started to move out of the way, but no

more than an inch separated them before Julie wrapped herself around him. She moved so fast, he had no choice but to sit back and hold her. She settled in his lap—and she felt very right there.

Mojo indicated that it was okay, for Clint to just stay put so she wouldn't get more upset. They both wondered if Julie was still a little in shock. She was too rigid, jumpy, alternately silent and then chatty.

And she hadn't mentioned her fiancé again since renouncing him.

After Mojo climbed into the back of the van with them, he pulled a narrow flashlight from his pocket.

Clint nudged Julie's chin with the edge of his fist. "He needs you to look at him a moment, Julie Rose."

She swiveled her head toward Mojo—while pressing closer to Clint.

Though she tried to hide it, Clint was aware of the tension rippling through her. He wished he could spare her, but they needed to see that she wasn't seriously injured, and they needed her to answer some important questions.

Red hit a hole in the road, and she jerked hard, startled beyond reason. Clint rubbed her back, her narrow shoulders, helping to ease her. Her softness drew him. Her vulnerability drew him. Her scent drove him nuts.

Mojo ignored the telltale reaction that proved her calm a facade. He took her wrist and checked her pulse rate, then slid his fingers around her wrist, her elbow. "Can you move your arms and legs okay?"

With him guiding her, she obediently flexed each arm. But when she went to rotate her right foot, she gasped, then quickly tried to cover it up. "Oh, it's a little sore. But not bad."

No one believed her.

Mojo touched her ankle, his brow furrowed with concentration as he pressed and probed. Julie grimaced, and her breath hissed out.

Sitting back on his heels, Mojo shook his head. "It's swollen. Not broken, I don't think. Probably just a sprain, but I can't be sure without an X ray." He looked at Clint. "Should wrap it in some ice as soon as we can and we'll see if the swelling goes down. No walking."

"I must have twisted it when I . . ." Her voice again trailed off. Clint noticed that despite her chattiness, she had a very hard time relating anything that had happened at the cabin. She'd have to talk about it sooner or later, if for no other reason than to clear away the demons.

He wanted her to confide in him.

The urge to reassure her, to comfort her, was strong. But he was only the man hired to retrieve her, not her confessor, not her lover.

Not her fiancé.

Then again, Julie Rose didn't need to share details for them to understand. They'd done more than one rescue, and each of them could visualize what she'd been through, how the bastards had mistreated her.

She said she hadn't been raped, and Clint

hoped like hell that was true. But sometimes women denied it out of a sense of unwarranted shame. If Julie Rose had been sexually abused, then all bets were off. He didn't care that his role in her life ended the minute he turned her back over to Robert. No way would he let it end without first finding all four of them again—and gaining his own retribution.

He made a sudden decision and didn't give himself a chance to reconsider. "Julie Rose, we can do one of two things here."

Her eyes were huge and watchful. An anticipatory stillness settled over Mojo and Red.

"We can call your fiancé and drive straight through. The two of you can decide what you want to do."

Red snorted and Mojo stirred restlessly.

Personally, Clint hated that idea, too, so he offered the next solution before she could give the first much thought. "Or we can stop for the night, and you can tell me anything you remember about those bastards. It's possible Red, Mojo, and I can figure out why you were taken, and who was behind it."

Julie bit her lip. Her chest rose and fell with deep, uneven breaths. "You'll keep me safe?"

"You have my word."

She nodded, rubbed at her tired eyes. "Let's stop for the night, please."

Chapter Three

Julie pulled awake with a wide yawn when the van stopped at a motel. How long she'd slept, she had no idea. The men had been quiet, the night dark. She'd dozed in fitful spurts, waking every so often with her heart in her throat, her stomach jumping. But Clint was always there, warm and solid behind her, and without a word, he'd calm her with his nearness.

Mojo had wanted to tend her myriad scrapes and scratches, but she'd put him off. She felt stretched to the limits and simply couldn't abide his touch any longer. He was a nice man—dark and silent—and she knew he wouldn't hurt her.

But logic wasn't a part of her reactions at the moment.

They'd run the air-conditioning in the van, and at first she'd been horribly chilled, cold deep down inside herself. The shivers had started after her decision not to go directly home, and she hadn't been able to still the quaking in her body.

Then Clint had wrapped both massive arms around her, and his heat sank right through to her bones. Sitting in his lap on the cargo area of the van, his hard body touching all along her side, she was able to get a little sleep.

It was the first rest she'd had since the kidnapping, when she'd been taken right out of her bed in the early morning.

"You were asleep, and we didn't want to wake you," Clint rumbled in explanation near her ear, "so we didn't stop for food. But we'll get something to eat in just a minute, all right?"

Her stomach growled an answer, making her blush. "Thank you."

Red left the van and went to the small glass-enclosed office. Julie watched him open his wallet, and guilt assailed her. Yet she had nothing with her, no money, no I.D. She'd make it up to them later.

The small motel was seedy, ugly, and mostly abandoned. An assortment of work trucks were parked in scattered disarray throughout the parking lot. What few patrons it boasted were likely congregated in the all-night bar and grill adjoined to the property. Half the security lights were out, leaving the lot in deep shadows. The only real illumination came from the neon signs in the bar and office.

Red returned, then pulled the van around to the back, close to the room he'd just procured.

Julie went carefully to her knees and watched through the window in awe. She'd never been to a place like this before, but the men didn't appear to see anything amiss.

Mojo slid from the front seat, stretched his long, hard body elaborately, then opened the sliding door on the side of the van. Clint helped her to her feet, holding her as if she had two broken legs instead of one sprained ankle. Limp with exhaustion and strain, Julie let him.

Mojo reached into the van for her, and because she couldn't stop herself, she shrank back.

Stupid, stupid, stupid, she thought.

He would be insulted, take her rejection personally, maybe even think she didn't like him when she liked him just fine.

It was over now. Thanks to Clint and his friends, she hadn't been raped, hadn't been hurt that badly. Mostly she'd just been scared out of her wits. She squeezed her eyes shut, trying to dredge up just a modicum of calm reason and courage.

But the idea of anyone else touching her made her skin crawl and her heart stutter. Ashamed of her reaction, she hid her face against Clint's chest. "I'm sorry."

"It's all right," he murmured. "Mojo understands." And somehow, being the amazing man he was, Clint got out of the van with her clinging to him like a sticky vine.

Her feet never touched the pavement. Clint swung her up into his arms as if it were expected of him. Red pulled a few duffel bags out of the van, and Mojo retrieved a large first aid kit. After locking the van, the three of them went to the door assigned them.

One door.

Julie gulped. Surely they didn't expect them all to share a room?

Mojo turned the lock and stepped inside to flip on lights.

The sudden glare after all the darkness made her shy. She knew she looked a wreck, and though logic told her it shouldn't matter, she hated to be seen so haggard. She wasn't a beautiful woman, but she always did her best to make a nice appearance. Her clothes were usually tidy, fit well, and her hair was always . . .

God, what was the use? At the moment she was filthy and sweaty and looked as if she'd been dragged through the dirt, her hair was so tangled. She peered up at Clint's rugged face, at the way his stormy green eyes watched her, and she managed a smile. "You can put me down now."

He walked over to one of the double beds and set her on the edge. Thankfully, the room appeared clean, if a bit tattered.

Mojo continued past them and opened an adjoining door. He placed two of the bags inside and set the other on the floor by her feet. Thank God, there were two rooms. But maybe that meant they would give her one on her own.

Without realizing it, she knotted her hands in apprehension. She was a grown woman, too old to be afraid of the dark.

But still her stomach cramped.

Clint stood there looking down at her. "You're awful quiet all of a sudden, Julie Rose."

Julie noticed her bloody, dirty knees, the grime on her naked toes. Her eyes burned and felt gritty. "I need a shower."

All three men stared at her.

At their prolonged attention, she shifted self-consciously. "You said we'd be here for the night, correct?"

Clint nodded. He still stood very close to her, and she appreciated that. "Yeah." He searched her face. "I thought you wanted to eat."

"I do. But I need to shower also." She could smell herself, and that was a truly appalling realization. Not only had she missed her morning shower, but the cabin she'd been taken to had been hot and stuffy and dirty. She'd sat on the floor, been pushed to the ground . . . Julie curled into herself, reliving those awful moments.

Clint interrupted her thoughts by giving her shoulder a gentle squeeze. "We also need to talk."

Yes, they had to talk. "All right. But after my shower."

He looked surprised at her ready agreement.

Red propped his hands on his hips. "We passed a Wal-Mart just a minute back down the road. Want me to go grab you a change of clothes? I'm not great with ladies' styles or sizes, but if you give me a clue, I can probably at least find you a simple dress and sandals so you've got something clean to change into after your bath."

Clean clothes sounded heavenly. "They're open all night?"

"It looked lit up."

Such a generous offer made her feel weepy again. What had she ever done in her life to deserve a rescue from such fine men? "That would just be so wonderful, Red." And not to push her luck, she couldn't help adding, "A toothbrush, too? And a hairbrush? And some lotion?"

Red took a step back. He looked at Clint, who shrugged, then to Mojo, who just pursed his mouth.

Red coughed. "Okay, uh, make a list. Mojo can grab us some food from the bar while I'm gone."

She turned to Clint. Her heart pounded in the now familiar fear. "You'll stay here with me?"

His eyes warmed and his voice gentled. "I'm not going anywhere."

Her relief was out of proportion, and she knew it. No, he wouldn't leave her. He'd come for her, saved her, carried her and protected her.

Clint found a pencil and pad next to the television anchored on top of the chest of drawers. He handed them to Julie, and while she wrote, the men watched her.

Attempting moderation, Julie scrawled down everything she might immediately need. A thought occurred to her, and she hesitated, then decided what the heck. Making sure the men couldn't see, she wrote panties, size five, at the bottom of the list, then folded it in half.

"Here you go. Be sure to keep the receipts and I promise I'll pay you back just as soon as I can."

Red tucked the note into his pocket without comment. He looked up at Mojo. "Grab me a sandwich and beer, will you? And cake if they have any."

Julie wrinkled her nose. Beer and cake?

She realized Clint still watched her and quickly switched to a smile. "A sandwich sounds wonderful. With chips and pickles and a Diet Coke."

All three men gaped this time, leaving her flustered and too warm. "What is it?"

"*Diet* Coke?" Clint snorted. "You should be drinking a milkshake or something."

Red shoved him, indicating that at least he realized she'd just been insulted.

Julie glared at all three of them. "Did I question your beers with cake? Did I? No, I did not. And for your information, my father drank everything diet, so I just learned to like the taste. It's not like I'm watching my weight."

Clint slanted her a sardonic look, and muttered, "Like you have any weight to watch."

Bristling, Julie looked at Red. "Well?"

"Well, what?"

"Aren't you going to shove him again?"

Red grinned. "Sure." And he slugged Clint on the shoulder, but Clint was barely jarred by the action. He just rolled his eyes.

"It's been a long day and I think we all have better things to do than play around. Mojo, go grab some food, and Red, don't spend all night shopping. She doesn't have to dress like a prom queen, so anything clean will do."

Julie started to object to his tone, if not his intention, and Clint stepped closer. "And you," he said, not two inches from her nose, "if you want your bath, get moving. Because I for one feel a little responsibility to your fiancé, whether you do or not. We really should give him a call."

Julie lifted her brows. That was at least one thing she could straighten out easily enough. "I'd agree completely if I had a fiancé. But I already told you that I do not."

Clint crossed his thick arms over his chest. He nodded to Mojo and Red, who took the hint and left. Then he faced Julie again.

"In that case," he rumbled, his eyes hot on her face, "I'd like to know who the hell hired me."

Robert was limp, sated, his every nerve ending still twitching in pleasure, when the distinctive ring of his cell phone made him jump. His home phone was set up to transfer calls to his cell phone. But who would be calling at this time of the night?

Marie was in the shower, singing her little heart out, happy as a lark after the amazing sex they'd just shared. She was so refined, so particular about her appearance—except when he made love to her. Then she was a complete wanton.

Naked, Robert stretched over the side of the bed, snagged his trousers, and managed to retrieve his phone on the fourth ring.

" 'Lo."

"Robert?"

Oh God. He bolted upright, his brain buzzing. *"Julie?"*

"Yes, it's me."

Thoughts whirled, too many too fast to grasp a single one. Relief, fear, confusion. He stared at the bathroom door, willing Marie to linger a little longer. "Honey, where the hell are you?"

"I'm safe now. We're in a small motel."

"We?"

"Yes. The men you hired got me away."

His mouth fell open. Dear God, did that mean Clint Evans had killed Asa, because he knew Asa wouldn't have given her up without a struggle. He didn't know how to ask. And he felt a little sick, imagining Marie's reaction to the loss of her brother. He rubbed his forehead, shaken to the core, overwhelmed with mixed emotions.

"I probably won't be home until the morning, though."

In the morning. Robert let out a breath of stark relief and tried to swallow down the emotions choking him. He didn't want Julie hurt, but Marie would be so upset if Julie came home now. She was insanely jealous of Julie, no matter how many times he told her that he loved *her*, not Julie.

He'd promised to end things with Julie, and so far he'd been successful in his deception. "I can't believe it. You're really safe?"

"Yes."

"Jesus." Incredible. Beyond incredible. What would Marie do without Asa? Would she thrive away from that dominating bastard, or would she fall into a decline? "Tell me what happened, Julie."

"I'm not sure what happened, but someone took me—I don't know who or why. Did the ransom note say why?"

"Money." Robert's tongue felt too thick, his words too heavy. "They said they wanted money. That's all."

The shower shut off, making him jumpier with the sudden quiet. He lowered his voice as he climbed out of the bed and reached for his slacks. "Julie . . ."

"Robert, why did you tell Clint that you were still my fiancé?"

He tripped trying to step into his slacks and banged his knee on the nightstand. "Goddammit."

"Robert?"

"Just a minute, sweetheart." Keeping the small phone caught between his ear and shoulder, he held on to the waistband of his slacks and half dressed, then stepped outside onto the veranda. The exposed aggregate surface irritated his bare feet. The sounds of insects droned in the night.

Silently, he closed the sliding doors and moved into the deepest shadows at the far end, beneath a lush flowering vine that scaled both stories of Marie's quaint home. He could see into her bedroom, but Marie wouldn't be able to see him.

"Julie." He tried to sound calm, reasonable. "Honey, the man I hired has a dangerous reputation. I don't want you to worry." He rushed to add, "I think you're safe enough with him for the night. But I wanted him to think we were still together, to protect you. Regardless of what has happened, I still care deeply for you. And you know . . ." He hesitated, not sure how far to push her. "Well, you know how I feel. For me, it wasn't much of a lie."

Silence greeted him. Julie could be so stubborn, so independent in her thoughts. Why couldn't she have just a little of Marie's loving, giving nature?

His tension grew, until finally she said, "I guess that makes sense."

Robert slumped against the railing and rubbed his face. The changing light in the bedroom alerted him. Marie opened the bathroom door and stepped out, enticingly wrapped in a white towel, her thick, dark hair piled on top of her head. She looked at the empty bed, frowned, and sashayed out into the hallway, calling Robert's name.

Robert gripped the phone hard. "Julie, is Evans there?"

"Evans?"

"Clint Evans."

"Yes, he's right here."

Memory of those cold, disturbing eyes made Robert shiver, even though the night was uncomfortably muggy. He kept his gaze glued to the bedroom to watch for Marie's return. "Why don't you put him on a moment, dear?"

"Why?"

Sweat began dampening his body, and Robert silently cursed. Did she have to question him on everything? "He's the expert, Julie. I want to hear what he has to say to me."

She hesitated, as difficult as ever, then answered with a shrug in her voice. "Okay."

Muffled sounds reached him before Clint's dark, ominous voice crackled over the line. "I got your fiancée for you, Burns."

He said that with a sneer, Robert was sure of it. Obviously, Julie had already explained that they weren't engaged. Not anymore. Had she told Evans everything? Had she told him that she dumped him when she discovered him in bed with Marie?

Robert hoped not. Not that it really mattered, he supposed. Evans had been hired to do a job, a job he'd accomplished, so he'd be paid, and his involvement ended there.

"Thank you. I'm stunned and relieved that you managed it so quickly." Gauging his words, Robert posed the concern uppermost in his mind. "You didn't give Asa my name, did you?"

"It wasn't necessary."

That told Robert very little of what had transpired, so he rephrased the question. "Did Asa . . . put up much of a fight?"

"No fight at all. In fact, he was cordial."

"But . . . that doesn't make any sense."

As if fed up with the subterfuge, Clint said, "He didn't have her, Burns. But he helped me to find her." And with a hint of glee, "I'd say you owe him for his assistance."

The phone slipped from Robert's numb hands, hitting the patio hard. He didn't have her? *Shit,*

shit, shit. Robert snatched the phone back up, took two deep breaths to calm himself, then put it to his ear. "You must be jesting."

If it wasn't Asa, then who? Robert felt certain Julie had been taken because of him, not for any other reason. The mystery of it left him scared spitless.

"I'm not a man given to jokes, Burns. Funny that you missed that during our meeting."

Robert almost groaned. "I didn't actually mean . . ."

"No, someone else had her kidnapped." Clint's voice lowered even more. "I'm curious as to why."

In the distance, Robert heard Marie approaching, still calling his name. It felt as though the world was closing in on him. He had to hurry. "Jesus, man, I don't know why. If it really wasn't Asa, then . . ." Inspiration struck, and he hurried on. "That's just it, don't you see? Until I can find out who'd do this to her, I don't think it's safe for her here."

There was only a moment's pause before Evans said, "I'll agree with you on that."

Thank God. Robert wiped his brow with a shaking hand. "Then . . . then perhaps you'll agree to keep her for a week?"

"Keep her?" Clint asked, and Robert heard Julie's immediate denials in the background.

He ground his teeth together, wishing that Julie would be docile and agreeable just once. Since falling in love with Marie, Julie and her pushy temperament had really rubbed him the wrong way. Still, he was relieved that she had survived. He was very fond of her, he just wasn't in love with her and never would be.

He needed her money, only he didn't want her dead for it. But if she wasn't home yet . . . Drew would surely give him more money for her ransom, more money to hire private investigators, more money for anything that was needed. Drew adored Julie, and worried about her as if she were his own. He didn't have to know that Julie was safe and sound. Robert could extort enough money from Drew to pay off Asa, to reward Clint Evans, and to cushion his departure from Julie's life.

Brilliant. He was absolutely brilliant. "Listen, Evans, you're the perfect man to keep her safe."

"Uh huh."

"It'd just be until I've had time to hire private investigators and to get some safeguards set up. New locks, new security system, maybe even a bodyguard. Not that Julie will like that idea. But she lives alone, damn it, insisting on her privacy no matter what . . ."

"I've noticed that she can be a bit stubborn." There was a rustling, and Robert heard Evans say, "Ow." Amazingly enough, humor infused that dark voice when he added, "And violent, too."

Robert froze. Oh, no. Surely Julie wouldn't antagonize . . . no, of course she wouldn't. She wasn't *that* headstrong. And she would be safe with Evans. The man couldn't get paid if he didn't deliver her back in one piece. "I'll double your pay."

"Double it, huh?"

Marie stepped back into the bedroom. "Robert?"

"I have to go, Evans. Tell me you'll keep her safe for me while I do some checking, try to figure out what the hell is going on."

"That could be dangerous for you, Burns."

Robert sighed, looking at Marie through the glass doors. "Yes, but I'm willing to risk it." He'd risk that and more for his Marie.

Evans grunted. "Yeah, I'll keep her safe."

Robert turned his back. "Good, that's good. Call me back in the morning and we can arrange . . ." Robert looked at the dead phone. Evans had hung up on him. "Well, hell."

The glass doors slid open with a hiss, and Marie stepped out into the night. "Robert? What are you doing out here?"

He turned to face her and held up the phone with a smile. "Business call. But I'm done now."

Her beautiful pale eyes narrowed in suspicion. "Business at this time of night?"

"Morning, actually. It's after midnight." In many ways, Marie's eyes were as notable as Clint Evans's, but for opposite reasons. Marie's exuded warmth and caring, not menace. "It was just a small problem. I got it taken care of."

"It wasn't that woman, your fiancée?"

He smiled at her jealous display. "No, darling, of course not. I told you that's over."

"It won't be over until you end the engagement."

"And I will. Soon now. I promise."

The total opposite of Julie, Marie didn't continue to question him. She smiled. "All right, then." Stepping into his arms, she rubbed her nose against his chest. "You are such a wonderful man, I can't believe she's letting you go." Her fingers trailed down his chest. "Come back to bed. The sun will be up all too soon and I'm not done with you yet."

Robert dropped the phone into his pocket and enfolded Marie in his arms. She was wary of every man, but him. She was feminine, luscious, and so sexy, she made his heartbeat erratic. He loved her more than he'd ever loved anything on earth.

If only she wasn't Asa's sister, and if only Asa didn't have it in for him.

"Robert." She groaned his name while kissing his shoulder, his throat, taking small love bites. "I want you to live with me. I want to go to bed with you at night and wake up with you in the morning and not have to count the hours." She toyed with his chest hair, one fingernail grazing his right nipple. "I want to know that you're all mine, and that other women, especially your fiancée, are out of the running."

Robert tugged her towel away and let it drop. Her large, dark nipples were already stiffened. He cuddled her lush ass, lifting her naked body up and into his. "There's no one but you," he panted, already on the ragged edge, even though they'd just made love less than an hour ago.

"Then let me tell my brother now. He wants me to be happy, he—"

"Sweetheart." Robert cupped her face, determined to make her understand. Everything depended on her being patient, on her abiding by his wishes. There was still a chance he'd be able to make everything work out, especially if he could get Asa paid back. Never would he let Asa think that he'd used Marie to even the score. But he knew that's the way Asa's mind would work.

No, Robert had to pay him his blood money, and until then, Asa couldn't know about them. "Your brother hates me."

"No."

"Yes," he insisted. "He does. I told you, we've clashed in business. But that won't always be the case." Robert cupped her neck, kissed her full mouth. "Asa will come around, you'll see. Then I can leave Julie and we'll get married and have babies and be happy."

She smiled up at him, her blue eyes hurt, but accepting. "We'll have everything."

"Everything." Guilt nudged at Robert, but he shoved it aside. He cared about Julie, hoped she would be spared. But didn't he deserve some happiness, too?

Marie took his hand to lead him inside. Robert held her close and fell with her onto the bed. Fate had intervened, and he'd be damned before he wasted the opportunity. He'd think of something. Somehow.

He had at least a week.

Clint replaced the receiver in the cradle on the wobbly Formica nightstand. He eyed Julie's anxious expression. "You're not engaged."

She waved that away as unimportant, when Clint knew it was anything but. "No. We used to be, but that ended a while ago. Robert was afraid you'd take advantage of me if you knew I was . . . available." She made a face. "Dumb, I know. But he thought if—"

"Not so dumb." Even now, seeing her there on the bed gave him ideas—ideas only a real bastard would act on. Clint stood, determined to put some space between them. "I'll run your bath. Sit tight."

"I'd rather have a shower."

"I'd rather you didn't try standing on your sprained ankle." He ignored her disgruntled rumblings and went into the miniscule bathroom. When he turned on the tub faucet, the water spat and sputtered and ran cold before finally settling in a warm, steady stream. He laid the bath mat on the floor, set out a towel and washcloth, and did his best not to picture Julie Rose's slim, naked body settling into the tub, lounging back, sleek and wet . . .

"Shit." He rubbed his face with both hands.

"Clint?"

"Nothing." He stepped through the doorway and surveyed her huddled form on the edge of the mattress. She looked exhausted, her eyes puffy, her shoulders slumped. Yet she tried so damn hard to hide it all.

The urge to lift her into his arms and pamper her shook him. "Why don't you soak until Red and Mojo get back? That way you can put on clean clothes when you get out."

"Clean." Her smile tilted. "I'll never again take the concept for granted."

Despite the roiling mix of emotions, Clint indulged his own smile. She was a trouper, fighting hard to hold herself together. He propped his shoulder against the doorframe. "You said you weren't engaged anymore. What happened?"

After folding her arms around herself, she looked away. Her shoulder lifted in a negligent shrug. "Robert was seeing someone else. I caught him at it." She made a small sound of humor. "Quite embarrassing for all concerned."

Clint went to her and helped her stand. He was thinking things he shouldn't, but knowing that didn't help clear his head. He gave up with a show of exasperation meant to hide the depth of his interest. "You don't look particularly broken up about it."

"No. I care for him and nothing will change that. He worked for my father, and now for my uncle and father's estate. I've known him a long time. But we weren't right for each other, not for marriage."

Lifting her to spare her ankle—or so he told himself—Clint cradled her to his chest and carried her into the bathroom. Julie Rose didn't object; she just twined her slim arms around his neck and laid her head on his shoulder.

Trusting. The woman was far, far too trusting.

"I'd already realized that marrying Robert would just be a convenience."

"A convenience how?"

She shrugged. "There wasn't anyone else I wanted to marry, and I'm getting older."

"You're still young enough."

"I'm almost thirty." She lifted her head with a sigh. "And my uncle approves of Robert, so it seemed an ideal situation."

Ideal for whom? Clint slowly lowered her to the tile floor. He bent to turn off the tub and gave in to his curiosity. "Why the hell would your uncle care one way or the other?"

Amused irony lit the darkness of her eyes. "He's my closest relative, and he was also my father's business partner."

"So now he's in charge of the estate?" Robert had told Clint plenty, but he wanted to hear it from Julie Rose, too, to get the truth in case Robert had lied.

Nodding, Julie said, "He's the one responsible for doling out my funds and trying to keep me on the straight and narrow. He teases me that it's quite a daunting task."

Robert had claimed Julie Rose was wild, indiscreet. Clint crossed his arms, affronted on her behalf and not yet ready to leave her to her bath. "Yeah? How so?"

"It's silly really." For just a moment, she looked lighthearted, free of the strain and hurt from the past day. "Uncle Drew is very old-fashioned, as was my father. He thinks a woman should be pampered and protected. And he's scandalized if a woman dates too often, parties too hearty . . ."

"Has sex?"

Her mouth twitched with that innate humor he'd first seen in her photograph. "Yes. Because I've had a few relationships but haven't yet married, he worries about my reputation, and about my trust fund. He thinks that men pay me attention to get my money." Her chuckle was husky, sexy, surprising Clint. "Not that I'm a femme fatale or anything. I mean, you've seen me."

Clint narrowed his eyes, and suddenly the memory of her velvet breast against his chest stirred the air between them. "Yeah. I've seen you."

Julie realized how that sounded, and she blanched. "That is, I mean . . ."

To save her from further ramblings, Clint reached out and brushed her downy cheek with the back of his knuckles. Every time he touched her, she went as still as a deer caught in his headlights—and for some reason, that turned him on. "Why should a sexy woman keep herself chaste? That's just dumb."

Her eyes widened. "You think so?"

"Yeah." He couldn't keep his narrowed gaze from drifting over her. "I think so."

A long moment of silence stretched between them before she found her voice. "Well, I'm hardly sexy . . ."

Clint could see her vulnerability, her desperate need for a compliment. It was strange, because he'd expected her to be jumpy around guys after what she'd just been through. And she was, just not with him.

Thumbs in his pockets, his stance as unthreatening as he could make it, Clint said, "You're sexy, Julie Rose."

Her eyes widened even more. She swallowed hard, turned pink, and got flustered. It was cute. She was cute.

He couldn't help but smile. "Don't go fainting on me again."

"No, I won't." Nervously, she crossed her hands over her middle. "Uncle Drew considers Robert an excellent catch. He thinks because we're from similar backgrounds, Robert will make me happy. And once I marry, the trust fund gets turned over to me and my husband. Robert already has money, so Uncle Drew knows he's not after my wealth." She sighed. "It did seem like a good idea. But then I found out that Robert hadn't been faithful."

A thousand questions buzzed through Clint's head. The more he knew about her, the easier it'd be to find her kidnappers. "You caught him in the act?"

"Yes, and got quite a rapid education." Her eyes twinkled, and she whispered as if sharing a scandalous confidence. "I'd had no idea that stuffy, proper Robert could be so kinky."

The hypocrite, Clint thought with annoyance, remembering how he'd accused Julie Rose. "So you broke things off?"

"Not immediately."

"Well, why not?" Clint didn't mean to sound so surly when he asked that question. Not that Julie Rose seemed to notice. She merely shrugged.

"I don't know. My life was sort of up in the air. I'd been subbing in this small, wonderful community, and I kept thinking how nice it'd be to teach there full-time. I realized that I didn't really love Robert, because the idea of moving away from him didn't bother me at all. But I do want to marry and have kids some day, and if I ended things with Robert, I wasn't sure I'd ever have another chance."

"But then you busted him in the sack with another woman."

"A really beautiful woman. She's everything I'm not."

"Meaning?"

"She's . . ." Julie held her hands out in front of her chest. "Voluptuous. Very fashionable. And sensual. I felt . . . I don't know. Insulted, of course, because we were engaged. But sort of hurt, too. Not because I loved Robert, but because he'd chosen another woman over me. Bruce encouraged me to free myself. He said I deserved better than Robert."

Clint's eyebrow lifted. Another man in her life? "I agree, but who's this Bruce? A boyfriend?"

She grinned as if his assumption pleased her. "No, of course not. Bruce is Bryan's twin."

"Bryan?" How many damned men did she know? "Who the hell is Bryan?"

"An ex–bounty hunter turned businessman. Bruce is his brother. They're identical twins. Bruce is also a preacher, and recently married. He's a wonderful man, but we're only friends."

Jesus. A bounty hunter, a preacher . . . But if Bruce talked her into breaking ties with Robert, then Clint had to respect him. To get her back on track, he said, "Okay, I'm with you so far. You and Robert aren't engaged anymore, but the two of you have remained friends?" If they weren't friends, that'd give him one more reason to suspect Robert.

"Very good friends. Uncle Drew thinks it's just a lovers' quarrel, that we'll get back together, but Robert and I both know that won't happen."

"I don't think Robert knows it at all."

"He does." She looked prim as she said, "I made it most clear to him."

"You made it clear to Drew, too?"

Wincing, she said, "I tried. But he worries so much. I hate to dissappoint him."

Drew sounded like a pain in the ass, to Clint. Was she surrounded by judgmental users and takers? "You should be careful about who you trust, Julie Rose."

Her lips parted. "You're not suggesting Robert was behind my abduction, are you?"

He narrowed his eyes and shrugged. "Honorable men don't cheat on women."

A smile brightened her eyes. "I agree, but he hired you to save me, yes?"

"Yeah but . . ." She wavered on her feet, making Clint curse softly. He caught her to him. "Damn it, I'm sorry. Here you are ready to collapse and I'm shooting the breeze." He dipped his head to see her face. "Julie Rose? You okay?"

"Yes, I just . . . I guess I'm hungrier than I thought."

That damn worry pushed at him again. He channeled it into anger, because anger he could deal with. It was more familiar to him than worry. "They didn't feed you at all, did they?"

She shook her head. "I received only a few drinks of water."

"Bastards." He held her shoulders. "Maybe you should eat first . . ."

Wrinkling her nose, she leaned back from him and said, "The bath is my first priority. Go. I'll be fine."

Still he didn't move. There were shadows under her soft eyes, amplified by the whiteness of her skin. "Do you want me to help?"

Her mouth fell open while color rushed into her face, making her less wan. *"No."*

"You're sure?"

She pokered up with insult. "I'm a big girl. I'll manage just fine."

"Big." Clint shook his head and cautiously released her delicate body. "Not quite." He headed for the door. "I'll be right outside. If you need me for anything, don't hesitate. You've been through an ordeal, so don't push yourself, okay?"

"Yes, sir."

Clint grinned reluctantly. "Smart ass." He went out, pulling the door shut behind him. Julie Rose had grit, he'd give her that.

A minute later he heard the soft splash of the bathwater, telling him she'd gotten in the tub.

Telling him that she was naked.

He closed his eyes, but that only made the images clearer.

Luckily, for his peace of mind, Mojo returned a few minutes later. He balanced a tray filled with sub sandwiches, a pitcher of beer, a can of Pepsi, and assorted snacks.

He set the food on the dresser, and his dark eyes went unerringly to the bathroom door. "She's in the tub?"

"Yeah."

"You talk to her fiancé?"

"Robert Burns." Clint practically snarled the name. "We talked. Only they're not engaged. The bastard lied about that."

"No shit?"

Clint nodded. "To protect her from me."

"Idiot."

"Yeah, he is. But then, I realized that right off." Which was why he'd bugged Robert's office. He'd call in first thing in the morning and listen to any conversations that might have transpired.

Mojo seemed to read his thoughts. "Think the recording will tell us anything?"

"I hope so. But I'm not taking any chances." Clint watched Mojo to judge his reaction to the altered plans. "I'm not letting her out of my sight till I know it's safe."

Mojo gave him a long look, but said nothing.

Ten minutes later, Red came in, toting a large bag fully stuffed. He closed and locked the door behind him, then looked toward the bathroom. "She still in the tub?"

Clint frowned. He knew damn good and well where his thoughts were, so he could easily guess what the others were thinking, too. He didn't like them picturing her naked. Hell, he didn't even like himself picturing her naked. "You know women. I suspect she'll be in there awhile." He nodded toward the bag. "You get everything?"

Red grunted. He upended the bag over the bed and dumped out the contents of light, feminine clothing. "She had me buy panties." He picked up a pair of miniscule nylon underwear and waved it at Clint. "Size five. Can you believe that? If Daisy sees the charge on our credit card, I'm going to have a hell of a time explaining."

Smiling, Clint took the underwear. "Daisy trusts you or she'd have divorced you by now."

They were chuckling when the soft sob struck them all at once. It was just a small muffled sound, but it was a sound that struck terror in most male hearts.

Clint jerked to attention, Mojo stilled as if he'd turned to stone, and Red frowned fiercely. Another small, nearly silent sob reached them.

"Damn." With a helpless expression, Red looked at the other two. "She's *crying?*"

Clint was at the bathroom door in an instant. He paused, shook his head with uncertainty, and tapped lightly. "Julie Rose?"

He heard sniffling, then a husky, "Go away."

Like hell. He said over his shoulder, "Wait here," and got a mute, horrified response from his friends.

He didn't wait a second more. Clint opened the door and walked in.

Chapter Four

Julie felt like a complete and utter idiot. One minute she'd been coping, concentrating on how good it felt to be clean, taking an inordinate amount of time to scrub her toes clean, then drying at a leisurely pace.

The next she'd felt the tears welling, the sob crawling up her throat, and she'd slumped to the floor like a wounded child. She tried to be quiet, to keep her grief private.

But Clint Evans wasn't a man to let much get by him. It was so mortifying.

She knew Clint stood there, a mere foot away, but she couldn't look at him, not while she huddled on the bathroom floor next to the tub, a towel wrapped tight around her body, her face blotchy from tears. She wanted to move, wanted to say something. But all that came out was a pathetic, strangled whimper of sound. A weak, girly sound.

Clint sat down beside her, uncaring of the water on the floor, of the awkwardness of the situation. He put his thick arms around her and pulled her back into his chest. "Shh, it's all right, baby. I've got you."

His crooning voice nearly melted her bones. "Don't call me that."

She heard his smile when he asked, "Why not?"

Julie knuckled away the tears from one eye. "It's demeaning." Her objection sounded weak and watery.

"It's affectionate."

She shook her head, making her partially braided, wet hair slap against his chin. "Go . . . go away, please."

"No."

Her hands fisted. She pressed her face to her knees, hiding. "Clint, I want to be alone."

"No, you don't."

No, she didn't. "I'm embarrassed."

He hugged her, his cheek against her crown. "Yeah, well, you'll get over it, won't you?"

A wobbly, broken laugh escaped. Such a stubborn, autocratic man! Everything he did, everything he said, overflowed with confidence. He told her she'd get over it, so she probably would. "I'm not dressed."

"I'm ignoring that fact."

An easy feat, no doubt. Despite his earlier compliments, she knew she wasn't exactly the type of woman to attract him. He'd made it clear he thought her skinny—and she was. Not sickly skinny, or at least she'd never thought so. But definitely thin.

Clint probably liked women with lots of curves. His attention . . . well, he had a job to do and he was doing it. She wondered how much Robert was paying him. Whatever the amount, it wasn't enough. She'd have to talk to her uncle to see if she could get him more.

She wiped her eyes again and sniffed. Clint loosened one brawny arm, reached behind him to snag some toilet paper from the roll, and handed it around to her. "Blow."

God, her whole life was upside down. Never in a million years had Julie ever thought to be sitting on a bathroom floor in a cheap motel, mostly naked, with a hunk of a hero holding her while she blew her nose into toilet paper.

She blew.

Clint lifted the toilet lid. "Throw it in."

He was so matter-of-fact about everything. Julie twisted a bit, aimed, and made a perfect shot.

"Good girl. Now, talk to me."

"I'm a grown woman, not a girl. A teacher."

"Talk to me anyway."

"It's stupid."

"I doubt it."

Her breath came a little easier with his presence. How or why that was so, she didn't know. But with him near, the awful feelings faded away. "I washed my hair."

"Yeah. It smells nice."

It did? She waved a hand toward the tiny bottle supplied by the motel. "I think it said jasmine, but anything would be an improvement, wouldn't it?"

He propped his chin on her shoulder, ignoring her question to ask one of his own. "You're crying because you washed your hair?"

That sounded plain silly, but the real reason wasn't much better. "No. I wanted to braid my hair, but I realized my hands were shaking too badly to get it done. I hate weakness, and I hate relying on others. That thought led to another and I just . . ."

He turned his face inward, and his breath brushed the side of her neck. "It's normal to be upset, you know."

His breath was so hot. "It's . . . it's weak and wimpy."

"Who says?"

More tears leaked out, and Julie swatted them away. "My father used to tease me, calling me an agitator and an activist. I've always taken care of myself and fought for what I believed in. I'm not used to crying and acting like a spineless wimp."

Clint indulged a moment of thoughtful silence. "You and your father were close?"

"Very. I loved him so much, it still hurts to know he's gone forever. And he loved me, too." Her lips quivered, and she drew a shuddered breath. "We butted heads all the time, you know, mostly over money. But if he were alive right now, he'd be so outraged." She gave a choking laugh. "He'd probably be calling out the National Guard. He was always very protective."

"He sounds like a good man."

"The best." Julie could feel the crisp hair on Clint's chest against her shoulder blades. He had the finest body she'd ever seen on a man, and his strength drew her for a variety of reasons. It exemplified his capability and his masculinity, making her feel very safe. After all she'd been through, that mattered a lot.

But he looked plain nice, too, very sexy and appealing.

Even after her ordeal, she wasn't immune. For her peace of mind, she hoped he donned a shirt soon.

"Robert told me you and your father had problems."

"Typical stuff, nothing serious. I never doubted his love."

"Robert gave a different impression."

Julie thought about that for only a moment. "Robert resented his protectiveness more than I did. It meant he couldn't ever make use of my money for anything, even after our engagement, without my father's approval."

Clint said nothing to that, but Julie could almost feel him digesting the information and sorting it in his mind.

His large hands clasped her shoulders. "Hold on to your towel."

"Why?" She stiffened, not afraid, but unsure of his intent.

"I'm going to turn you to the side a bit. I can finish your hair for you while you talk."

That surprised her enough that she went limp

while he readjusted her. She almost lost her towel, and it did slide up far too high on her thighs.

A tap sounded on the bathroom door, and Red called out, "Everything okay?"

"She's fine." Clint tugged on her hair. "Leave her clothes and the first aid kit there by the door, and you two go ahead and eat."

"Will do."

Julie peeked at Clint. He had an intense look of concentration on his face as he worked on understanding her braid. Normally, she took care of herself and refused help from anyone. She'd gotten stubborn about such things with the way her father had tried to buy her way through life. But now, she was interested enough in seeing Clint manage a braid that she didn't refuse.

"Tell me what happened at the cabin."

When she curled tighter into herself, he cupped her chin and brought her face around. "I've retrieved men from similar situations, Julie Rose, and they've been as shaken as you, sometimes worse. It's nothing to be embarrassed or ashamed about, just proves you're human. But it does help to talk about it, to get it out of your head."

Julie felt as though she could sink into Clint's consuming gaze. He didn't just look at her; he looked into her, seeing her soul. No one had ever done that before. Most men looked only on the surface—and saw a strict teacher with less than outstanding looks.

Robert saw a means to an end. She knew that,

just as she knew her father and Drew saw her as a princess who needed to be protected.

And the men who'd abducted her had seen her as a plaything, a way to pass the time with cruel games.

She swallowed hard and peered down at her hands, still trembling but now clean. Her nails were a ragged mess.

"It was six in the morning. I was still in bed, trying to wake up and thinking about what I had to do that day." She frowned in stark remembrance of the moment she'd realized she wasn't alone. She never ever wanted to feel that kind of shock again. "For some reason, the security alarm didn't work."

Clint's head lifted. "You have a security alarm?"

"Well, yes. A good one—or so I thought."

Clint appeared troubled by that, confusing Julie. "My father had it installed when I insisted on living alone several years ago. But apparently, it didn't go off when they entered. One minute I was half asleep, and then there was something over my mouth and hands were on me everywhere and men were dragging me away."

The panic renewed, clawing through her until she took several deep breaths, until she clenched and unclenched her hands. Clint gave her a quiet moment to collect herself, then went back to work on her hair.

"I screamed," Julie admitted in a small, helpless tone. "It was a really startling sound, too, but there wasn't anyone to hear and he—one of them—hit me."

She touched her cheek where the bluish bruise could be seen. Her first glance in the bathroom mirror had been staggering. She wasn't just a mess, she was a fright.

Using her braid to tug her closer, Clint pressed a light, tender kiss to the mark, then brushed it with his fingertips. "Go on."

Julie held her breath and stared at him. He'd kissed her a couple of times now, small, impersonal pecks that made her feel so much better. She wondered if she'd ever get used to it.

She wondered if he'd give her the chance to get used to him.

"I was so afraid I could barely breathe." She shivered with that ugly admission and pressed a fist to her chest. "My lungs hurt. I couldn't seem to focus. I don't ever want to be that afraid again."

"We'll make sure of it."

The verbal commitment to her safety surprised her. She glanced again at Clint, but all his considerable concentration was on twisting her hair into a lopsided, uneven braid.

"They put me in the backseat of a car, down on the floor, and they drove for what felt like a long time. They wouldn't tell me anything except that I should be quiet and not fight them. Then they'd laugh. Every so often they . . . messed around with me. Pawing me, making me think they might rape me." Clint's busy hands stilled in her hair, and she could feel his surging anger like the static before a storm.

"Petie seemed to be the one in charge. He . . .

he grabbed my breast and I slugged him, but I know I didn't hurt him. He just laughed and ripped my gown and he held me down while he went ahead and mauled at me and the others laughed . . . Oh, God." Her voice had risen with the retelling, sounding as panicked and shaken as she'd been at the time until, with a gasp, she bit her lip and fell quiet.

Clint pressed his face into her neck, and Julie realized he was trembling, too, but not from fear. No, his reaction was pure rage.

On her behalf.

She tried to choke down the emotions, but still she cried. Her words were broken and raw, depicting her continued fear, her remaining terror. "They said they would rape me," she whispered, "and I wanted to die. Only they didn't. We got to the cabin, and they tied my hands, and then they just got drunk. Petie said something about having to wait." She let out a shaky breath. "He said once the ransom was paid, no one would know what he did until it was too late."

"He never mentioned any names? Didn't give you any time frames or how much money he was talking about?"

She shook her head, almost dislodging her hair from Clint's fist. "Mostly he just toyed with me. But if they did talk, I'm not sure I'd have remembered much. I was busy trying to think of how to get away, where I'd go if I got out the door, how I'd stop them if they tried to rape me."

Clint looked grim, holding the end of her braid out straight. "How do you expect this to stay put?"

"Oh." Distracted from the memories, Julie lifted the strip of material she'd torn off her ruined nightgown. She pulled the braid over her shoulder and tightly tied off the end. "My hair is bone straight, but if I braid it wet, then it at least has some body the next morning. I'll still put it up, but it won't seem so flat and . . ." Julie realized she was babbling and closed her mouth.

Clint looked troubled—or as troubled as a big warrior could look. At her sudden silence, he drew himself out of his private thoughts and smiled. "If you say so."

"Clint?" Julie figured they might as well get it all out in the open. "I need to know who was paying Petie, don't I?"

"Yeah, we do."

This time she couldn't resist. "We?"

If she'd expected a declaration of some sort, he dissuaded her from that notion. "Robert doubled my pay to keep you safe for a week. The only way to keep you safe is to find out who had you taken and why, so I can make certain it doesn't happen again."

"Oh. Yes, of course." They were still sitting on the floor, and she started to stand. Her ankle hurt, but then, so did her shoulders, her neck. Her eyes burned, and her nose was stuffy. The soap from her bath had made her more aware of every scrape and cut.

"Sit tight." Clint pressed her shoulders until she

subsided. Then he stood and fetched the clothes and first aid kit outside the door. He knelt back down by her. "I want to put some medicine on those scrapes. You say the cabin was dirty, so there's no reason to take a chance on infection."

"I can do it."

"I can do it better."

Arguing with him didn't seem worth the effort. Julie stretched out her legs and waved a hand at him. "Knock yourself out."

Clint eyed the length of her legs for a moment, then soaked a cotton ball in medicine and, with intense focus, dabbed at her knees. Julie hissed out a breath.

"Sorry. I know it stings." He bent to blow on her abraded skin. Julie looked at the top of his dark head, at the breadth of those remarkable shoulders, and felt breathless for an entirely different reason.

It took Clint ten minutes to treat each small mark on her body. By the time he finished, Julie wasn't sure what she felt. Given the men from Visitation, she'd known plenty of males who were big and strong and capable, but none who had been so incredibly gentle, so careful, *with her.*

It was a special form of intimacy. At least, in her limited experience with men, it seemed so.

Clint was gruff one moment, tender the next. He was her hero.

Clint eased her upward, keeping his gaze averted from her slipping towel. "Now, let's get you dressed."

"*That* I can most definitely manage on my own."

"I'm not taking any chances."

His determination battered her. But Julie could be just as determined. She held out her hand without a word. Clint hesitated, but finally draped the nightshirt and panties over her arm. "Stubborn," he muttered.

"Modest," she countered. "Now, turn your back."

"All right, but if you so much as breathe wrong, I'm helping."

"Your confidence in my abilities is staggering."

"The confidence is there, Julie Rose, make no mistake. You're a strong woman and I respect that. But anyone would be off kilter right now. You've been through a hell of a lot; you're injured and still shaky."

She felt vulnerable enough to add, "And you want to make sure you get me home in one piece, so you'll get paid?"

His green eyes narrowed, glittering with intent. "You got your sass back with a vengeance, didn't you?"

Julie noticed that he didn't deny wanting his money. Well, what could she expect? She was a job, and she should be glad that he did his work so well. "Turn around, Clint."

He did, but not before scrutinizing her for a long, heart-stopping moment.

Keeping a close watch on Clint's back so that he wouldn't peek, Julie pulled on the clothes, then glanced in the mirror to make sure she was decent. The baby blue nightshirt hung to mid-thigh, and the material was thick enough to conceal her meager curves. It would do.

The braid, however, was a sight to be seen. While the part she'd braided hung smooth and straight, the one Clint had finished bent in the middle, sticking out at a funny angle, sort of clumpy. She almost laughed, but she didn't want to hurt his feelings. He'd tried.

"All right. I'm finished."

Slowly, Clint turned to face her. His gaze went to her feet and crept upward before finally reaching her face. "Everything fits?"

"Yes. Your friend, Red, did a wonderful job."

Clint reached out for her hand. "How's the ankle?"

"I can hobble out of here, if that's what you mean."

"I don't mind carrying you."

Resolute, Julie shook her head. "Not necessary." Teeth gritted, Julie took a cautious step and was proud of her success. Without a word, Clint picked up the first aid kit with one hand and put his free arm around her waist, half lifting her, helping her through the door and to the bed.

Rather than retreating to their own room, Red and Mojo had propped up in the opposite bed. Mojo was drinking beer and watching television. Red was on the phone, apparently speaking with his wife, given the kissing noises he made before hanging up.

Empty food containers filled the small waste can by the door, proof that they'd already eaten.

At her appearance, both men froze, staring at Julie with comical expressions that she didn't understand until she remembered her hair. She wrinkled her nose and fingered the braid. "Clint helped me with it."

The comical looks transferred to Clint. Red gave an ear-splitting grin. "Now, that was real nice of him, huh?"

"Shut up, Red."

Chuckling, Red got up and moved to the only chair in the room. Mojo also stood and, without a word, went to the adjoining room to steal the chair from there. He dragged it through the doorway and in front of the TV.

Watching them rearrange themselves for her amused Julie, and touched her heart.

She smiled at Red. "Thank you for the clothes. They're perfect."

"The rest of the stuff is there on the dresser, including the lotion and toothbrush."

Lotion. Funny how the small things suddenly became so precious. "Thank you."

Clint rolled his eyes. "Quit thanking him."

"Why?"

"Because it's not necessary."

Red smiled. "It really isn't."

"Still, all the same—"

Her words broke off as Clint lifted her, set her in the bed, then helped her get settled.

"You wanna eat now?" he asked.

"Yes, but I hate having you wait on me."

He grunted.

What kind of reply was that? Julie wondered. And she supposed if she thanked him, he'd take exception to that, too.

Using the tray Mojo had carried the food on, Clint served her a sandwich, the can of Diet Pepsi, chips, pickles, and a slice of chocolate cake.

Mojo lounged in the straight-backed chair, his long jeans-covered legs stretched out before him, his lean hands, still holding a can of beer, braced on his middle. He didn't look away from the television when he spoke to Clint. "There's ice in the bucket."

"Oh, no, I like it like this." Julie lifted the Diet Pepsi and took a cautious sip. She felt conspicuous enough as it was. Everyone else drank out of a can, so she would, too.

Clint shook his head. "He means ice for your ankle, not for your drink." He got two towels from the bathroom, folded one to put beneath her leg to keep the bedding dry, and filled the other with ice cubes. With ultimate care, he put it around her swollen ankle. It wasn't very comfortable, but Julie kept her winces and her gasps to herself.

Clint moved to the first aid kit and returned with three small pills. "Here, take these."

"What are they?"

"Two tablets for pain, and an over-the-counter sleeping pill."

Julie hesitated, unsure if she really wanted to sleep. As tired as she felt, she was still wired and anxious and . . . afraid. Sleeping meant nightmares, and she'd had enough of them during her ordeal.

Clint enfolded her hand in his own. "You need sleep, Julie Rose."

He had that implacable look again, and she'd managed to draw more attention from Red and Mojo. She tossed the pills down with a drink of her Pepsi.

Satisfied, Clint put the tray in her lap and went for his own food, settling himself on the opposite bed. The sandwich looked delicious, and Julie dug in, hoping to ignore her own misgivings about the coming night. She tuned out everything other than appeasing her hunger.

She had just finished her last bite of cake when she realized that while the television still played, all three men were watching her instead of it.

Her face warmed as she dabbed her mouth with a napkin and lifted her brows. This was getting ridiculous. "Is something wrong?"

Red shook his head. "You must have an incredible metabolism."

She saw that Clint was still eating, but she'd already cleared her plate. Her face burned even more. "I always eat more when I'm nervous." And for some reason, though she trusted the men, she got more nervous by the second.

Clint said, "You must live a secure life free of worry, then."

Her temper frayed. She felt so frazzled, she needed a reason to release the tension. Clint made a great big solid target. "Is that another crack about me being skinny?"

He looked surprised at her waspish tone. A reluctant grin seemed to catch him unawares. "Yeah, I suppose it is."

Well! He'd actually admitted it! Now what?

Forestalling her response to that, Mojo got up with an elaborate stretch and turned off the television. "I'm gone."

Red groaned. "Same here. I'm dead on my feet."

Clint popped his last bite in his mouth. "Give me a second to shower." He topped off the garbage with his paper plates, picked up his duffel bag, and strolled into the adjoining room without a word to Julie.

Her heart sank, and the fear she'd been trying to ignore blossomed.

Red and Mojo moved around her, taking her tray, locking the deadbolt on the door. Mojo checked the ice in the towel, replaced it, then bid her good night with a mere nod of his head.

Red paused in the doorway. "You need anything else?"

She needed company.

But she couldn't admit that to him. She'd look weak and silly, and besides, the sun would be up in a few hours, and she had to let them get some sleep. She shook her head. "Thank you, no."

He smiled. "All right. G'night, then." He flipped off a wall switch, leaving the room dark except for the lamp beside the bed. The shadows seemed to expand and grow, squeezing in around Julie.

The door closed behind Red, and she was alone.

Fighting off an absurd sense of hysteria, she looked around for a distraction—but found none. The silence struck her like a roar; the darkness spread.

Well, she scolded herself, while curling her hands in the sheets, *what did you expect, Julie Rose? That they'd all sleep in here with you?*

Now, that'd be a scandal that'd send Uncle Drew through the roof. Julie Rose, sleeping with three men. She could just imagine the conniption he'd have.

When she realized her own thoughts, she frowned in disgust because Clint now had her calling herself by both names. *Way to go, Julie. You're definitely losing it.*

Forcing herself to move, she leaned up in bed and removed the painful ice pack. There was still some swelling around her ankle, but she'd manage. Evidently, she had no choice. She couldn't start believing in boogeymen now, just because she'd had a bad experience.

She was a grown woman, not a child, and she would not be more of a burden on these wonderful men than necessary.

As drained as she felt, they had to be exhausted, too. They'd probably been called as soon as Robert knew she was missing. Petie had told her the ransom note was sent to Robert immediately.

Her head throbbed with unanswered questions and her own sense of desolation, so Julie knew she wouldn't sleep. She slid her legs off the side of the bed, then hopped—with some pain—to the dresser. She found the lotion and the toothbrush and toothpaste Red had purchased for her, resting among a colorful sundress, flip-flop sandals, and more panties. It took only a few minutes to brush her teeth and smooth her skin with the lotion.

And still she was antsy.

Despite the pill Clint had given her, she resigned herself to a sleepless night. Leaving the bathroom light on to chase away some of the demons, she crawled back into the bed and propped herself up against the headboard with the sheet pulled to her chin. She found the television remote and turned the set on, keeping the volume off so she wouldn't disturb the others. Without cable, it was difficult to find a channel, but she finally located an old black-and-white western.

It beat staring at the walls, and it beat her own turbulent thoughts.

Clint cracked the door open just to check on her and saw her huddled in a tense ball on the bed. Her hands gripped the remote so tightly, he wondered that it hadn't cracked. The television was on, but she stared beyond it, her eyes big and dark and haunted, her soft mouth pinched tight.

Well, hell.

He'd taken his shower in record time and

shaved so fast he had three nicks for his trouble. He'd worried about her and, strangely enough, hadn't wanted to leave her alone with Red and Mojo. Not that he didn't trust them, but if Julie Rose got upset and needed to be held, he wanted to be the one to hold her.

Not any other man. Not even his best friends.

"Hey." He spoke in a soft whisper so he wouldn't startle her.

She jerked, looking up at him in shock. She swallowed convulsively. "I thought . . . I thought you went to bed." Her voice was a high whisper, filled with a barely suppressed panic that she couldn't hide. Not from him.

Her eyes, watchful and wary, tracked Clint as he sauntered into the room and closed the door behind him. This worrying crap was for the birds. He hated it. And if he didn't want to worry, then there was only one thing to do.

He stopped beside the bed, leaned down, and pried the remote from her stiff fingers. He switched off the television, then went to the bathroom and turned out the light.

"What are you doing?" The words were shrill in her uncertainty.

Clint hadn't bothered with a shirt, donning only clean shorts and jeans before coming to her. Now he pushed the jeans down and off and tossed them to the other bed.

Julie Rose stared so hard, he felt burned— but he ignored her attention the same way he'd ignored so many other things. He pulled back the sheets, slid into the bed, and patted her hip. "Move over."

Breathless, she scrambled quickly out of his way. "Clint?"

"Shh. Let's get some sleep, babe, okay?" He flipped off the bedside lamp, and the room was thrown mostly into darkness. Where the curtains didn't quite meet over the window, a single beam of moonlight intruded, not quite touching the bed. Clint could see Julie Rose's eyes shining in the darkness, and he could feel her nervousness feathering against him like the wings of a trapped butterfly.

"You're . . . you're sleeping with me?"

The hopefulness in her voice contradicted the appalled expression he was sure she wore. "I'm sleeping with you."

He stretched out in the bed and tugged her into the cradle of his body, her bottom to his lap, her back to his chest. Deliberately, he had one arm under her head, the other resting across her waist, enfolding her, protecting her.

She lay rigid, her breath coming too fast. It felt like hugging a skinny pole. "Relax, Julie Rose."

A shiver ran through her, but not from the air-conditioning. This room was moderately warm, especially compared to the room the other men slept in. Her fingers fretted the blanket, and her feet kept shifting.

Finally, she whispered, "You knew I didn't want to be alone, didn't you?"

"I knew."

She squirmed a bit more, and Clint had to bite back a groan as her soft rump pushed against his groin. He flattened his hand on her belly to still her.

"What will the others say?"

"Red and Mojo?"

The top of her head bumped his chin when she nodded.

"They know me."

She twittered a nervous laugh. "Meaning, they know you're honorable?"

Right. Honor was a sketchy thing, meaning different things to different people—or so he'd learned. "They know I'd never take advantage of you."

They'd also know the torture of sleeping with a sexy woman whom he couldn't touch. They'd give him hell about it later, ribbing him, but they wouldn't say anything in front of Julie Rose.

Minutes stretched by, and Clint hoped she was falling asleep. He knew she wasn't when she touched his hand that rested on her stomach. "You saw me."

She'd said that in the bathroom, too, so apparently it preyed on her mind. He intuitively knew what she meant, but asked anyway. "When?"

"Back at the cabin, when my gown was torn." He could hear her breathing. "You saw my breast."

Her delicate fingers were busy tracing his, from his knuckles to his fingertips and back again. Though he doubted she realized it, the erotic imagery was so vivid it made him nuts. He'd love to feel her soft fingers on his cock, tracing it the same way.

Shit.

Clint caught her hand and pinned it to her stomach beneath his. He could almost feel her mind working. "Yeah, I saw you."

"What did you think? When you saw me, I mean."

She asked the strangest questions. "A lot of things."

"Like what?"

He sighed. "Julie Rose."

"What?"

Knowing she wouldn't give up, Clint said, "I thought about killing all four of them. I thought about what I was going to do when I found the guy who'd hired them to take you." He gave her a squeeze. "Mostly I thought about getting you safe."

"Oh." A load of disappointment filled that one single word.

"And I thought that you were far too pretty and petite to be mauled by those animals."

She held silent for a few moments, then teasing, she whispered, "You thought about throwing up, too."

"Brat." Her silent laughter could be felt, and some of her tension eased. "No. I don't think about that. It just happens."

"Did you think I looked pitiful? Or pathetic?" She made that sound like the worst thing imaginable.

"Pathetic?" He grunted. "You'd just spit on Petie as if you weren't tied and helpless," he reminded her. "I thought you looked very brave." Foolishly so. He'd moved to put himself in front of her before Petie could retaliate, which Clint had known he would. "I ignored your nakedness, Julie Rose, because it wasn't important. Getting you safe was."

She wiggled again, but quickly stilled. Her breath caught and held. She trembled.

It was a stupid question, but still he asked it. "What's the matter now?"

Her voice dropped with shyness, with something more. She spoke so low he could barely hear her. "You're . . . well, you have a . . ."

Hard-on. Didn't he know it. "Yeah, but I'm ignoring that, too."

She made a choking sound and teased, "Because it's unimportant?"

"Because it doesn't mean anything. I'd have to be dead to not have a boner right now, but I'd have to be a major bastard to want to do anything about it. You don't need to be afraid of me."

He thought he might have heard her snicker, but wasn't sure.

"No, I'm not afraid."

"Can you sleep, then?"

"Not yet."

Clint started to groan, but caught the sound in time.

"You feel awfully big."

Hell. Normally he enjoyed it when women

noticed his size. But not now. He damn sure wouldn't discuss it with Julie Rose. "Listen . . ."

"Do you rescue people for a living?"

A change of topic. He didn't know if he should be relieved or annoyed. "Used to. These days I'm mostly a retrieval agent."

"What does that mean?"

Clint carefully masked all emotion. "A repo man. People stop paying on property, I take it back for businesses."

"Oh. Is it dangerous?"

Instead of disdain in her voice, he heard fascination.

"Sometimes. Depends on how expensive the item is, and how determined someone is to keep it, even if he hasn't paid for it."

"What kind of things do you repossess?"

"Anything. Everything. Most recently we took back a two hundred thousand–dollar directional drill. It's a big, awkward piece of machinery, so even after locating it, getting it back wasn't easy."

"Did you have to beat anyone up?"

His mouth quirked at the way she asked that, as if she'd enjoy a gory fight story. "No. Not that time."

"Oh."

He should have had this damn conversation sitting up, with the lights on. But he'd honestly thought she would sleep. She had to be exhausted, and she'd taken the pill. It wasn't strong, but she was so slightly built, it should have had some effect on her.

"What do your parents think of your work?"

"I don't have parents."

She twisted her head back to look at him. "Well, for heaven's sake, everyone has parents."

Clint shrugged. "Not me. Not anymore. My mother left when I was a kid, and Dad died from lung cancer when I was almost eighteen."

"I'm sorry." She resettled herself. "My mother passed away when I was young. It was just me and my father."

Clint gave her a squeeze of sympathy. No little girl should be without her mother.

He could almost hear her chewing over her thoughts before she asked, "Were you close with your father?"

Thinking back, Clint said, "He worked a lot, but I don't have any complaints. He kept me fed and dressed, and we had a decent house."

"I bet he'd be proud of you now."

Clint lifted his head to see her. "For being a repo agent?"

"It's an honorable job requiring a lot of skill."

"How do you know?"

"Logic tells me that you couldn't hire just anyone to retrieve equipment of that value. You'd need someone qualified and very capable. But actually, I meant saving people. I'm here now, so you must still do rescues sometimes, too?"

He didn't want to share his entire life, so he settled on saying, "When the pay is good enough."

That was a partial lie; he'd never turned down a job, because the minute he knew someone needed his help, he felt driven to try to give it. Dumb as it was, he always got too involved. Even the episode two years past hadn't taught him his lesson.

"You've rescued women before?"

Memories intruded, ugly and hurtful. He pushed them aside. "Yeah. A few. Mostly it's men, though. And a kid or two."

Several heartbeats passed, then, "Have you ever slept with any other women?"

The workings of the female mind were a thing of wonder. Clint reached up and pinched her chin. "Like I'm sleeping with you? Or do you mean have I had sex with them?"

Not the least intimidated, she half turned toward him. "Have you?" Her gaze searched his in the darkness. "Had sex with them?"

That wasn't what she'd been asking. He'd put the idea in her head and he cursed himself. "No."

"Oh." She turned back around. "Have you slept with them like this?"

"Once before."

"Will you tell me about it?"

Why not? Maybe the story would put her to sleep. "She was a television personality, taken by some rabid fan. By the time we found her, she was injured and too weak to be moved, so I stayed with her, and Red went for help. It was during a damn vicious snowstorm, and it took till the next day for him to get back with doctors. She damn near died on me. I was afraid to be more than an inch away from her."

"She's okay now?"

"Last I heard, yeah. She's since left showbiz, married, and has a baby, too."

Julie rolled to her back to see him better. Clint was so aware of her, her scent, the soft feel of her skin, her feminine curiosity. It shouldn't have, but it felt right to be with her like this, in the darkness, sharing intimate talk.

Damn. "Go to sleep."

"Where'd you learn to fight?"

"Julie Rose . . ."

She ducked her face into his chest. "I'm sorry. I'll be quiet now so you can sleep."

Meaning she wouldn't sleep. He came up on one elbow over her. "I'll answer this question, but that's all, okay? Then you'll close your eyes and think nice thoughts and go to sleep. Agreed?"

Her small hand flattened on his chest, inciting his lust, pushing his control. "Agreed."

He held her hand to keep her from stroking him. "I learned to fight in a lot of places. The army first, when I was still mostly a kid. I got out and needed more money, so I entered some fighting competitions."

"Boxing?"

"Less structured than that." *Less legal than that.* "You just fight, any way you can, no holds barred. I won a few, lost a few, got a few broken bones, and I learned as I went along. But because it was profitable and I enjoyed it, I eventually paid more attention to techniques. I got better."

"You got good."

"Very good." No bragging, just truth. He was incredibly good and when necessary, lethal.

"So how'd you end up rescuing people?"

"That's a whole new question, but I'll give you the short end of it. Someone who'd watched me fight had need of my help. His daughter was in a cult, and he couldn't get to her. Being a public figure and all, he wanted to avoid scandal, so he couldn't go to the police."

"You saved her?"

"I got her out. Emotionally, it was an ugly place. Her parents had reason to intervene. It took about four weeks before she got back to her old self, and then she contacted me to thank me. She moved back in with her folks and finished up college."

"A job well done."

Julie Rose had a killer smile. The urge to kiss her mouth, to taste that smile and share in her simple happiness, churned inside him. "It happens occasionally."

"More often than not?"

"Thankfully." He touched her cheek and, unable to stop himself, bent to kiss her forehead. Damn it, he *had* to quit doing that. "Now sleep, woman. That's an order."

"All right." This time he went to his back, and Julie cuddled into his side as if she'd been doing so forever. She pillowed her head on his chest and put her arm around him. "Clint?"

He gave an aggrieved groan only partly feigned. She was so soft and warm, so female, that if she didn't go to sleep soon he'd start howling in sexual frustration.

"I'm thinking very nice thoughts. I just wanted you to know." Her serenity seemed to waft around him, and she whispered, "Thank you."

"Anytime."

A few minutes later, her breathing evened into sleep. Clint smiled into the darkness. God, what had he gotten himself into?

And would he ever be able to get out?

Chapter Five

Clint woke slowly, aware that something wasn't quite right. He felt strangely at peace, but then, he'd just had a very restful sleep for the first time in ages. Usually, personal demons plagued him the moment he closed his eyes. But last night, his dreams had been darkly erotic rather than full of menace.

Predictably enough, he had morning wood. He also had his arms full of woman—a slight, pain-in-the-ass woman who had factored into those sexy dreams in a big way.

Against his closed eyelids, Clint detected sunlight coming through the curtains.

Almost at the same time, he felt Julie Rose's body shift against his. Her scent, spicier after the warmth of being cuddled all night, filled his head. Cautiously, he opened one eye.

She wasn't asleep now.

No, Julie Rose was half propped up over him, and she had the top of the covers in her fingertips, lifting, so she could look beneath. At him.

She stared at his lap.

Well. Considering his state, the little darling got an eyeful. Clint didn't know if he should laugh, groan, or take her to her back and kiss her silly.

In a voice still rough and froggy, he whispered, "Hey."

After a small startled yelp, Julie dropped the covers and twisted to face him. "You're awake."

"Guilty." He didn't move. He had one arm behind his head, the other under Julie's waist, and his legs were slightly parted. Her hair was a mess, going every which way, more out of her braids than in, and her cheeks were rosy, her eyes still heavy from sleep.

She looked good. Damn good. Like a woman who'd just been fucked hard—and enjoyed it.

Though his heart pounded in heavy beats, Clint merely watched her, waiting to see if she'd make excuses for what she'd been doing.

She cleared her throat. "I guess you caught me."

"Is that right?"

Mouth going a little crooked in chagrin, she admitted, "I was sneaking a peek."

That threw him for only a moment; she was too damn honest for her own good. "No kidding?" He half smiled. "I never would have guessed."

She watched him so intently, Clint felt naked.

She cleared her throat again. "I should apologize, I suppose."

Clint shrugged.

For a few seconds, she worried her bottom lip, then huffed out a breath. "I've never seen anyone as impressive as you, so I was curious. I woke up, but you were still asleep, and the covers were sort of tented . . ."

"I do understand." He cleared his throat. "No big deal."

"Is that a sexual pun?" Then, before he could reply to that, though God knew he had no idea what to say, she added, "You have some scars."

She said it as if confiding a secret. "I know."

Her cool fingertips touched the side of his nose, moved to his eyebrow, his chin.

Uncomfortable with her tender touch, Clint felt compelled to explain. "I broke my nose twice fighting. The second time I didn't bother going to the doc. I just put it back in place myself. It shows."

Julie touched his nose again. Her eyes were big and dark and velvety. "It looks fine. You have a strong, handsome nose."

It was crooked as hell, and they both knew it.

"How'd you get this scar on your eyebrow?"

"A kick. It split the skin."

"Ouch." She trailed her fingers over his upper lip, making him a little nuts. "And this one?"

Her voice went husky and deep, and Clint wanted to take her fingers in his mouth, suck on them a little, tease her a lot . . . but he didn't want her keeling over on him again.

"Why do you ask?" His voice was rougher now, too, and it had nothing to do with sleep because, thanks to Julie Rose, he was wide awake.

"Aren't most women curious?"

Clint shook his head. "No. Fact is, no other woman's come right out and asked me about my scars."

"Really?" She seemed genuinely surprised by that. "Why not?"

She stared at his armpit while asking that question, confounding Clint. "I suppose they wanted to get laid and didn't want to offend me."

Her gaze softened. She reached out, trailed her fingertips over the exposed underside of his arm, along his biceps down, then dropped her hand. "Am I offending you?"

"Look at me when you talk to me, Julie Rose."

She took her time obeying that order, allowing her gaze to linger on his upper arm, his chest, his throat, and finally his face.

Clint sank deeper by the second. Convictions, even honor, faded beneath a fusion of lust and caring. He shouldn't touch her. But God how he wanted to. "Just what the hell's going on here, Julie Rose?"

Her expression turned prim. "I don't know what you mean."

"Yeah, you do. Last night you were shaken, so I stayed with you. But I was careful not to get too familiar. I was careful not to offend you. After everything you've been through, I know the last thing you want is my attention."

Her brows drew down. "I like your attention."

The woman could learn a little discretion. Her upfront honesty wasn't making this any easier for him. "I mean my sexual attention, Julie Rose." She continued to watch him, so Clint made it real plain. "You don't want me coming on to you, grabbing at you, or trying to get in your pants—"

"I'm not wearing pants."

"You think I haven't noticed that?" Christ, she was going to make one comment too many, and he'd lose it. He couldn't be more aware of her slim bare legs, or the fact that no more than a nightshirt and panties shielded her.

"I don't want to be grabbed."

Of course she didn't. Clint tried to hide his frustration because grabbing her right now seemed like one hell of an idea. At least it did to his less-logical body parts; his brain knew she wasn't ready for that yet. Hell, he wasn't ready for it, either. He never, ever, got physically involved with the women he rescued.

Up till now, that resolution hadn't been a big deal because truthfully, up till now, *until Julie Rose,* he hadn't even wanted to.

Now he did. In a big way.

He was trying to convince himself to let it go when she said, "I like when you touch me, though." Her hand opened on his chest. "And I like touching you, too. You're solid and safe and very warm."

A man could only take so much, Clint told himself, and she more than begged for it.

She pulled the covers down, farther and farther until the top of his boxers showed, leaving his abdomen—rigid with restraint—on display. "What about this scar?" Her small, soft hand, cool against his fevered skin, traced the scar that ran from his ribs to his hipbone.

Strangling on his own lust, Clint growled, "A knife wound."

"I'm sorry. It looks so painful."

Pain was lying in bed with Julie Rose while she innocently checked him out. But at least her comment gave him a different path for his thoughts. "Might've hurt at the time, I don't remember." All he really remembered was pure, red-hot rage that the weasel he'd confronted had dared to pull a blade on him. Clint had lost his temper, and his control. He'd beat the man so badly that he'd spent well over a week in the hospital before he could be questioned by the cops for domestic violence.

It was the case that had nearly ruined Clint, and not just professionally.

His morbid thoughts got shattered when Julie lowered her head and lightly brushed her lips over the old wound. She'd put herself into a damned suggestive position, with her head over his lap, her lips way too damn close to where he'd really like them to be.

His imagination had no problem picturing the covers and his boxers long gone.

Her silky, lopsided braid trailed over his skin,

and her breath was about the most erotic thing he'd felt in too many months.

Fighting the urge to take her, right here, right now, he stiffened.

Julie lifted her head. Her cheeks were flushed and she skimmed her tongue over her lips, as if tasting him. "Did I hurt you?"

God, she looked as turned on as he felt. "No." Her hair was more out of the braid than in, and Clint tucked a long hank of brown silk behind her ear. "You didn't hurt me."

"Then do you mind if I kiss you?"

Ah, hell. That did it. Forget his self-made rules. Forget caution. One little kiss couldn't hurt, right? It wasn't like he'd let things get out of hand.

It wasn't like he'd strip her naked and crawl between her slim thighs and sink into her . . . No. He wouldn't do that.

His mind made up, Clint leisurely brought his arms down so that he could clasp her waist. "Come here, Julie Rose."

She stilled, but when Clint eased her over his chest, she didn't fight him. Her legs tangled with his. Her soft belly flattened against his boner.

All breathy and excited and maybe even hopeful, she whispered, "What are you going to do?"

Slowly shaking his head, Clint said, "Not a thing. But you're going to kiss me." When he had her settled atop him, he released her and stacked both his hands behind his head so she wouldn't feel threatened or overwhelmed, and so he wouldn't get carried away.

No matter how badly he needed her, he wouldn't allow himself to forget what she'd been through. He wouldn't let himself forget that he'd been hired to rescue her, or that he'd only known her a few hours.

Julie breathed hard. "I was already kissing you."

"Try kissing me on the mouth."

Her chest rose and fell with her uneven breaths.

"Come on," Clint taunted. "You know you want to."

Julie licked her lips. "I do, but . . . This isn't very proper."

And sneaking a peek at his boner while he slept was? He didn't voice that thought because he didn't want to embarrass her. Instead he said, "So? I heard you weren't all that proper anyway."

Her face paled at what she saw as an insult, even as her eyes darkened with anger. She was such an intriguing contradiction.

"Who told you that?" Julie demanded, stiffening her arms so that she loomed above him. "Robert?"

"Yeah." Julie Rose might be a spinsterish schoolteacher, but when she got riled, she bloomed with passion.

"And you believed him?"

"No." Clint wanted to kiss the sour expression off her face. "Your friend Bobby is a liar and a cheat, and you're better off without him. But you, Julie Rose, have this mischievous twinkle in your eyes that tells me you enjoy being a rebel every now and then."

"Oh." Her expression softened, and a nervous smile appeared. She leaned down and kissed him very gently. "That's true."

"I know."

She stared at his mouth. "I was thinking . . ."

"About?"

"About the plans I'd made."

So now she wanted to talk instead of kiss? Fickle woman. "What plans might those be?"

Her gaze lifted to his. "I wanted to start living, to make up for lost time and have fun and just be me."

Lord help him. "Is that right?"

"Yes. I recently resigned from my job at a stuffy private school and signed on at a public school in Visitation, North Carolina. It's much more . . . stimulating."

He had a feeling the last thing Julie Rose needed was more stimulation.

"I was in the process of looking for a place to live there, away from relatives and people who knew me in only one way."

"As a prim and proper schoolteacher?"

"Exactly. I was going to really cut loose and do all the things I'd never had a chance to do."

"Then you got kidnapped?" Clint wondered if the two were related, if her plans for a new lifestyle had left someone—maybe good old Robert—feeling threatened.

"Yes." She looked at his mouth again and leaned a little closer.

Clint didn't know if she planned to give him another chaste kiss or the killer kind he craved.

"Jamie warned me that things would happen, that I should be careful. But I didn't believe him."

That bald statement had Clint scowling. He turned his head before her mouth could meet his. "Jamie? Who the hell is Jamie? Another man in your life?"

"Jamie Creed." She caught his face and held him still, then kissed him, a little longer this time but still with closed lips, a nice, tidy, dry kiss when what he wanted was the wet, deep kind, with a lot of tongue play and some moaning thrown in.

But this was her show, and he'd go at her pace if it killed him.

She lifted her head and sighed. "Jamie isn't really in anyone's life. He's something of a hermit, very withdrawn and mysterious. He lives up on this tall mountain in Visitation."

Disgusted, both with his escalating need and the admiration in her tone, Clint said, "You sound smitten."

"Most of the women who meet Jamie are. But truthfully, he scares me a little. Jamie often knows things before they happen. He definitely knew about my kidnapping."

Clint's muscles pulled tight. "The hell you say? Maybe I should talk to him."

"It wouldn't do you any good. Jamie can't be intimidated, and he can't give iron details."

With evil relish, Clint said, "I could make him give details."

She patted his chest, then began smoothing her hand over his left pectoral muscle. "Down, boy. It's not like that. Jamie's a good man. A kind man. He's just very different."

"Different how?" If she didn't stop stroking him, Clint wouldn't be able to stay in control.

"He has feelings—like premonitions or visions—about things."

"And he had a premonition about you?"

She nodded. "He warned me, but I didn't listen. I didn't want to listen because I'd just broken things off with Robert and I'd made the decision to start living the way I wanted."

"What about your Uncle Drew?"

She put both hands on him, feeling his skin, her fingers tunneling into his chest hair. "I told him to keep his stupid money."

"Your money."

She shrugged. "Whatever. He uses it to try to control me, and I can't stand that anymore."

"No," Clint agreed, and he could have sworn he felt his heart actually softening. "You wouldn't like being controlled."

"I don't want money that's doled out to me like I'm a child. I get by on my teacher's salary, and the rest just isn't important. Not to me."

He believed her. As to everything else she'd said . . . He decided he'd meet this Jamie Creed fellow and draw his own conclusions about what he knew and what he divined—*what bull crap*—before he let Julie go.

And thinking of letting her go . . . Clint lifted a brow. "Are you going to kiss me the way you really want to, or are you going to talk me to death?"

She frowned down at him.

Clint thought she'd deny it, but he should have known better. Julie Rose had guts and a healthy curiosity—a dangerous combination for a guy trying to resist her.

"I did make a vow to live a little."

"Yeah, you did. You can start by giving me a real kiss." And with any luck, he'd survive it.

She stared at him for an excruciatingly long time before leaning down and putting her mouth to his again.

Just that, the simple press of her lips. She didn't move, didn't open her mouth. She didn't even seal the kiss much. Her lips barely touched his, hovering there, light and tentative and sexy as hell.

Clint smiled that such an innocent touch could affect him so much. Against her mouth, he said, "You're not really into this, are you?"

He felt her indrawn breath. "You don't like it?"

"Sure, I do." He held her gaze with his. "Do you?"

Determination showed in the set of her shoulders. *"Yes."*

She took his mouth again, this time with her soft lips opened, and she gave him a little tongue: a flick here, a lick there. Absurd, how quickly she got him primed.

Panting now, she moved back and waited.

"Not bad," Clint rumbled.

Her eyes were heavy, her face warm. Staring at his mouth, she whispered, "You taste so very nice."

"You can taste me anywhere you want to,

honey." The second the words left his mouth, he groaned. *Damn it.* Clint decided he had to have masochistic tendencies for putting that idea in her head.

His arms strained with the need to hold her, and he laced his fingers tight to contain himself.

Her eyes flared. She drew two deep breaths, then whispered, "I think I'd like that."

Jesus. He waited, his muscles coiled tight enough to break, his eyes closed in an effort to shut her out.

"I . . . I was just thinking."

Maybe she'd save him by backing out. "You decided this is a bad idea?"

"Oh, no. Just the opposite." She cupped his face and wiggled against him in a tantalizing way. "You said I'll be with you for a week?"

It was a dangerous game to play, but he couldn't call a halt. "That's right." His eyes narrowed. "At least a week."

Her hips pressed in, wringing a growl from deep in his throat.

"I trust you, Clint Evans. I like you and I find you very attractive."

Shit, shit, shit. That sounded too serious by half, and a lot like hero worship, which wasn't uncommon under the circumstances. He'd let things get way out of hand, and now he had to set her straight. "Listen, Julie Rose . . ."

Before he could finish, she blurted, "May I experiment with you for the time that we're together?"

Clint cursed. He was already on the brink and now, with her suggestive question, he felt ready to implode.

As if to convince him, she rushed into more speech. "Nothing too risqué, I promise. But we're going to be together anyway, correct? And you don't seem to mind kissing me."

She sounded so unsure of herself, Clint couldn't lie to her about it. "Kissing you is not a problem, Julie Rose."

Her face lit up. "Wonderful. So there's no reason some heinous kidnappers should interrupt my plans to start over, now, is there?"

"No." But she sure as hell shouldn't be starting over with him.

"And being with you is convenient."

"Convenient?" Why that pissed him off, he couldn't say for sure.

She nodded. "Because you're so trustworthy."

"You don't know me well enough to make that call."

"And you're very sexy, too."

Under the circumstances, he didn't feel all that complimented. "Right."

"You see? It's the perfect opportunity for me to have fun, to live my life to the fullest." Her smile was falsely bright and full of hope. "My plans don't have to be interrupted at all—as long as you're willing to cooperate."

She'd put him in one hell of a position. If he knew Julie Rose—and Clint figured, even with such short acquaintance, he knew her better than Robert or Drew did—then she'd be doing her experimenting one way or another. If not with him, then with some other bozo.

And that thought burned like acid.

Despite what she'd just been through, she didn't shy away from him. Being in bed with him, knowing he was turned on, hadn't frightened her at all. Hell, she'd been bold enough to take advantage of him in his sleep.

Still, she was naturally reserved, not at all like the outrageous flirt Robert had described. He had to play this carefully, protecting her feelings without crossing the line.

Alert to any signs of withdrawal, Clint brought his arms down and around her. She was so slight, so fragile against him, that the lust got tempered with protectiveness. He'd rather engage in another knife fight than hurt her feelings.

With one hand, he cupped the back of her head, urging her closer. "I'll cooperate," he promised her. At least as far as kissing went. When he gave her the full brunt of his lust, she'd naturally back away on her own. He'd show her how a man wanted a woman. He'd show her a man's greed, his power.

He'd kiss her the way he'd wanted to kiss her ever since first seeing her picture in Robert's library, and he'd probably shock her down to her proper little schoolteacher toes in the process.

"Thank you," Julie whispered, and then his mouth was on hers, hot and hard, his tongue sinking deep, his hands keeping her close so she couldn't retreat.

But she didn't even try to pull away. Her

mouth opened, her fingers clenched in his hair, and she moaned.

Julie didn't back away. No, sir. In fact, she nearly pushed him over the edge.

Julie knew she was smart. And she was definitely educated. So how come she hadn't known a kiss could be so . . . *incredible?*

As Clint's tongue curled with hers, hot and wet and hungry, she heard herself moan.

She, Julie Rose, moaning out loud.

It was wonderful. She didn't even care if she was too noisy.

Apparently, neither did Clint, given that his erection flexed beneath her belly and he deepened the kiss even more.

It was so nice the way he held her close, not grabbing at her the way Robert used to, but *feeling* her, touching her all along her back, her upper arms, her hair, her nape.

Her bottom.

He groaned as his hands settled around her backside, kneading, squeezing. Surprised and aroused, Julie stiffened her arms, pushing her upper body up and away from his so she could see his beautiful face. But the position only drove her lower body into closer contact with his, reminding her of his size.

A hot bubble seemed to expand inside her, filling her up. Breathless, seeing Clint through a haze, she managed to explain, "I haven't seen many erections."

Clint's eyes were narrowed, his cheekbones flushed. He gripped her hips and ground himself up against her. "Is that a hint?"

"*No.* I mean . . ." She closed her eyes and moved against him, enjoying the thrill that gave her. On a sigh, she said, "I don't have much experience with size and all that."

He hesitated, appearing torn. Then his hands slid to the backs of her thighs and spread her legs so that she straddled his lap. His erection touched her in *just* the right place, stealing her breath, making her skin burn and her stomach tumble.

"I'm a little bigger than average," Clint rumbled in a low, rough voice. "But I'm not so big that I'd hurt you."

He held her in such an intimate position, Julie could barely speak. If they were both naked, he could be inside her right now. Picturing that increased the heat, until she felt feverish.

But she wanted to make one thing perfectly clear. "I told you that I trust you. To protect me and to keep me safe."

He went still. His hands loosened on her hips. "Yes, I'll keep you safe."

Julie moved against him. "I know you would never hurt me."

He cursed low.

"Touch me again, please?"

His jaw locked. "I shouldn't."

"I really need you to." She couldn't bear it if he stopped now. "Please?"

He hesitated, his gaze locked on hers, and finally he dragged his hands up her legs, under her nightshirt, under the elastic leg bands of her panties and onto her naked flesh. Julie caught her breath. His palms were hot, a little rough as they cuddled her.

Staring into his eyes as he stroked her was both exciting and deeply intimate.

Feeling brazen and sexy, Julie whispered, "More?"

Clint's expression was so hard, it was almost frightening. His eyes burned, and he looked furious, hot, torn. Still holding her gaze, he pressed his right hand lower, between her legs. Through gritted teeth, he ordered, "Open up, Julie Rose. Spread your legs more for me."

Such talk shocked and thrilled her. Heart pounding, she adjusted her legs, and felt one thick finger glide over her, press in—

"Hey." A rap sounded on the door. "You guys up yet?"

At the verbal intrusion, Julie screeched, launching herself to the side of Clint. In her haste, she forgot that his hands were trapped beneath her panties. She frantically freed herself and darted under the covers.

Clint groaned, muttered a few colorful expletives, then snapped, "Give us a minute."

"Sure thing," said Red. And even Julie couldn't mistake the note of amusement in his voice.

The room fell into a strained silence, and Julie lowered the covers only to find Clint on his side, watching her. Even now, with her heart still in her throat and her face hot with embarrassment, she noticed how incredibly sexy he looked stretched out on the bed.

She cleared her throat. "I'm sorry. I think that was just a nervous reaction."

For long moments Clint didn't say anything. He didn't smile, didn't show any softness at all. "I had no business touching you like that."

Julie's heart slowed, and her stomach cramped. "But I liked it."

He shook his head. He had the most incredible eyes she'd ever seen, heated one moment, cool the next. Now they looked very resigned. "If I had any sense," Clint murmured low, "I'd stay the hell away from you."

Panic hit her, both from the idea of being alone, without Clint's security, and at the thought of losing him so soon. "You can't." She tried and failed to keep her voice calm. Her heart hammered hard, and her lips quivered. "You promised to protect me."

His gaze traveled over her, from her fists clenching the top of the blanket, down the length of her well-concealed body. "I know." His attention came back to her face. "But who the hell's going to protect you from me?"

He was such a good, honorable man. In a whisper, Julie said, "I don't want to be protected from you."

He touched her lips, very absorbed in thought before dropping his hand. "You don't know what you want, Julie Rose. Hell, you're probably still dazed from yesterday."

"I'm not an idiot. And I'm not that fragile."

One side of Clint's mouth lifted. "Yeah, baby, you are."

He said that so sweetly, with so much understanding, Julie couldn't take exception. She just sighed. "When Jamie told me my life was about to change, I never imagined it'd change this much, and I never, in my whole life, imagined a man like you."

Without a word, Clint pushed out of the bed. He paced away, but before he reached the door he turned and stalked back to her. Bending down, one big fist on either side of her hips, he growled, "One question."

Julie reared back. "What?"

"When you were doing all this planning on cutting loose, who the hell did you intend to fuck?"

Chapter Six

Annoyed and taken off guard, Julie swatted at him. "Your vocabulary is atrocious."

"Is that right?" He didn't move away. "If you can't say it, angel, how the hell are you going to do it?"

Julie studied his expression—and knew he wanted to scare her off. It annoyed her enough that she flattened both hands on his chest and shoved. She would have made a regal exodus from the bed, except that Clint didn't budge. Even using all her strength, she couldn't push him back a single inch.

"Quit trying to intimidate me."

He snorted. "If I was trying, you'd probably faint again."

"That was from hunger, not fear!"

Clint rolled his eyes and gave her a little space.

Not much, but at least she could move without bumping her nose into his.

He still glared at her. "Now, answer my question."

Refusing to let him see how affected she felt, Julie lifted her chin. "I thought we'd make love, not . . . the other."

Aggrieved, Clint snarled, "Not that question. I meant, who did you plan to *make love with* before you met me?"

"Oh." Julie shrugged. "I don't know."

Wearing a sneer, Clint said, "One of your buddies from Visitation? The spook, Jamie, or maybe the preacher's twin?"

"Bryan?" Julie was amazed he remembered all the men she'd mentioned. "Oh, no. Bryan's married already, too. In fact, all the really hunky guys in Visitation are married. Well, except Jamie, but I don't think I could even find his home up on the mountain, much less talk him into—"

Clint's eyes narrowed. "*Hunky* guys?"

"Whew, yes." She fanned her face. "Visitation is practically overrun with dominant males. The testosterone hangs so thick in the air, it's a wonder the women don't all go insane."

"You don't say."

Julie nodded. "It was bad enough when Joe Winston first showed up. Now, Joe's a man with a capital M. A self-proclaimed bad boy and pretty dangerous in a very sexy way . . ."

"Are you trying to piss me off, Julie Rose?"

His voice went all soft and low in a way that told Julie he didn't like the subject matter. She patted his chest, trying to soothe him. "Joe married Luna, and they moved to Visitation. He's not available. Bryan sort of followed him there because some maniac wanted to kill Joe, but together they got the miscreant and put him away."

"A killer?"

"He was no match for Joe and Bryan. They're both much like you, except for the throwing up part. But what I mean is, they're very capable and full of bravado, and they seem to think they're invincible, and somehow they convince everyone else of that. Except maybe for Scott, the local deputy who's pretty sexy in his own right. He lent a hand in capturing the man who was after Joe, and the pimp who tried to get Shay, and the crazed lunatic who tried to kill Cyn."

"Did you say you moved to Peyton Place?"

Julie smiled. "Actually, Visitation is a very peaceful place, full of wonderful people."

"You've certainly convinced me."

"Now, don't be sarcastic."

"Was there a point to this story?"

"Yes. I was trying to explain how so much masculine perfection ended up in Visitation. You see, once Bryan visited the area, he kept coming back. It seems most people do that. There's just something about Visitation that makes you want to settle there."

"Could be all the killers and pimps and crazy people."

She laughed. "Naturally, when Bryan decided to stay, his twin brother, Bruce, followed. They're very close."

Clint moved away from her, sat on the side of the bed, and put his head in his hands. The pose wreaked of masculinity. His broad back was bare, thick with muscle and divided by a deep furrow. His shoulders were bunched with frustration. His derriere in the snug boxers looked very fine.

She could spend a happy week just looking at him.

Without raising his head, Clint said, "You're staring a hole through me, Julie Rose."

"Oh. Sorry." Trying to give an accurate depiction of Visitation and the denizens, Julie continued. "Jamie was there before any of them, although I don't think he was born in Visitation. There's something very mysterious about his past—"

"That's enough."

"It is?"

Clint looked over his shoulder at her. "I asked you who were you going to sleep with?"

"You."

His mouth flattened with annoyance. "Before me, damn it."

She scooted across the bed until she could kneel beside Clint. She liked being close to him; it made her feel somehow more confident. "That's the thing. Before I met you, I wasn't sure I'd find anyone. I'm not a prude, but I would not sleep with a man unless I found him very appealing on many levels."

Clint stared at her. Hard.

Trying to feel encouraged despite his lack of response, Julie ticked off what she considered his best qualities. "You're strong and very capable, but not cruel."

"I can be cruel."

"Only when necessary, I'm sure."

Clint sighed.

"I feel safe with you." She smiled and put a hand on his shoulder. "You're very honorable."

His eyes went cold and distant, shutting her out. "Don't be naïve."

"I'm not."

"Like hell. At least see me for what I am, Julie Rose."

As a teacher, Julie had dealt with enough insecure children to know vulnerability when she saw it. Beneath her hand, Clint's shoulder had gone rock hard, giving away his tension. "You're a good man."

He shoved to his feet, rejecting her touch. "I'm a mercenary."

"You still saved me."

"Because I was *paid* to."

She shook her head. She didn't believe that was the only reason. She wouldn't believe it.

"Shit." Clint rubbed his face. "Stop looking like I've slapped you. I just want you to see the truth."

"You're being crude again."

"I *am* crude. Crude and unscrupulous, and ten times more dangerous than your buddy, Joe."

"Joe might be dangerous, but he's also honorable. Just like you."

His hands curled into fists. "No, goddammit, I'm not."

"Stop yelling at me."

He looked ready to detonate. "I'm trying to make you understand what a mistake it'd be to—"

Another rap sounded on the door. Red cleared his throat. "You two planning to emerge soon or what? We're starving over here."

Clint turned away from her. "Get dressed, Julie Rose. You've got ten minutes." And without another word, he stormed through the door, but shut it very softly behind him.

He wasn't that far away, and Julie still felt abandoned. Rejected. Even lost. She sat there for a full two minutes, not moving, hardly breathing. He'd been so . . . sweet, so caring—right up until she wanted to care back.

She went over their conversation, everything they'd done, and tried to order the events into some sort of rationale. But no matter how she tried, she didn't understand him. He wanted her, she couldn't be wrong about that.

Whatever reasons Clint had for trying to warn her off, her reasons for wanting to know him better were stronger. She wasn't a woman to turn tail and run at the first sign of difficulty. One way or another, she'd get Clint Evans figured out.

He might be a hard-edged, fully capable mercenary, but *she* was a schoolteacher, and that meant she had the advantage.

Clint felt like putting a hole in the wall as he stalked past Mojo and Red. Because they were friends, they didn't heed his dark look as most sane men would have. No, if anything, they showed their annoyance by staring.

"*What?*"

Mojo just continued to glare, but Red got right in his face and hissed, "What the hell is the matter with you?"

Knowing he had it coming, disgusted with himself for letting things get out of hand, Clint crossed his arms over his chest and waited.

"We heard every fucking word, and you," Red accused with a mean but hushed snarl, "were being a complete bastard."

No shit. He'd damn near taken her. If he'd had five minutes more, he'd probably be coming right now, buried deep inside her. "I lost control. It won't happen again."

Red's face pinched up even more. "She *wants* it to happen again."

Doing a double take, totally disbelieving, Clint snapped, "Don't be a fucking idiot."

"It's better than being an abusive jerk."

"Abusive?" Incredulity rang in his voice. He'd walked away, goddammit, when walking away was about the hardest thing he'd done in years.

"We heard you, Clint. You were downright mean to her."

Clint thought his head might explode. "I was trying to clue her in. She's goddamned naïve and—"

"*Keep your voice down.*" Red grabbed his arm and hauled him to the far side of the room, like that afforded any privacy.

Rather than punch one of his best friends, Clint went along.

"She's a real sweet woman, Clint."

Red's quiet words, filled with admiration, rubbed him on the raw. "She's pushy."

"She's smart."

"Not about men."

"You like her."

Clint locked his jaw. "No, I want her."

"Oh, for God's sake." Red leaned around Clint to see Mojo. "Do you believe this bullshit?"

Mojo shook his head in a very pitying way.

Red faced him again. "Listen to me, Clint. That little lady in there"—his finger pointed in the direction of the other door, where he'd left Julie Rose looking as though her favorite puppy had just been run over—"went through hell yesterday, and regardless of how tough she wants to think she is, or what kind of front she puts on, right now, you're her lifeline. Not me, not Mojo. *You.* So quit giving her such a hard time."

Clint bunched his shoulders and braced his feet apart. His eyes narrowed. "So if you'd been her lifeline, you'd be in there fucking her right now?"

Red's face turned nearly purple, and Clint braced himself for an attack.

In a fury-filled whisper, Red said, "You sorry son of a bitch."

Mojo sat up, ready to intercede if necessary.

"Shit." Because Clint didn't want to fight with his friends, he took a step back and ran a hand through his hair. "That was out of line."

"You're damn right."

Knowing his point was valid, Clint said, "But listen to yourself, Red. You're suggesting that after all the trauma she's suffered, I should've given her some jollies in bed, like that'll make everything all right."

Red, too, backed down a little. "You know how women are. Maybe that's what she needs right now to help her settle down."

"For the love . . . If she heard you say that, if any self-respecting woman heard you say that, you'd probably be castrated."

A little uncomfortable, Red shrugged. "It may have escaped your notice, but women are different from men. And as far as that goes, no two women are alike."

Clint looked at Mojo. "Now that he's married, he's an expert on womankind?"

Half smiling, Mojo shrugged.

"I'm serious here, Clint. Whenever Daisy's feeling sad or frazzled, it works with her. Not just the sex part, but the cuddling and stuff. Women like the closeness. It makes them feel more secure, and that little lady in there could use some security."

"I can damn well keep her secure without stepping over the line."

Mojo said, "You already slept with her."

Like he'd ever forget? Holding Julie Rose throughout the night had somehow given him a sense of peace that had been missing from his life for a good long while. Considering he'd known her only hours, the closeness he felt was bizarre—but true all the same. "Right. We *slept*."

"Now she wants more." Red held out his hands. "Where's the harm?"

"You're both morons."

"At least we're not cowards."

Clint jerked around to face Mojo. A muscle ticked in his jaw. "What. Was. That?"

Not the least intimidated, Mojo pushed out of the bed. His obsidian eyes were unflinching, his posture relaxed. "No man scares you, Clint. We know that. But women—"

"Good women," Red clarified.

"—always send you into a tailspin."

Jaw tight, Clint struggled to control his unreasonable anger. "The last *good* woman I tried to help damn near destroyed me. She ruined me financially and came close to landing me in jail."

"This isn't at all the same. That broad had some real problems."

"And you think Julie Rose doesn't?"

"Nothing you can't fix."

Forcing an incredulous laugh, Clint threw up his arms. "I was hired to get her away from the kidnappers, not to *fix* her."

"You weren't hired to sleep with her either," Red pointed out. "Or braid her hair, or help her dress, or any of the other shit you've done. And it's those things that have her thinking a little more is in line."

Clint decided he'd had enough of the ridiculous conversation. Truth was, he hadn't known that many good women. And the ones he thought were had turned quick enough when it mattered most. Julie Rose would probably be no different.

But even as he thought that, he knew it couldn't be true. "If you two were so hell-bent on getting the lady laid, why'd you knock on the door?"

Mojo rolled a shoulder. "Didn't know what you were doing then."

Red nodded. "It wasn't until afterward, when you started giving her hell, that we figured out what we'd interrupted."

And thank God they had, Clint thought. Otherwise they'd probably be telling him to propose. "If we're done dissecting my psyche, can we get on with business?"

Red started to object, but a small tap sounded on the door that divided the two rooms, and a second later, Julie Rose stepped in. She'd brushed her hair into some absurd matronly bun that seemed doubly out of place with the colorful sundress Red had bought her.

It was yellow with splashy pink flowers. The elasticized top fit snug to her small pert breasts, and the skirt fell loose to a few inches below her knees. Her narrow feet were slipped into flat pink sandals.

Shoulders straight, head held high, she carried the shopping bag, filled with her other things, in one hand, and leaned on the doorknob with the other.

Her expression was distant, her gaze flat. She

looked emotionally wounded, her feelings as battered as her body. "I'm ready."

Clint soaked in the sight of her. Her brown eyes wouldn't meet his, and her mouth was pinched. Had she overheard their conversation? Probably.

"How's your ankle?"

She stared at the far wall. "I'll manage."

His eyes narrowed and his muscles felt stiff. "That's not what I asked."

Lifting her chin another notch, she glared at him. "You can see it's still a little swollen, and it's sore, but I can walk on it as long as we move slowly." She gave her attention back to the wall. "I won't be a burden to you today."

Clint struggled with himself, wanting to apologize, wanting to hold her, but knowing it might be best to just let it go. So he stood there like an idiot while Red reassured her, saying, "You weren't a burden," at the same time that Mojo sauntered over to her, went to one knee, and lifted her foot.

Watching her face, Clint saw the way she tried to hide her pain. It infuriated him. "Mojo?"

"She shouldn't be on it." Then, taking both Clint and Julie Rose off guard, Mojo easily lifted her up against his chest and took the two steps to the bed. With infinite care, he set her on the edge of the mattress.

Red poured her a cup of coffee made from the in-room coffee machine. When he looked at Julie Rose, his expression was gentle. "We'll grab some breakfast on the road, but this'll help for now."

Very prim, Julie thanked him and accepted

the disposable cup. Her eyes met Clint's over the rim as she took a small sip.

Just as quickly, she looked away.

Damn it, Clint didn't want the others catering to her. He sure as hell didn't want them touching her and smiling with her . . . He stalked across the room and opened one overnight bag to withdraw the small cell phone. If he kept his mind on business, then maybe he'd get through this.

"Who are you calling?" Julie inquired, and she sounded both suspicious and worried.

"Your fiancé," he replied, deliberately nudging her temper because he could handle anything better than her current hurt, reserved disposition.

In her best teacher's voice, she said, "You must learn to pay closer attention, Clint. Robert is *not* my fiancé." And then, under her breath, "Whether you want him to be or not."

Clint sat in a chair. "He's damn lucky he's not."

"Why?" Julie asked.

And Red, grinning like a fool, said, "Because then Clint would probably kill him."

Since that wasn't too far off the mark, Clint didn't respond. "I need you all to be quiet." Using the cell phone, he dialed in a number.

"What are you doing?"

Red leaned close to Julie—too damn close as far as Clint was concerned—and explained how the phone worked. "Anything Robert has said or done within range of the recorder will be played back for us to hear."

Julie shot an accusing glare at Clint. "You *still* suspect Robert?"

"I suspect everyone. Now hush."

The phone beeped, once, twice. Clint pushed another button, and all conversations from Robert's office began playing back. By setting the phone onto the nightstand and opening the volume, they could all listen.

A male voice, not Robert's, spoke. "Have you found her?"

"Drew! I wasn't expecting you." A few shuffling sounds, then, "I thought you were going to wait for my call."

"I detest waiting. Surely you know something by now?"

"Uh, no. Not yet. But we agreed you'd wait at your house. What if the kidnappers call you—"

"Why in God's name would they call me? The note was sent to you. The demands were made of you." Drew's voice rose in panic as he spoke. "You haven't heard *anything*? You're sure?"

"I've been right here, waiting."

Something smashed to the floor, making Julie jump and Clint frown. "Dear God," Drew raged, on the verge of hysteria. "This doesn't make any sense. You should have gotten a call by now." There was a pause; then Drew whispered, "The note said that they'd contact you with the place to pick her up. We've followed their orders. We didn't call the police. *Where is she*?"

"Drew, perhaps it's time to think of hiring someone . . ."

"She's been gone for too long. Something's wrong. I can feel it."

"Calm down, Drew. It'll be okay."

"Okay? How can it possibly be okay when Julie is being held hostage, when even right now she could be . . ." His voice faded away to a soft, tortured groan. "We have to do something."

"Exactly. Perhaps I should hire someone to seek her out."

Aghast, Drew whispered, "But that could get her killed."

"I don't think so," Robert soothed. "It's probably someone she met, someone she got involved with who found out she has money. She's not at all discreet."

Clint thought he might kill Robert after all.

Drew's voice grew strained and harsh. "God, I pray you're right."

Clint saw Julie put a hand to her throat in regret. "Why doesn't Robert tell him—"

"Shh." Red squeezed her hand. "Just listen."

"This is my fault," Drew said. "I should have protected her. I should have—"

"Nonsense. You've been very good to her." There was the clink of crystal, and Robert said, "Here, drink this. It'll help you calm down."

"I don't want a damn drink! I want Julie back. You're her fiancé. What are you doing to help her?"

"Like I said, I've considered it, and I think we need to hire someone." Robert cleared his throat. "If you could extend me another ten thousand—"

"I gave you the ransom money. I thought you'd pay it and we'd have her home by now, where she belongs."

"That's what I'm trying to make happen."

"No, it's too risky. Someone will call and you'll give them the cash and Julie will be fine."

"I don't know, Drew . . ."

"I have to go." Something toppled, maybe a chair. "I have to do something to help her."

"Drew, wait! You can't go to the police—"

"No, no I won't. And don't you either. Just stay by that damned phone and call me the minute you hear. Do you understand me, Robert?"

"Yes," Robert said wearily. "I understand."

A door slammed, more crystal clinked, and then Robert sighed.

A tiny beep indicated a break in the time frame. The next sound was a ringing phone, and then Robert's weary voice. "Robert Burns."

"You motherfucker."

Clint sat up a little straighter. Both Mojo and Red leaned forward.

The wheezing of Robert's breath was the only sound.

"Don't you dare pass out on me, Robert. You need to hear every goddamned word I have to say to you."

"Who is this?" Robert demanded.

"What the fuck did you do?"

"I . . . I don't know what you mean."

"The hell you don't. You were supposed to send the money in exchange for the bitch. But you didn't follow the rules, did you? Instead, you sent some fucking maniac to kill all of us, didn't you? *Didn't you, Robert?* Only I'm alive. Alive and very pissed off."

"Jesus."

"Praying's not gonna do you no good. He took the woman, Robert, do you hear me? He took her, and now I have jack shit. No woman and no money. But don't think that'll save your ass. I kept my word."

"Your *word*?" Gaining some backbone, Robert said, "You're a kidnapper! Your word means nothing."

"I did what I was paid to do." There was a moment of throbbing silence, then the caller, in a more collected tone, growled, "And you, you jackass, were supposed to pay me for her safe return."

"How did I know you wouldn't kill her once you got the money?"

"Start worrying about your own ass, Robert, because I'm coming after you. And you fucking well better have my money when I get there."

The line went dead, and Robert let out an agonized groan. "Ohmigod. Think, think . . ." He continued to mutter to himself for a few moments, then the office door opened and closed, and the recording ended.

Clint waited, but when the line remained dead, he turned off the phone, dialed in a few numbers to set it to record again, and got up to put the phone away.

He didn't want to look at Julie, but he couldn't stop himself. As if she'd only been waiting for his attention, she stared right at him, her eyes enormous and bruised.

"Julie Rose—"

She lurched awkwardly to her feet. "I have to call Uncle Drew."

Shaking his head, Clint blocked the phone. "No."

She tried to step around him, but stumbled on her hurt ankle and gasped in pain. Clint caught her up against his chest. And damn, it felt good to hold her again. He'd been cold without her.

Not on the outside, but on the inside.

Her hands clutched his shoulders, her nails biting into his skin. "I have to call him, Clint. Please. You heard him. He's afraid and worried sick. It's cruel—"

"Shh." Clint stroked her hair and in the process loosened the offensive, old-biddy bun. "Listen to me, baby." He forgot that Mojo and Red were interested observers. He forgot everything he'd just told himself about keeping his distance.

"Please . . ."

He couldn't bear to hear her beg. "We don't yet know what's going on. And until we do, you can't talk to anyone."

"But . . ."

Clint pressed a finger to her lips. "You heard him, Julie Rose. Someone hired those bastards to take you. Maybe Robert's innocent, but maybe he's not. Until I know for sure, I'm not trusting anyone."

In a whisper, she said, "I can't bear it."

Clint held her closer, pressing his mouth to her forehead. "I know it's rough, babe. But look at it this way. Robert asked me to keep you, right? He had to have a reason for that."

"He wants you to keep me safe until he can find out who took me."

"Maybe. But what if he set the whole thing up? If Drew finds out that Robert hired me, it could put him in danger."

The motel room door opened and closed, and Clint looked up to see that his friends had gone out, giving him some privacy. And damn them both, they knew that privacy was the last thing he wanted right now.

He could feel Julie Rose shaking and scooped her up to set her on the bed. "Stay off that ankle while I clean up real quick. Then we'll get on the road."

Staring down at her hands, she whispered, "I hate this."

Clint actually felt his heart hurting. "I know." He saw her squeeze her eyes shut, and then she lifted her face, her expression once again impassive.

Somehow, that hurt him even more.

Backbone straight, she asked, "What are we going to do?"

Damn, but she was a trouper. "We need to head out. The longer we stay in one place, the riskier it is." He leveled a look on her, trying to make her understand, hoping to alleviate some of her guilt. "I know it's not easy, and believe me, we'll tell your uncle everything as soon as we can. But until then, you're going to have to trust me."

Julie stared at him, unflinching, her eyes big and dark and accepting. "You really do have a problem paying attention, don't you?"

Clint leaned against the bathroom door frame. "How's that?"

She pushed to her feet and hobbled to the door. When she opened it, Clint saw Mojo and Red lounging there, waiting for them. "I already trust you, Clint Evans." She stepped out into the sunshine. "More than anyone I've ever known."

Robert felt ill. A sleepless night had brought no answers. Soon, Julie would return home—he couldn't expect to keep her away forever. Then Drew would want his money back, leaving Robert between a rock and a hard place. The kidnapper would come after him, but he wouldn't be the only one.

Somehow, his problems were piling up, higher and higher until they seemed insurmountable. If he didn't start setting things right, and soon, he'd lose Marie forever. He'd lose everything.

He'd start with his most immediate threat. Asa.

Driven by new determination, Robert ran up the stairs to his bedroom, moved the heavy framed painting to the floor, and opened the wall safe. The thick envelope holding the money Drew had given him to pay Julie's ransom was right where he'd left it. He'd hoped to keep it all for himself, but Clint had failed to kill Asa, damn him.

Once again, Robert had no choice.

Opening the envelope, he counted out half the bills—a sizeable amount, but not enough. Not enough to save Julie, not enough to save him.

But maybe, just maybe it'd buy him some time.

He stuck the folded bills inside his suit coat and grabbed the keys to his Jaguar off the top of the mahogany armoire. His mind buzzed with problems and probable solutions as he hurried to the garage. With the push of a button, the garage door rose, flooding the enormous, dim interior with sunlight that glinted off the silver hood of his car, nearly blinding him.

He unlocked the driver's door and slid behind the wheel. He had just put the key in the ignition when a young man, dark and menacing, strode into the garage wearing a smile. While Robert sat mute with fear, the man opened the passenger door and seated himself.

"Drive."

Robert swallowed down his terror. The inevitable had happened. He only hoped he had enough money to put off his own death. "I was going to see Asa."

"Yeah? Well, how about I ride along, to make certain you get there safe and sound?"

Knowing he had no choice, Robert didn't object. "Where to?"

"You know the Road Kill Saloon?"

Robert's head throbbed. "It's down by the river."

"Yeah." And with an evil grin, "Asa will see you there."

Knowing what would happen, Robert whispered, "I don't have all the money yet."

"Your problem, buddy, not mine. Now drive. Asa doesn't like to be kept waiting."

It took twenty minutes to reach the disreputable saloon. With each mile that drew them nearer, Robert's uneasiness grew. He remembered Clint Evans, his unnatural calm, his forbidding confidence. If only he had a little of that man's ability. But he hadn't been raised as a thug. He was an educated man, genteel, polite, suave.

Even with the air conditioner on, sweat dampened Robert's back and chest and palms. His hands felt slippery on the steering wheel. He couldn't seem to get enough air into his lungs. *Marie, I'm sorry.*

"Park right there, next to that truck."

Robert knew his fear was palpable, and he also knew the young man beside him enjoyed witnessing it. He turned off the engine, sat only a moment, then opened his door. Hot air, tainted with the stench of poverty and sour liquor, poured in, suffocating him all the more.

As they crossed the lot into the dank interior of the all-night, all-day bar, Robert fought to maintain a steady gait, to appear indifferent to the situation, rather than terrified.

Asa wasn't in the front of the saloon, but then, he wouldn't be. You couldn't kill a man with a half dozen witnesses, never mind that they were all so boozed up they probably didn't remember their own names.

He followed behind Asa's man, across the room and through a warped wooden door half covered with peeling paint. A steep stairwell led to a cellar, lit only by one bare bulb.

Going down that stairway to hell, something strange happened to Robert.

His fear melted away.

His nervousness got replaced with indignation.

One mistake. One miserable, measly mistake he'd made, and he was supposed to pay for it with his future? No, by God.

Not anymore.

When he reached a closed door, Robert waited. Asa's man stepped around him, pushed the door open, and motioned for him to go inside.

As was usually the case with Asa, his immediate surroundings had been improved to the point of absurdity in the rest of the squalor. Fluorescent lighting made the room bright, showcasing the heavy leather furniture, cheery paint, and plush carpeting.

Asa himself sat in a big easy chair, smoking a cigar and watching some sporting event on a large-screen TV.

"Robert. What a wonderful surprise."

At the sound of that coarse voice, disdain filled Robert, but he merely nodded. "Asa." He started to reach inside his suit coat for the money, and the cold prod of a gun barrel jabbed into his spine.

Slowly, Robert withdrew his hands and raised them. "I have money for you. Inside my jacket."

Asa nodded to the man who'd ridden with Robert. "Take his money, Davy. But don't shoot him. Yet." He smiled at Robert.

Sick to death of the games, Robert smiled back.

That surprised Asa, as Robert had intended. If he could keep him off guard, maybe he could maneuver into the unexpected. "I don't have it all. Not yet."

"A pity," Asa said, while counting the money. "Where's the rest?"

"I'm working on it."

"How long?"

Robert shrugged. "A few weeks. Two, maybe three, tops." By then he'd have Julie back, and perhaps he could extort more cash from Drew in the guise of comforting her.

Asa's eyes widened, then he threw back his head and laughed and laughed. "Weeks? You think you have weeks?"

Knowing he didn't, Robert simply shrugged again. "There's no point in lying to you. If I could get it sooner than that, I would. But there haven't been any big deals."

All signs of humor disappeared from Asa's face. "I had a deal, until you fucked it up."

"I told you I'm sorry about that."

"And I told you, I want what you cost me. You told me you could recoup that money within days. That was many, many days ago."

"I have no excuses, at least none that you'd care to hear." He'd invested every dime he had in his plans to extricate himself from Drew's control, so he and Marie could start new some-

where else. "I've done all I can." What an understatement. "But most of my money is tied up."

"You better untie it, eh?"

"I'm working on it." If he made too many financial moves, he had no doubt Drew would hear of
it. Julie's uncle was a suspicious sort, as well as
an exceptional businessman. He'd cut Robert
out in a heartbeat if he thought he wasn't suitable for Julie. But Robert could hardly convince
Marie to leave her brother if he was penniless,
with no way to support her.

Robert was counting on Drew for the money.
Drew owed him, whether he realized it or not.
He just had to keep juggling the balls in the air
long enough to let everything play out.

While staring at Robert as if in deep thought,
Asa thumbed through the money again and
again. Finally he smiled. "I'll give you one more
week."

Robert still held his breath, waiting for the
other shoe to drop.

"But just so you don't forget about me . . ."
He nodded to Davy, who turned to Robert with
a large, anticipatory grin. Yes, the man enjoyed
hurting people. And he'd enjoy Robert now.

A massive fist smashed Robert's face. He managed to turn a little to the side so that the blow
hit his temple and cheekbone, rather than his
nose.

Pain exploded, and Robert would have
dropped to his knees except that Davy held him
up by his dress shirt and tie, nearly strangling
him. Another blow landed in his gut, then on his

chin. Robert tasted his own blood, but still, the fear was gone.

Two more strikes, and Davy let him fall, but he wasn't finished. No, he used his feet, kicking, stomping, until finally, after what seemed an eternity, Asa called a halt.

Robert couldn't move. He couldn't even moan.

No one looked up from their drinks as Davy dragged him back through the saloon and outside, where he deposited him in his car. Strangely enough, Robert's thoughts were on the blood and how it might ruin his fine leather seats. He had to laugh at that. Maybe the stress had caused him to lose his mind.

Or maybe, just maybe, he was finally toughening up a bit.

Chapter Seven

They didn't drive that long, but they turned so many corners, took so many back roads, that Julie lost track of time and place. Even though Clint sat in back with her, she refused to lean on him, and he ignored her.

She was lost enough in her own thoughts that she didn't mind.

They'd stopped for a drive-thru breakfast, but she wanted real food, if only a cheese sandwich. When Clint noticed that she'd eaten only half of her ham and egg biscuit, he nudged her.

Julie spared him a glance, then looked away again.

"What are you thinking about?"

She shrugged. "My future." What if they didn't find the person who'd had her kidnapped? What if, after Clint's designated time frame of a week, they were no closer to the truth than they were now? Would she be left on her own? It seemed likely, given that Clint wanted nothing more to do with her. He'd been very plain about that.

As he'd said, it wasn't his job to "fix" her. He'd been more than generous, and she'd been pathetic long enough.

Clint stiffened beside her. His fingers caught her chin and turned her face toward him. Julie was surprised to again see anger in his eyes.

"You're thinking about your next little seduction, is that it?"

Appalled that he'd say such a thing, and not in a whisper either, her gaze swung to the front of the van, to Mojo and Red. They already knew that Clint had rejected her. Wasn't that humiliation enough?

"Oh, hell no." Clint's arm pulled her tight into his side and his face lowered to hers. "Do not even think it."

Disgruntled, Julie shoved him away from her. "Think what?"

"Mojo and Red are off limits."

She gasped hard and felt her face flaming. "I wasn't thinking any such thing!"

"You were eyeballing them."

If she were a violent person, she'd pop him right in the nose. Instead she sat perfectly erect and gazed at him with loathing. "I looked at them because *you're* being rude and I don't want them to hear."

Glancing over his shoulder, Red assured her, "We're not listening."

Julie appreciated Red's attempt at gallantry,

but she felt compelled to point out the obvious. "Of course you are. If you weren't listening, you wouldn't have commented just now."

Red said, "Hmmm," and turned back to face forward.

Julie was so furious with Clint, she wished she had the option of walking away. Not for good, because she still wanted him, but at the moment she was afraid she'd say something she'd later regret. Being that he was so close, and still frowning at her, it wasn't easy to maintain her composure.

In a lower voice, but not low enough, Clint growled, "So then, who are you thinking about?"

"I was thinking about *me*, actually, if you really have to know."

Clint watched her suspiciously. "I have to know."

"Fine. I was wondering what'll happen if I don't get this figured out. I've never had an enemy. I've never known of anyone disliking me so much that he'd want to do me harm. It's not a very comfortable feeling."

Clint's expression softened; his hold became comforting. "We'll find the bastard." He caressed her shoulder. "I promise."

Julie heaved a sigh. "You've given yourself a week to accomplish the impossible, but there are no guarantees that we'll know anything concrete by then."

For some reason, Clint looked insulted. "If it takes longer, it takes longer."

"Damn right," Mojo added.

Julie twisted to face the men in the front seat. "But you all have busy lives. You can't—"

"I *can*," Clint told her. "Now, quit worrying."

As if that settled it, everyone fell silent, so Julie did, too. She wouldn't talk if they didn't want to hear her. She wouldn't show her worry if that would make them worry, too. And she definitely wouldn't ask Clint for anything more.

Another ten minutes passed before Clint put his lips near her ear. His breath was hot, his words more growled than otherwise. "So, do you have other prospects?"

The caress of his breath sent a shiver down her spine. Julie did her best to hide her reaction. "For teaching?" She was set on living in Visitation, and no stupid kidnapper would ruin those plans.

Clint shook his head. "I'm talking about this seduction business of yours."

How dare he bring that up again. The nerve. He'd already rejected her, and everyone in the van knew it.

Julie slanted him a searing glance. But since Clint continued to watch her, waiting, she folded her hands in her lap and tried to look serene. "That's really none of your business. Not now."

"The hell it isn't. Maybe you did flirt with the wrong guy, as Robert suggested. Maybe—"

Julie rounded on him. Fury brought her to her knees and within an inch of Clint's startled face. She totally forgot about Mojo and Red. "I *didn't*, all right? There was just you, Clint. But since you're not interested, the matter no longer concerns you. Period."

Very slowly, Clint's expression cleared of anger, and instead, he looked sympathetic and understanding. His big hands cupped around her neck. He brought her closer still, until she was practically in his lap. "I'm trying to protect you, honey, like I promised. You don't really want me. You just think you do because I saved you."

"Don't be absurd. Mojo and Red helped, and I don't want either of them."

Mojo laughed and Red coughed.

Julie glared at the backs of their heads. "Oh, be quiet, both of you. Since Clint insists on airing this where there's not an ounce of privacy to be found, then fine. But I don't need added comments that aren't helpful."

"Sorry," Mojo said.

"My apologies," Red added.

Julie didn't have a single doubt that they were both grinning—at her expense. She took her frustration out on Clint. "You think I have some misplaced hero worship going on? You think you're so big and strong and unique that my feeble little mind just can't grasp it?"

"I never said—"

Julie poked him in the chest. "For your information, Joe Winston is as big as you, and he's just as strong and twice as handsome."

"Good for him."

His sarcasm only fueled her temper. "Both Bryan and Bruce are fine specimens, too. Tall and handsome and very amusing. And I can't forget Scott Royal or Jamie Creed."

"I remember." And with utter disdain, Clint

mimicked, "The town drips testosterone, and the women all go insane with lust."

Forgetting that she was an educator with a higher moral standard than most, forgetting that she detested violence of any kind, Julie slapped his shoulder. "I said it was a wonder they *didn't* go insane, not that they did."

Red turned in his seat. "You admire all these guys?"

Still ruffled, Julie subsided back against the side of the van. Her ankle throbbed and so did her head. Her heart felt like it'd been ripped into little pieces.

Sitting close to Clint wasn't helping. "Very much. They're wonderful men, very heroic, and I consider them good friends."

"They're all boyfriends?"

Why these men insisted on thinking she ran a male harem, Julie couldn't guess. "No, they're all married now. Except Jamie and Scott."

Clint worked his jaw. "Jamie frightens her."

Shooting him a look of accusation, Julie said, "You didn't have to tell that part."

"What about Scott?" Red asked.

"He's great." Then wrinkling her nose, Julie added, "But being a deputy and everything, he's pretty . . . controlling. I've had enough of controlling men to last me a lifetime. Not that Scott has ever paid me much attention anyway. Other than as a friend, or as the local law who wants to keep everyone safe."

Red grinned at her rambling responses. "So

you don't think any of them could have been involved with your kidnapping?"

She shook her head hard. "No. Absolutely not. I have not a single doubt that any one of them would be more than willing to help me now if they knew what was happening. As I explained, they're heroes, not villains."

Red met Clint's gaze. "She's pretty convincing."

"Maybe."

Julie didn't like the way Clint said that. "Clint, do not even think about going to Visitation to bother my friends. I mean it."

"I'll do what I think is best."

"If you bother them," Julie threatened, "I'll tell Robert not to pay you."

Clint had the audacity to shrug, as if he didn't even care about the money when he'd already been clear that money was his sole motivation. "You didn't object this much over Robert."

"Perhaps you should take notes, so that you don't keep getting confused."

Red snickered, Clint narrowed his eyes, and both reactions satisfied Julie. "We've already determined that Robert is a cheater, and while I honestly don't think he'd ever do me harm, one bad character trait could—if I stretch my imagination—indicate other bad traits. But the same isn't true of Joe or Bruce or—"

"Yeah, yeah. Visitation's finest. I get it already." Clint moved across the van to settle next to her again, so close that their thighs touched, as if he hadn't realized she wanted some space. "They're all saints without an evil thought."

"Oh, they have evil thoughts, believe me." She chuckled, just thinking about some of the encounters they'd gotten into. "I wasn't there when it happened, but I heard that Bruce almost beat a man to death for trying to hurt his wife."

"Bruce the preacher?"

"Yes. And Joe put his knife in the guy who tried to hurt Luna and his children. Bryan—"

Clint held his head. "We're almost there."

"There, where?" She leaned forward and looked out the window. All she saw was a heavily wooded area with a big black truck parked among the brush. "Where are we?"

"Back in Ohio. Mojo left his truck here."

"Why?"

Clint didn't look inclined to explain, so Red did. "It's better to have more than one out. Not that we wouldn't notice it if we were followed, but we don't take chances."

"That's ingenious." Julie realized how careful they were, and again, it reassured her. "So you leave your vehicles in different places, and then if you need a ride, or need to switch cars, you have more than one option."

"Exactly."

Mojo pulled the van beneath a large tree, but left the engine running. He started to get out, and Julie said, "You're leaving? Now?"

Mojo paused, taking the time to turn and face her. He nodded.

Julie bit her lip, then reached into the front

seat and put her hand on his forearm. "Thank you so much, Mojo. For everything."

He patted her hand. His eyes were dark, but gentle. "It'll be all right. You'll see."

She nodded, and Mojo and Red both got out and walked to the front of the van.

Clint cupped the back of her neck, turning her face up to his. "Sit tight while we make a few plans. I'll be right back."

"What plans? I want to know what you're doing."

His thumb brushed her cheek, lingering for a long moment. "Just stay put."

Julie caught his wrist. "You can be a very condescending man, Clint, do you know that?"

"Yeah, I know it." He pulled loose and slid the side door open, then shut it behind him. The three men gathered near the black truck, talking softly. Julie tried to read their lips, but couldn't. By the time she'd crawled into the front passenger seat and rolled down the window, Mojo had turned away, and Red and Clint were returning.

Well, darn. She had no clue what their infamous plan might be.

No one mentioned the obvious fact that she'd been trying to eavesdrop. Red got behind the wheel, then leaned to the passenger seat and rolled the window back up to keep out the hot June afternoon air.

Clint merely waited until she moved into the back again, then he joined her. They rode along in silence.

Less than five minutes later, they stopped again,

this time in the packed parking lot of a popular grocery store. Clint slid the door open and reached for Julie's hand. "Let's go."

"The van isn't yours?"

Red answered her. "It's mine. The jeep is Clint's." He got out, too, but again left the motor running.

Not giving her a chance to object, Clint scooped Julie up into his arms and carried her to the side door. Having retrieved her bag of possessions, Red unlocked the door and opened it. Luckily there were no shoppers in the lot to witness her weakness.

After Clint had set her inside and rounded the hood, Red leaned in to put her bag at her feet. There was already a crowbar and a wooden stick of some sort on the floor, leaving her little room for her feet. She shuffled around and finally decided to use the bag to cushion her injured ankle.

Still leaning in, Red pressed a quick kiss to her cheek. He lingered, his mouth near her ear. "Hang in there, kiddo, and trust Clint."

No one had ever called her kiddo before. It sounded very affectionate, coming from Red. Julie nodded. "I do trust him." She put her arms around Red's neck and gave him a hug. "I hate saying goodbye."

Red returned the embrace. "You'll be seeing me again."

Clint turned the key and the engine roared to life. *"Goodbye,* Red."

Holding up his hands and grinning, Red said,

"I can take a hint." He began backing away. "Hey, Julie Rose?"

"Yes?"

"Take it easy on him, okay?" He winked. "Clint needs a clear head now, and you're confusing the hell out of him."

Clint put the jeep in gear and started forward.

Julie leaned out the window. "Thank you, Red!"

Clint said, "For God's sake, Julie Rose. Close the damn window and put on your seat belt."

Julie subsided into her seat with a sniff. "I will—but only because I was going to anyway. You should understand right now that I don't take well to orders."

"I noticed." Clint glanced in the rearview mirror, paused at the main drag, then eased into traffic. Once they were under way, he asked, "How're you holding up? Your ankle okay?"

"Perfectly fine, thank you." And then, just to annoy him, she tacked on, "You need not concern yourself."

Julie watched his hands tighten on the wheel.

"Knock it off, Julie Rose."

"I have no idea what you mean." She knew *exactly* what he meant.

"Yeah, you do." He glared at her for an instant. "You're trying to shut me out."

"Au contraire." She turned to face him, bumping her sore ankle against the stupid crowbar. If he kept picking at her, she just might use it on his head. "*You* shut *me* out, and you weren't even polite about it."

"Bullshit. Just because I don't want to take advantage of you during a difficult time doesn't mean—"

Holding up an imperious hand, Julie halted his lame excuses. "I've heard enough, thank you very much. More explanation would only be superfluous."

"What the hell does that mean?"

"It means you've already made yourself quite clear." Julie's brows came down, and she wagged a finger at him. "But for your information—"

He smacked the steering wheel. "I *knew* you were stewing, just waiting to blast me. Anytime a woman's silent, it's because she's building up steam."

"—I do *not* require fixing." The hurt welled up again, threatening to choke her. She blinked hard and firmed her chin. "I'm a perfectly acceptable woman just as I am."

"I agree."

"I'm intelligent, independent, loyal, and while I know I'm not beautiful, I've never been dissatisfied with my appearance."

"I already agreed."

"Your actions would say otherwise."

"Drop the teach-talk, will ya? It doesn't even suit you."

Her mouth fell open. "Well, of course it does! I'm first and foremost a teacher."

"No way. You're a *woman,* and you're pissed because you think I rejected you."

"I *know* you rejected me. I was there through the whole humiliating thing, and unlike you, I do pay attention." And then with sarcasm, "But of course, no one paid you to sleep with me."

The words no sooner left her mouth than the jeep veered sharply off the road, skidded to a halt with a stirring of gravel and dirt, and Clint had his seat belt off, reaching for her. Her feet got tangled in the stuff on the floor, the wooden stick, the crowbar, her stupid bag of meager belongings.

Startled, she screeched—and the sound got muffled by Clint's mouth. Fingers held her skull so she couldn't retreat, and then he kissed her senseless. His mouth was hot and hungry, his tongue searching and exciting.

It was a ravenous kiss, one maybe of anger, but definitely of passion.

When Clint finally came up for air, Julie struggled to get her eyes open. "Mmm. Okay." She licked her swollen lips and tried to get her brain to function. "And that was . . . ?"

Busy smoothing her skin and sort of smelling her neck, Clint murmured, "Proof that I want you."

"I see . . . no, I don't."

Clint eased back. "Did I hurt you?"

"No. I rather enjoyed it."

He grinned—then eyed her hair. "I hate this, this . . ." He gestured at her. "Old-biddy bun thing you stuck on your head. How do I get your hair loose?"

He was the oddest man. "I don't want my hair loose."

Determination intensified the green of his eyes. "I do."

A diplomat of the first order, Julie said, "Share your plans with me, and I'll take it down."

Settling back, Clint studied her for a long moment, then nodded. "Fair enough. We're going to my place. I'm going to leave you there while I take care of a few things."

"What things?"

"Things."

"Not good enough, Clint." She began tucking the strands he'd loosened back into her bun.

"All right, already. No reason to torture your head." He worked his jaw. "I'm going to go see a few people. Robert first, then Asa."

Robert and Asa? But why? Asa had nothing to do with anything, and Robert . . . well, despite Clint's suspicions, she really didn't believe Robert would hurt her on purpose.

She hated to see Clint waste his time on dead ends. Opting to cover her most immediate worry first, she forged ahead. "You won't hurt Robert, will you?"

One brow lifted. "Hurting him isn't part of my plan. But I can't make any promises." He refastened his seat belt. "If he insults you again, or tries to lie to me, yeah, I might smack him."

"Clint!"

"Just once or twice," he soothed. "He'll be okay."

Her savior obviously had some barbaric tendencies. "That is *not* acceptable." Frantic, Julie tried to think of some way to control a male of Clint's size. If he were a student, she could give him extra work, take away his recess, maybe threaten to call his parents.

But Clint wouldn't be easily reined in.

"Robert's not like you."

"Now, there's an understatement." He glanced at her. "I don't cheat and I don't lie."

"I know," Julie said with a smile. "But I meant he's not hardened the way you are. He's . . ."

"Soft?"

"Yes. In body and temperament. He's a businessman. Striking him would be like hitting me."

Clint made an exasperated sound at that comparison. "Take your hair down." He put the jeep in drive and merged with the traffic again.

Taken off guard, Julie automatically reached up to do as instructed. She hadn't had much to work with when she'd fixed her hair at the motel, so it was fastened mostly by the efficient means of a cheap ink pen. She'd twisted her hair tightly and then worked the pen through the bun to anchor it in place.

Now she pulled the pen away, and her hair tumbled to her shoulders.

"Better," Clint told her, and he even reached across the seat with his right hand to work his fingers through her hair to her scalp, gently massaging. It felt good. "You have nice hair, Julie Rose. You shouldn't pinch it back like that."

"It gets in my way."

"You look sexier with it down."

She needed to deal with the issue of him hurting Robert, but still she said, "Looking sexy serves no purpose if you're not willing to cooperate."

Through his teeth, Clint said, "It improves my mood, all right? That should be reason enough."

"Your moods don't scare me, Clint Evans. Well, except that I want you to promise you won't hurt Robert."

He took a ramp off the highway and onto a rural road. "No can do, babe."

Unacceptable. Julie thought quickly and decided hard measures were in order. "Clint Evans, either you swear to me that you won't hurt him, or I'm firing you right now."

He shot her an incredulous look. "You can't fire me. You didn't hire me."

"I can certainly decide to walk away. I can refuse your help. I can—"

"No."

"What do you mean, no?"

"I won't let you leave." His face darkened and his eyes narrowed, but his voice remained calm and sure. "I mean it, Julie Rose. You're not going anywhere, so you can get that lame-brained idea out of your head right now."

She fell back in her seat. "So now *you're* kidnapping me?"

"No! Damn it, just be reasonable." He turned down yet another road lined with shabby apartments. "I told you I'd keep you safe, and that's what I intend to do."

"Then promise me that you won't hurt Robert."

Under his breath, but not under enough, he muttered, "You are such a pain in the ass."

Refusing to let his complaint hurt her, Julie said again, "Promise me, Clint."

"Yeah, whatever." He swung the jeep into a parking garage, his movements jerky with annoyance. "I won't hurt him."

"Wonderful. I'm so glad we got that settled." When he turned off the engine, Julie released her seat belt. "Now explain to me why you're going to see Asa?"

"So you do know him?"

"I've met him, yes. He's a product of his society. Very sad."

Clint looked apoplectic. "He's a gang leader, a criminal, and possibly involved in your kidnapping."

"Why would Asa want to kidnap me?"

"Robert claims you flirted with him."

She dropped her head back with a laugh. "Dear God, according to Robert, I'm out to enflame all of mankind."

Leaning toward her, Clint slipped his hand behind her neck. "I'm beginning to think you could."

Her eyes opened. He was very close and staring at her mouth. "Truly?"

"You've sure as hell enflamed me." And then he kissed her again.

Julie would never tire of his mouth or his taste or his wonderful scent. His hand on her neck tipped her head back more, and he deepened the kiss with a groan.

What kind of game was he playing with her? He was more fickle than any person she'd ever met. When Julie turned her face, his mouth went to her throat, and that was almost as exciting. He drew her skin in against his teeth, and Julie felt it everywhere, especially in her breasts and between her legs.

"Clint?" she said on a whisper of sound. "Are you going to keep doing this?"

"No. It's wrong." He kissed her again, briefly this time. With his forehead to hers, his breath fanned her lips. "But I can't stand having you think I don't want you."

"Because you do?"

"Damn right."

Julie smiled. As far as admissions went, she liked that one a lot.

In the next instant, Clint's door opened, and he got yanked out and onto the concrete parking floor. Taken by surprise, he landed flat; Julie heard the impact of his head with the hard ground. Two men loomed over him, both of them clearly set on malicious intent.

Enraged that anyone would try to hurt Clint, especially when his current duty was to protect *her,* Julie instinctively reacted. She groped on the floor of the jeep, found the wooden stick, wrapped her fingers around it, and then launched herself out of the car and onto Clint, protecting him with her person.

She'd keep him safe, or die trying.

Chapter Eight

When he landed flat on his back, Clint lost his breath, then lost it again when a soft, warm weight bounced onto his abdomen. His guts felt smashed. His brains felt scattered. And a dull ringing filled his head.

Surprise faded, and it took him less than five seconds to realize he'd been attacked, and that Julie could be at risk.

Not about to let anyone hurt her, he dismissed his pain, shoved up to his elbows—and found himself staring at Julie's ramrod-straight back while she straddled him, crouched atop his lower chest, her legs on either side of his ribs. She wielded the Hanbo as if she actually knew how to use it.

Peering beyond her, Clint saw that one man had a gun aimed right at her.

Rather than retreat, Julie shouted in a mean,

believable voice, "You won't hurt him! I won't let you. Now go away."

Clint wondered if the knock on his skull had left him delusional. "Julie, move."

"I can't." She kept her gaze on the man in front of her. "He wants to shoot you."

Clint narrowed his eyes and summoned his own dead-serious tone. "If he doesn't get that fucking gun out of your face right now, he'll be damn sorry."

Smirking, the man glanced at Clint—and Julie used that moment to whack him hard in the thigh. The Hanbo, a martial arts weapon made of laminated wood thirty-six inches long and one inch in diameter, required special training for proper use.

That didn't slow Julie down. Her aim was dead-on, and the bastard with the gun let out a yell as his leg buckled.

Taking advantage of his painful distraction, Clint tossed Julie to the side. She yelped, but with her out of his way, Clint swept his right leg across the man's feet to knock him off balance. He dropped the gun, and it skidded out of reach. As he stumbled, Clint planted his boot in his face to finish him off.

The poor schmuck went down in a boneless heap.

Driven by adrenaline and a need to protect Julie Rose, Clint bounced to his feet and snatched up the .45 semiautomatic. Still somewhat unsteady, he stuck it in the back of his jeans and regarded the other man, who looked wide-eyed with awe and ready to bolt.

Clint shook his aching head. "Don't even try it. If I have to chase you, it's really going to piss me off." He put a hand to the back of his head and discovered an enormous goose egg. Damn it, he didn't have time for this.

The guy backed up. "We wasn't gonna shoot ya. We jus' wanted yer wallet."

Shit. Brought low by a two-bit punk. Disgusted, Clint barked, "Well, you're not going to get it now, are you?"

Climbing awkwardly back to her feet, Julie held the Hanbo aloft over her shoulder. "Want me to hit him?"

The guy scrambled farther back.

Clint said, "No," and with one quick grab caught the man by the front of his shirt. Before the queasiness set in, he needed to secure the scene. He jerked the guy forward to throw him off balance, at the same time pulling the front of his shirt up and tucking it over his face so that it caught on the back of his head. Holding him by the back of the neck, Clint retrieved a piece of rope from the jeep and quickly tied his hands. Unable to see and without the use of his arms, the man was hobbled enough to satisfy Clint.

He tossed his cell phone to Julie and relieved her of the Hanbo. "Call 911." He gave her his address to relay to dispatch.

After shoving the second man down to sit by the first, Clint leaned on the jeep, willing his stomach to settle. If he puked now, he'd never live it down.

After several deep breaths, he still felt a little unsteady and a lot stupid. Talk about getting taken off guard . . . If he didn't watch it, his distraction with Julie Rose would be the death of him.

He heard her say, "Oh, yes, it's under control. Clint kicked him in the face and took his pistol. No, Clint won't shoot anyone. He doesn't need to. Yes, of course the man is bleeding. Actually he's knocked out. Clint is very good at this sort of thing."

He forgot about his weak stomach. Damn. Maybe he shouldn't have had Julie call after all. She might end up getting *him* arrested.

She continued, saying, "Well, I hit him first. Yes, with a stick." She nodded, smiled, and said, "Thank you."

Clint held his head. This was incredible to the point of being bizarre. Julie Rose was unlike any woman he'd ever met—and that might not be a good thing.

"They're on their way." After disconnecting the call, Julie limped over to Clint and put a hand to his jaw. Her eyes were warm, her brow drawn in worry. *For him.* "Do you need to be sick?"

Oh, for the love of . . . Looking at her made Clint uneasy, so he gave all his attention to the two punks. "No."

"Are you sure?" She didn't look at all convinced. "There's a nice grassy spot right over there."

"I'll live." He dropped the Hanbo back into

his jeep. No need to go flaunting specialized weapons to the cops—not that they'd necessarily recognize it as a weapon. But Julie apparently had. "How about you? Did I hurt you? How's your ankle?"

She mimicked him, saying, "I'll live." Then she added, "But *you* landed on the ground awfully hard." Her fingers brushed past his ear, and she stretched up to touch the back of his head. "Oh, Clint," she whispered, her normally strident voice filled with concern. "You have an enormous bump back there."

"It's nothing a few aspirin won't fix."

"It must be terribly painful."

"It's not," he lied.

"You need some ice. You should be sitting."

Emphasizing his words, Clint said, "I'm *fine*." He caught her hands and put them away from him. "Quit fussing."

If he looked weak to the two bozos on the ground, they might try rushing him. He could handle them, no problem, but he really just wanted to stand still until the pounding in his brain subsided.

As if reading his mind, Julie turned to glare at the men. The one Clint had kicked was just coming around with a lot of groaning and moaning. His nose was quite obviously broken.

Damn. Clint pressed a hand to his lurching stomach and breathed through his nose.

The other guy, still hidden beneath his dirty shirt, just hunched his shoulders and muttered to himself.

Propping her hands on her hips, Julie glared at them both. "You'll get no sympathy from me. If Clint hadn't hurt you, I would have. How dare you threaten him. Maybe this will teach you that crime doesn't pay."

The injured guy opened one eye, took in Julie Rose's display of fury, and rolled to his side—away from her.

Clint rubbed the bridge of his nose, feeling a bitch of a headache coming on. "Don't torment them, Julie Rose."

She made a credible fist, shaking it toward them. "I'd like to strike them both again."

To spare his attackers, Clint pulled her into his side. "Hush, baby. Leave them be." He realized Julie didn't seem the least bit flustered or upset. He didn't know what the hell to make of that. His mind churned with a tumultuous mix of emotions. Shock that Julie would try to protect him led the pack. She couldn't weigh more than one-fifteen, but she'd deliberately put herself between him and danger, with only a Hanbo for protection.

Rage tempered the shock, because the little ditz could have been shot in her absurd efforts. Didn't she realize she was a scrawny schoolteacher with no experience in fending off goons?

But even as Clint told himself she'd been foolish, he admired her bravery and quick thinking. Most women would have cowered in the jeep, screaming and crying and carrying on.

Not Julie Rose. She wanted to protect him. She wanted to mother him.

She definitely wanted to sleep with him.

Still in defensive mode, Julie kept her gaze on the two men. Riding an adrenaline high, she looked ready to jump them if they moved too fast.

Clint shook his head, caught between a moan of pain and rib-tickling amusement. He gave Julie a one-armed squeeze and smothered both reactions, but he couldn't smother the rise of sexual awareness.

The fact that Julie wasn't falling apart made him doubt his earlier assessments on her delicate sensibilities. Maybe she hadn't been all that devastated over the kidnapping. Sure, she'd been upset—any intelligent person would have been. But totally, emotionally devastated?

Thinking back, he remembered that she'd only cried that once, and since then she'd been a real trouper.

Even during the worst of the situation, when she'd been tied up with Petie harassing her, she'd had the backbone to spit on him. Imprudent, but damn gutsy all the same. Definitely not the act of a frail woman.

So maybe, just maybe, she really did want him—*just for him*—and not because she saw him as her rescuer.

Police sirens split the air, intensifying the pain in Clint's head and making his stomach roil. Seconds later two patrol cars pulled in behind the jeep. Four cops swarmed out, guns in hand, but at least things were nearing an end. As Clint put his hands in the air, he thought about get-

ting Julie Rose alone. He wanted to kiss her
again. He wanted a whole lot more—like everything.

He accepted that they'd eventually end up in
bed. How soon that'd happen was still up in the
air.

Slurring a curse, Petie Martin shielded his eyes
from the late afternoon sunshine as he staggered from the bar. The thick, muggy air closed
in around him, adding to the sour state of his
temper. A nasty scowl on his twisted face warned
drunks and sober men alike to stay out of his
way.

Thanks to that son-of-a-bitch who'd attacked
him, almost got him arrested, and royally fucked
up his plans, he'd have his jaw wired for several
weeks. Reduced to sucking whiskey through a
straw made it damn difficult to get rip-roaring
drunk, but he'd managed. The doc warned that
his jaw would bother him for months, that chewing and even the weather could make it ache,
when it hurt enough now to make his hands
shake.

The booze, mixed with his pain meds, helped,
but not enough. Nothing would help except re-
venge. And when he located the bastard who'd
done this to him, he'd be smart enough to sneak
up and shoot him in the back. He deserved no
better.

If smiling didn't hurt so much, Petie might
have grinned over the image of the big man hit-

ting the ground face-first. Before drawing his last breath, he'd know that Petie Martin had escaped the cops through the woods. He'd sacrificed his friends, left them behind to be handcuffed and booked, so that he could find the man responsible and make him pay. He might have gotten the better of Petie back at the cabin, but Petie always got even.

Digging his keys out of his pocket, Petie stumbled and staggered to his car. Just as he reached it, a slight human form took shape in the alley at the side of the old run-down saloon. Holding back, the figure was disguised by heavy shadows. Petie stared harder, and as recognition came, he stiffened with outrage.

"You," he hissed from between his wired teeth.

Graceful even now, the individual avoided contact with the rusty metal Dumpster and the crumbling brick wall of the building, silently waiting for Petie to approach.

Shaking with rage that amplified with each agonizing throb of his jaw, Petie stalked forward.

"Where are the others?" Petie was asked. "Where are the men you worked with?"

"All in jail!" Petie wished he could open his mouth and raise holy hell, but he could barely squeeze the words out around all the metal on his teeth. "Because you set us up," he accused, crowding closer, hoping to intimidate. "But not me. I got away. And believe me, it wasn't easy, not with my jaw broke and my body on fire."

"The others might talk. They might tell the police about me—"

"And get hit with a kidnapping charge?" Petie laughed. "No, your ass is safe. From them."

A sigh, then, "Good. That's good." Very little emotion showed in the gentle face that Petie had stupidly trusted.

Petie's eyes narrowed. "But if I don't get my fucking money,.I might start talking."

"You didn't follow directions."

"You didn't pay me my goddamned money!" Petie didn't bother to point out the obvious: he'd lost the choice to follow directions.

"We made a deal." The words rang with icy fury.

Petie drew up short, appalled by the uncharacteristic loss of composure when normally all he got was moderate, almost shy, instructions.

Something had gone seriously wrong.

Once stylish clothes were now disheveled, the usual flawless appearance marred by strain. Petie took in the pale face and saw the biggest change in the eyes, now bloodshot and filled with worry.

"Jesus H. Christ," Petie muttered. "What the fuck happened to you?"

"If everyone else got arrested, then where is she?"

Petie scowled. Did he look like a fool? "Where's my money?"

"You didn't follow orders. I *told* you to follow orders . . ." Sounding defeated and distraught, the individual sighed—and produced a .38, fitted with a silencer.

It pressed into Petie's gut.

"What the fuck?" Petie yelped, stunned spitless by the turn of the situation. He hadn't figured this one to be the violent type. "Where the hell did you get the gun?"

Blank eyes met frightened ones. "The same place that I got you, Petie. Off the street."

"Now, wait a minute!" Panic raced through Petie. "Just hold up a second. I can explain—"

The slugs hit him before he realized the gun had been fired. One in the gut. Another in the chest. Ah hell. Stumbling backward, Petie fell to his ass. Blood oozed everywhere. His vision blurred.

The gun was now held in both hands, aimed at Petie's head.

Dear God. *"No, wait—"*

"You should have followed orders." With no emotion whatsoever, manicured fingers squeezed the trigger. Petie never heard the shot that ended his miserable life.

By the time the cops left with the confiscated pistol and the would-be thieves in tow, Clint's stomach had settled. His head wouldn't ease up anytime soon, but at least he wouldn't puke.

With Julie Rose fussing at his side, they climbed the long flight of stairs to his second-floor apartment. He wanted to carry Julie, to spare her ankle, but even if she hadn't refused him, he couldn't trust himself to manage it.

Carry her? He snorted at himself. She limped along beside him, bracing her shoulder under his arm as if she'd somehow be able to steady his weight if he went off balance. She'd even wanted to carry his bag and her own, but he'd won that tug-of-war.

More than a little aware of the peeling paint in the hallways and the rickety stairs, Clint fell silent. A few years past he'd had a prosperous life.

But that was before the incident.

Now he lived in near squalor, and though he knew he had a shitload of money in the bank, almost enough to start over, Julie Rose wouldn't know it.

Strangely enough, she seemed unfazed by her surroundings. Even when three rough, chain-wearing, tattooed youths came barreling down the stairs toward them, she didn't appear uneasy. She just tried to shield Clint with her body so that he wasn't jarred.

Clint had hoped to make it inside without any confrontations with his colorful neighbors, but it wasn't meant to be. And Marlin, Dwayne, and Emilio were more colorful than some.

The teens stumbled to a halt. Dwayne bumped into Marlin, and Emilio bumped into Dwayne. They stared. Dwayne, the youngest one, about fifteen going on fifty, suddenly sported an ear-splitting grin. His gaze on Julie, he drawled, "Hey, dude. What's up?"

"Nothing." Clint tried to take another step, but they blocked him.

Julie shooed them away. "Go on now, children. Clint can't visit right now. He's hurt, and he needs to lie down."

They stared at her like she'd just grown another head. No one had called them children in years. For all intents and purposes, they weren't kids. They were punks in the making—but Clint had tried to change that.

So far, he had no idea how successful he might have been.

Marlin was the tallest and had the most tattoos. They twisted up and down his arms, onto his neck, and even over the left side of his face. Normally he looked very intimidating, but now he wore an expression of comical shock. "No shit?" His dark-eyed gaze moved to Clint. "You got whacked?"

"Watch your language," Clint warned. "Not in front of the lady."

"Yeah," Emilio said, elbowing Marlin hard. "Clint's got a lady. Make nice."

They all snickered.

Julie rolled her eyes. "Oh, please. Clint has said much worse in front of me, so he has no right to lecture. But it's a fact that foul language is a sign of an empty mind. And children especially should refrain from profanity."

Emilio pulled back. "She's insultin' us."

"No," Julie countered, "I'm instructing you."

Clint gave Emilio his patented *don't-go-there* smile. "Thank her, boys."

With varying degrees of disbelief and antagonism, they muttered, "Yeah, thanks."

"Sure, yeah."

"Right."

Julie nodded. "Being that you're all so friendly,

might I ask that you stop forcing Clint to loiter in the hall? He hurt his head, and he needs some rest."

At the end of his rope, Clint expanded on a deep breath. Too many more deep breaths and he'd pop. "For the tenth time, Julie Rose, I'm fine."

In a conspiratorial whisper, Julie addressed the boys. "He insists on being macho. You understand. But I'm afraid he might have a concussion."

"Ain't possible. Clint's head is made of stone." Flashing a gold tooth, Marlin reached for the bags. "I got these." He wrested them right out of Clint's hand and began backtracking up the steps.

"Spill the lowdown, Clint." Emilio kept pace with his friend. "Someone got the sneak on you?"

"Don't get any ideas," Clint warned.

"Not me." He held out both hands. "I like wearing my head on my shoulders, instead of up my ass."

The boys all chortled again and even shared a few high fives.

"Language," Clint reminded them wearily, knowing it wouldn't do him any good. But the offender did offer a fast apology.

"So spill it. You were fighting one dude and another sucker punched you?"

"They hit ya in the head with something?"

"I bet Clint did some ass-kickin', for sure."

They were at his door now, and Clint tried to ignore their enthusiasm as he fished his keys out of his pocket. He knew the boys suffered something close to hero worship, and he'd tried to use it to influence them for the better. But sharing ass-kicking stories with them wouldn't convince them to live on the straight and narrow. "It was nothing."

Julie puffed up with pride. "I struck one of them."

"No shi—er, no kidding?"

Dwayne said, "You protected Clint? Now, ain't that sweet."

Knowing a barb when he heard one, Clint rolled his eyes.

"I couldn't let him be hurt," Julie explained. "It happened quite fast, and I didn't have time to think things through. Otherwise, you understand, I'm against violence."

"Ain't we all," Dwayne drawled with a grin.

"How'd they get him? Clint usually knows everything that's going on."

Julie cleared her throat. "Well, you see, Clint and I were . . . necking, I suppose you could say."

Three pairs of jaded eyes blinked. Dwayne screwed up his mouth, trying not to laugh. "Makin' out, huh? Where was this?"

"In Clint's jeep."

The boys all looked at Clint. Marlin winked. "Smooth moves, dawg."

"Then," Julie said, regaining their attention, "someone grabbed Clint, and he got pulled out of his vehicle and onto the ground, and he hit his head quite hard. It made a horrible sound."

"Probably cracked the concrete, too."

For that clever quip, Marlin and Emilio slapped hands in another high-five salute.

Julie smiled with them. "I grabbed a stick from the floor. I knew it was there because it had made my trip most uncomfortable. I couldn't get my feet settled."

Clint frowned at her. "If you were uncomfortable, you should have said something."

Chin in the air, she sniffed. "I didn't want to talk to you then." She turned back to the boys. "Anyway, they had wanted to steal Clint's wallet. I used the stick to wallop one of them, and then Clint took over and made mincemeat of them, and finally four police officers arrived to haul them away."

Clint turned the key in the lock and shoved the door open. "Inside, Julie Rose."

She held out her hand to the boys. "Thank you for your help."

Flustered by her, the boys each shook her hand.

They were almost inside when Dwayne said, "You want Carmen to take a look?"

Clint said, "No," at the same time Julie Rose inquired, "Carmen?"

"Yeah. She was a doc back in the day. Still looks after most of us when we get banged up."

Seeing that Julie wanted to accept, Clint took her arm and pulled her into the apartment. "Thanks, guys, but there's no reason to bother Carmen. I'm fine." He started to shut the door, then thought to ask, "Where're you headed, anyway?"

Guilt flashed on three cynical faces. Marlin said, "Just hanging out."

Knowing he lied, Clint kissed Julie's forehead

and said, "Give me a minute." Then he stepped back into the hall and pulled the door shut. Because he knew Julie would try to open the door, he held onto the doorknob.

And she did try.

Holding the knob secure, Clint asked, "Where are you really going?"

Dwayne curled his lip. "Just a party, man. No big thing."

"Right." Clint marveled that the boys' parents never seemed to keep tabs on them. They had far too much time to get into trouble. "There'll be drugs there? Booze?"

Emilio shrugged. "We'll have a few beers, that's all. No need to freak."

"It's mostly the trim we're after anyway," Marlin added with a sly grin and bobbing eyebrows.

Clint's stomach churned. "You've all got protection?"

Dwayne laughed. "I'm carrying my knife."

Clint wondered if he should confiscate the knife. But hell, in this neighborhood, they might actually need the thing. "You know that's not what I meant."

"Rubbers. Yeah. I got it covered." Then Dwayne glanced at the closed door and grinned. "Why? You need to borrow a couple?"

Clint caught Dwayne by the front of his shirt and rattled him a little just to get their attention. "I'm serious. Do I need to drag your sorry asses down to the clinic to show you what STDs look like? Do you want to be pissing through a Grinch ornament?"

"Shit no, man."

"Then take my word for it, some chances aren't worth taking. Even with a rubber, if you don't know the girl or she looks like she's giving it away too easy, pass on it." He tapped Emilio on the forehead. "Think with the big head, because it's the one that should have the most sense."

Dwayne pulled away and straightened his shirt. "Damn, dude, lighten up. It's just a party."

But they all three looked more somber.

Clint shook his head, then smacked Marlin on the shoulder. "Why the hell I care about you sorry sacks, I don't know. But you've grown on me."

"Like a wart?" Dwayne teased.

"Exactly." He considered all three again and knew he didn't have the right to harangue them too much. "If you get into trouble, give me a call."

"You're the man."

Emilio didn't immediately follow his friends. He studied Clint and then held out his fist. "Thanks."

Clint tapped it with his own. "Just stay out of trouble and think before you do anything."

Emilio nodded. "Keep it real."

Feeling like a damn grandpa, Clint watched him go. He opened the door and found Julie Rose in tears. "What the hell?"

She threw her arms around him and squeezed him with all her puny strength. Her lips brushed his throat as she babbled. "I could hear every word."

Unsure of her mood, Clint gingerly put his arms around her waist. "Yeah? Sorry about that."

"You were very good with them." She sniffled, and Clint felt her tears dampen his flesh. "What's a Grinch ornament?"

Grinning, Clint said, "You remember the Grinch?"

"Yes. A holiday character. Skinny and green . . . Ewww. That's disgusting."

He laughed. "I know. I just hope they got the picture."

"I think they did. They respect you. That's plain to see."

Did they respect him enough to avoid the temptations of their environment? Clint didn't know. "So why are you in here sniveling and carrying on?"

She laughed, sniffled again, and wiped her eyes. "Because you're wonderful." She pulled back and touched his face with shaking fingers. "The most wonderful man I've ever known."

And according to her, she knew some real paragons of machismo.

Clint's head hurt. Bad. But at that moment, with Julie Rose smiling up at him, her big brown eyes liquid, her soft mouth quivering, he couldn't pay any attention to the pain. He wanted her mouth—under his mouth, on his flesh, sucking, biting . . .

A teasing rap sounded on the front door. "The doctor is in. Open up."

Clint groaned.

In a whisper, Julie asked, "Who's that?"

"Carmen." He released her and stepped back. "Brace yourself, babe. Carmen is probably different from any of the women you've known."

That was all the warning Clint gave her before opening the door. Carmen burst in, her arms open to embrace him, her body more uncovered than otherwise. She wore skin-tight black slacks and a barely buttoned sleeveless white blouse that did nothing to conceal generous breasts and dark nipples.

Dainty sandals covered her feet, and her toes and fingernails were painted fuchsia. Her dark exotic looks made her a showstopper. Her proclivity for drugs and prostitution made her a woman to be pitied.

At least to Clint.

He allowed her the embrace, but turned his face before her mouth could find his. "Bring it down, doll. I clunked my head and it hurts like a son-of-a-bitch."

"I know, poor baby." She pursed her red lips and cooed at Clint. "That's why I'm here. I saw Emilio on my way in, and he told me all about it."

Julie stepped forward. "Hello." She held out a hand.

Carmen gave her the same look she used for insects. "Who are you?"

Still smiling in sweet welcome, Julie said, "A friend of Clint's. The boys told me you were a doctor. I'm glad you're here. I'm afraid Clint might have a concussion, but he's flatly refused to go to the hospital."

Cautiously, briefly, Carmen took Julie's proffered hand. "The boys?"

"Emilio, Marlin, and Dwayne." Julie softened her voice. "They are boys, you know. I doubt any of them are eighteen yet."

Feeling unaccountably proud, Clint put his arm around Julie. "Emilio will be eighteen in a few more months."

She leaned toward Carmen. "Doesn't matter. You know how boys are—they mature much slower than females."

Carmen raised one carefully drawn brow. "Yes, they do. They can be fully grown and still be little boys."

"And this one"—Julie hugged Clint's arm—"he's like all males, stubborn and too proud. He's definitely hurt, but doesn't want to admit it."

Carmen made a tsking sound. "Macho, all of them."

"True, true."

Clint couldn't believe his own eyes. Damn, but Julie had made fast friends with Carmen when usually Carmen pulled out the claws on other women. Men, she loved. Women, she saw as competition. But despite Julie's obvious claim on him, Carmen behaved.

"So," Carmen said, "let's go have a look at you."

A little dazed by the female bonding process, Clint led the way to the kitchen. He pulled out a chair, turned it backward, and straddled it. "I just got dinged, Carmen. It's no big deal."

Julie shook her head and proceeded to the refrigerator. She located a bag of frozen peas.

Carmen smiled. "I'll see for myself—oh, my. That's one impressive ding." She pressed and prodded, then moved to the front of Clint and stared at his eyes. "Any blurred vision?"

"No."

"Dizziness?"

"Nope."

"Did you lose consciousness when you struck your head?"

Julie said, "Yes," as Clint said, "No."

Gasping, Julie said, "You did, too!"

His back straightened. "Don't call me a liar, Julie."

His dark tone left her unfazed. "Then don't lie."

"I'm *not.*" His head probably ached more from gritting his teeth than being conked. "I had the wind knocked out of me, that's all."

Carmen's gaze went back and forth between them. "Interesting." She gave her attention back to Clint. "The symptoms of concussion are amnesia, loss of consciousness, headache, dizziness, blurred vision, attentional deficiency, and nausea."

"All I've got is a headache."

She nodded. "Headache, of course, isn't confined to concussion. Other symptoms that shouldn't be ruled out are irritability—"

"He's often irritable," Julie muttered.

"—impaired coordination, sleep disturbance, noise or light intolerance, lethargy, behavioral disturbance, and altered sense of taste or smell."

"I'm hungry, not the least lethargic, and I can smell your perfume just fine."

Carmen grinned. "Then I suppose you'll live." She turned to Julie. "But if any of the other symptoms should show, I'd get him to an emergency room whether he wants to go or not. Better safe than sorry."

Like a soldier taking orders, Julie all but saluted. "I'll see to it. Thank you."

Rather than leave, Carmen strolled to the sink and began making coffee. "So, while I get some coffee brewing, you can talk to me. What's the story with you two?"

"Story?" Julie pressed the frozen veggies gently against Clint's skull. It felt good. He hadn't been pampered in . . . well, never. But Julie seemed content to stand there behind him, holding the icy bag in place, so he let his head drop forward and sighed.

Carmen pulled a pack of cigarettes from the waistband of her slacks and struck a match. She puffed—

And Clint, without lifting his head, said, "Not here, doll. You know better."

"You are such a stick in the mud."

"Coffee, cola—but no smoking. Take it or leave it."

She wrinkled her nose at Julie while stubbing out the cigarette in the sink. "He does like to lay down rules."

"I've noticed that." Julie frowned. "But he's correct about the smoking. It's very bad for you."

Carmen laughed. "God, I can see the two of you will get along just fine." She slanted Julie an appraising look while putting her cigarettes away. "You two an item?"

Julie opened her mouth—and Clint squeezed her knee in warning. Julie tended to be far too trusting, and while he cared for Carmen, she was an addict and that made her impossible to trust.

Julie caught his hint and fell silent. Clint said, "She's a friend of the family."

"I didn't know you had any family."

"What?" Clint asked. "You think I crawled out from under a rock?"

Carmen shrugged. "So, she's staying with you?"

"Temporarily. Her belongings got snatched during her travel. She lost everything, and she doesn't want to finish her trip until the cops recover her stuff."

With the coffee preparations complete, Carmen rejoined them at the table. "That explains the awful dress."

Julie looked down at herself. "I rather like it."

"Oh, please. Was your make-up stolen, too?"

Julie blinked, and admitted a bit sheepishly, "Actually, I never got the hang of make-up."

"Ohhh. Uncharted territory." Carmen rubbed her hands together. "Trust me, honey, I can do you up right. We'll have a blast."

Alarmed by the idea of Julie changing, Clint said, "Now, Carmen—"

Julie beamed. "That sounds wonderful. Thank you."

Clint said, "Shit," but the women ignored him.

Settling back in her chair, Carmen eyed Julie up and down. "You're not that far from my size, either, so I could probably loan you some of my old clothes."

"Really?"

"You'll need a padded bra, though."

"No, she does not."

Smiling, Carmen propped her head on her fist and winked at Clint. "So defensive over a mere pal?" She laughed. "Trust me, honey. If she wants to fill out my blouses, she'll need some help. That's all I meant."

The coffee finished sputtering, and Carmen got up to pour three cups. A hostess by nature, despite the debilitating effects of the drugs, she set a mug in front of Clint and one in front of Julie, along with sugar and a carton of milk.

"I'm taking mine home with me, so Clint can rest." She saluted him with her coffee. "But, Julie, honey, give me a call tomorrow and we'll do a makeover. Clint has my number."

"A makeover on me? Really?"

"Head to toes. It's long past due." She wagged her fingers at Clint. "Too-da-loo, love."

Julie handed the frozen vegetables to Clint and went hobbling after Carmen to the front door. Clint groaned. Julie might not realize it, but her personality made her potent enough already. Carmen's idea of a makeover would no doubt emphasize Julie's sexuality, and that'd be more than he could take.

He pictured Julie in the getup Carmen wore,

and his head swam. Damn. He heard the front door close and knew he was all alone with her now.

"Lock the door, Julie Rose." For the next few hours, he didn't want any interruptions.

Chapter Nine

"**I** don't know why you thought I might not like her," Julie said as she reentered the kitchen. "She's charming."

Julie Rose was definitely unlike any other woman he'd known. Rich, but she didn't look down on Carmen. Skinny, but with more spirit and backbone than most two-hundred-pound men. "She's an addict and a hooker."

"I didn't realize she had a problem with drugs. That's so sad." Julie took her seat opposite Clint and reached for her coffee. "But I've known other hookers."

Clint fell back in his chair. "Come again? No, wait. More of the sterling specimens from your beloved Visitation?"

Julie grinned while sugaring her coffee heavily. "Visitors to Visitation, actually. Well, except for Cyn. She married Bruce and stayed."

"A preacher and a hooker . . . never mind. I don't want to know." He reached across the table and took Julie's hand. "Listen to me. Carmen is nice enough when her head is clear. But her entire existence is desperate, and desperate people can't always be trusted. You're not to tell her anything about being kidnapped, about who you really are or where you're from."

"All right."

Clint's eyes narrowed. "Are you humoring me?"

"Of course not. I'm not stupid, and I already told you I trust you. If you don't think it's safe, then I don't think it's safe." She patted his hand. "There's no reason for you to fret."

"Women fret, men do not."

"Oh? Then what would you call it?"

"I'd call it trying to keep your sweet ass out of trouble."

Her gaze lowered, but he could see the smile on her mouth and the flush in her cheeks. "Do you really think my, er, ass is sweet?"

Everything about her was sweet. Sweet and sexy. "Yeah. So don't let Carmen go wild on you, okay? You don't need to change."

Her rebellious look had him worried. "It could be fun to spice up my image some. As Carmen said, it's long past due. And it could go hand in hand with my plans for enjoying life a bit more—"

Groaning, Clint closed his eyes and rubbed his forehead.

Instantly concerned, Julie leaned toward him. "Clint? Would you like some aspirin?"

"I'd like you to promise me that you . . ." The words stuck in his throat.

At his hesitation, Julie tipped her head. "What is it?"

Damn it, if he said it, there'd be no going back. Did he even want to go back? Not really.

Julie pushed out of her seat and, still favoring her ankle, came to him. "Clint?"

He'd done enough fighting for one day. Tossing the frozen bag of peas aside, Clint scooted back his chair and stood to tower over Julie. She was so petite, but with so much grit and twice as much heart. He cupped her face. "Promise me you won't change." He bent, put his mouth to hers in a gentle, undemanding kiss. "Don't let Carmen make you into someone you're not, because who you are is pretty damn special."

Julie's gaze softened. Her lips parted. And she whispered, "Whatever you say, Clint."

Julie reveled in the way Clint kissed her now. She could tell the difference; this was a kiss meant to seduce, a kiss of foreplay, a prelude to making love.

And it was wonderful.

When Clint kissed her throat, she summoned enough sense to ask, "Your head is okay?"

"Better by the second." His lips moved to her ear, and his breath teased her seconds before his tongue touched her lobe, then licked inside.

Breath catching, stomach flipping, Julie

moaned. "My goodness." Who knew ears were so erogenous?

She laced her fingers in his dark hair and held him closer. His hand crept down her back and onto her bottom.

He lifted her to her tiptoes. "Tell me if I hurt you."

She knew he never would. She opened her hands on his chest, enjoying his heat, the thundering of his heartbeat, the solid feel of bunched muscles. Clint was so physically strong, but it was his strength of character that really drew her. He cared about people, even ragtag kids and a drug-using hooker.

While he ravaged her neck and throat and shoulders, Julie felt him everywhere she could reach, over his back, down the deep furrow of his spine, around to his rigid abdomen.

Clint stilled in suspended anticipation.

Against her belly, Julie could feel the solid rise of his erection caught beneath his faded, worn jeans. Curiosity got the better of her, and she cupped her hand over him.

A rough, rumbling groan erupted from deep in Clint's throat. He caught her hand—and pressed it tighter to him. "Hell, yeah." Near her ear, he rasped, "You are so full of surprises, aren't you, baby?"

Julie wasn't quite sure what he meant by that. She was breathless with excitement and very much enjoyed exploring his body. "I suppose curiosity is a side effect of being an educator."

That made him laugh, until she squeezed him through his jeans. He was so big, so thick. She trailed her fingers up and down his length, measuring him, marveling at the power of him.

"Keep that up, and I won't be able to control myself."

"Really?" Julie looked up at him—and was struck by the savage heat in his gaze. "You have the most remarkable eyes."

He choked. "Eyes, huh? Forget my eyes." And he closed them while issuing a small groan and pressing himself tighter into her hand.

Julie wrapped her fingers around him as much as she could—and stroked. "Clint?" His eyes opened, leaving her caught once again in their depths. "Will you promise me something?"

Going very still, Clint assessed her. Julie saw the cynicism he didn't bother to hide, the way he curled his lip. "Still worrying about me hurting poor Robert?"

"What?" That was so far away from what she'd been thinking, she drew a complete blank.

Clint caught her wrist. "You figured now was the best time to exact a promise from me?"

"Well, yes. But it has nothing to do with Robert."

"Uh huh. So what, then?"

She used her other hand to cup his testicles and leaned her breasts into his chest. "Promise me you won't stop, and that you won't regret having sex with me."

His eyes flared.

"Please? It's important to me."

"Ah, shit." Clint pulled away from her, but scooped her up into his arms.

"Your head!"

"Isn't helping me out much right now. Let's go to bed, babe. I want you naked."

"Oh." Julie wrapped her arms around his neck. "You'll get naked, too?"

As he started out of the kitchen, he pressed a kiss to her forehead. "It usually works better that way."

His apartment was miniscule, only the front room, the kitchen, a small bath that they passed in the hall, and one bedroom. It didn't take Clint too many steps before they were standing next to his bed.

Julie looked around, absorbing the sight of the male domain. His bed was full sized, but without a headboard or footboard. One painted dresser and a mismatched nightstand were the only other pieces of furniture in the room. On his nightstand sat a clock and a phone. The room was tidy, not a single piece of clothing out of place, but not decorated at all.

Plain beige curtains hung at the one window, and there were only blankets on the bed, no bedspread.

"Not exactly what you're used to, is it?"

Julie realized Clint had been watching her. She stroked his cheek. "There's a bed, and you're here. That's all I care about."

That got her a brief, tight hug, and a muttered, "You are such a sweet-talker."

She smiled. It was easy to be sweet when Clint held her. But now she wanted more than sweet. She wanted hot and gritty and slow and deep. She wanted Clint, all of him. "If you put me down, I can take this dress off."

For two seconds longer, he kept his face tucked into her throat, and his arms contracted a bit, squeezing her. Then slowly, carefully, he let her slide down the length of his body. Julie felt the thick ridge of his erection and deliberately pressed her belly flush to him as her feet touched the floor.

Clint's hands held her waist. "You're not shy, are you?"

She tipped her head back, smiling up at him. They'd done so little, but still sexual excitement gripped her. It seemed a look from Clint could do more to arouse her than a hundred touches normally would have. "I'm not a virgin, but I'm hardly a seasoned veteran of intimacy either. The thing is, we can't proceed until we're naked."

"Yeah, we can." He brought his hands up to hold her face. "Keeping some clothes on will help us go slow. And we're definitely going slow, so I can savor this." And then his mouth took hers in a long, leisurely kiss. His tongue explored, his lips moved on hers, and he even used his teeth, nipping her bottom lip and giving her a thrill.

"Kissing is good," Julie said breathlessly when he moved to her throat. At the same time she began pulling his white T-shirt from his jeans. She'd seen his chest, touched him and felt his heat, his heartbeat, but that was before she had leave to explore him as she wanted to. Now was her chance.

"Hold on." Clint stepped back and in one smooth movement stripped off his shirt. He tossed it aside, stepped back to her, and crushed her to him. His mouth covered hers again and his hands went to her bottom, stroking, caressing.

He lifted her up and moved her against him, pelvis to pelvis so that his erection rubbed along her cleft, almost like sex, but not quite.

Julie tangled her hands in his chest hair and moaned. It was incredible, definitely not what she was accustomed to, but she felt herself climbing toward a climax.

Then Clint altered the movement, and she moaned again, this time in disappointment.

"Clint . . ."

"Shh." One of his big, rough hands covered her breast. "Let me play with you a little. God knows I haven't thought about much else the last couple of days."

"Play with—*mmm*." His thumb circled her nipple, rubbing back and forth, teasing. She wanted her dress off, *now*, so that he could touch her bare flesh.

Sinking her fingertips into his rock-hard shoulders and putting her mouth to his collarbone, she tried to muffle her heavy breaths. "I . . . I want you to touch me, Clint. Not through my dress."

"I will. In time." He kissed her forehead. "Relax."

Relax? He had to be joking. "Are you out of your—"

Taking her by surprise, he scooped her up and placed her on the mattress, then came down beside her. "You like being bossy, Julie Rose, but not here. Not in my bed."

"You're just teasing me, though," she complained.

He grinned, and it made him look younger and very roguish. That special look, one she hadn't seen before, all but melted Julie's heart.

"Trust me, baby. You'll like the way I tease. Now, just hush and hold still and let me have some fun. You think you can do that?"

Quite honestly, Julie said, "I don't know."

Everything she'd learned about men, what she'd experienced herself and what she'd read in books and seen in movies, told her men were impatient for sex. They wanted it fast and hard. Clint was definitely turned on—she could see the proof of that in his steel erection, in the brightness of his hypnotic eyes, the darker color on his cheekbones, the deepness of his breath.

But at the moment, he seemed content to rest his hand on her belly and stare at her stiffened nipples, visible beneath the bodice of her sundress.

"I'll help you, then." And he caught her hands, raising them above her head. Loosely chaining them there with one big fist, he kept her still. Then, with another killer smile, he slid his other hand up under her dress.

Julie pressed her head back on the mattress

and closed her eyes . . . until she felt his fingers between her legs. Her whole body bowed.

"You're hot, Julie Rose. And already wet."

His fingertips traced up and down the crotch of her panties, too light to give her what she needed, but enough to add to her urgency. Determined to do as Clint wanted, she swallowed her complaints. Disappointing him wasn't an option.

Unless he took too long getting on with it.

"I'm going to kiss your nipples."

Never in her life had she heard a man talk so much during sex. But she didn't complain, not when his mouth closed around her left nipple, hot and damp and gently pulling. The dual assault almost did it. If only he'd press his fingers more firmly against her. If only he'd lower the dress so she could better feel his tongue.

He moved to her other nipple, and when Julie strained against him, he firmed his hold on her wrists, reminding her that he was in control.

She parted her legs and dug her heels into the mattress, lifting into his fingers. It didn't do her any good. He adjusted to her every move, keeping the pressure light, making her sexual need climb until she didn't think she could bear it.

"Clint."

"Let's get rid of the panties." One-handed, he stripped them down her thighs, but left them at her knees. He pressed his palm to her mound and touched his mouth to hers. "How do you feel?"

Seeing him through a haze, Julie licked her

lips and swallowed. "Like . . . like I'd hit you with that stick if it was handy right now."

"Yeah?" He grinned. "Does this help?" His finger moved over her, parted her swollen lips, and sank inside.

"Oh, God." She caught her breath. "Maybe. I don't know."

"How about this?" He began gliding that finger in and out, not deep, but shallow and slow.

Julie twisted. Her muscles squeezed around him. In a voice so faint, she barely heard herself, she pleaded, "Harder please?"

He watched her intently. "Like this?"

She was close, so blasted close. "I need . . . I don't know."

"But I do." He brought his hand out from under her dress, then released her wrists just long enough to pull her dress down to her waist. He scrutinized her, his gaze burning, his nostrils flared. "Christ, you're sexy."

With the opportunity there, Julie grabbed his head and pulled it back to her aching nipples. Clint obliged her, taking her in his mouth, wet and hot, and sucking strongly so that she cried out.

"I like hearing you, Julie Rose." He moved to the other nipple, licked, nipped with his teeth, then tugged.

Her back arched, and he tugged again, more insistently, filling her with a heated rush of sensation.

Still at her breast, he inched her dress up, higher and higher. Julie had one moment of un-

certainty, wondering at how she looked with the
flowery material balled up at her waist, her panties
twisted around her knees. And then Clint's fingers were there again, two of them pressing inside her, deep, firm, and she didn't care how it
looked. She needed a climax, more than she
needed her next breath.

"Oh, please," she whispered, her eyes squeezed
shut, her knees spread open.

"All right." His thumb came into play, moving
slowly, rhythmically over her distended clitoris,
and less than a minute later Julie felt herself
convulsing.

Her thighs clenched, her belly tightened,
her breasts throbbed. She seemed to have no
control over her body, how she moved and the
low guttural cries that were forced from her
lungs. It went on and on, and Clint was relentless, tasting her, stroking her, keeping her at the
peak longer than Julie had known was possible.

She couldn't say for sure when it ended, but
at some point she became aware of Clint over
her, balanced on one elbow, watching her with
an expression that was both tender and hot.

His fingers were still pressed inside her. Her
nipples were wet and sensitive to the air-
conditioning.

"Oh, God." Cautiously, she opened her eyes.

As if he'd been waiting for just that sign of
life, Clint bent to her lips, indulging in long, soft,
deep kisses, eating at her mouth with hunger
and gentleness combined.

Julie was too limp to do more than accept his

attention. She gave a quiet moan of pleasure and tipped her head for a better fit. She *loved* Clint's kisses.

In another form of torture, he dragged his fingers from her swollen sex. Out of her, up and over her still-quivering clitoris. Julie caught her breath.

Their eyes met. Clint held her gaze as he lifted his hand and put his fingers in his mouth. His eyes half closed, and he gave a low growl as he tasted her.

Julie had never seen such a thing. Equally fascinated and aroused by the gesture, her lips parted, and heat flushed her face.

Without a word, Clint sat up and wrested the wrinkled dress from her body. "Lift up." Julie raised her hips, and Clint removed her twisted panties.

Struggling for coherent thought, Julie said, "I'm naked, and you're not."

Clint didn't reply. He put his hands, fingers spread, on her shoulders and began feeling her all over. Down her arms, lingering over her breasts, skimming her waist as if measuring her, across her hipbones, her pelvic bones. When he reached her knees, he pushed them up, then open, leaving her legs sprawled wide.

To help fight off her embarrassment, Julie turned her head to the side and closed her eyes. She was very aware of Clint's fingers clenching on her inner thighs, almost as though he fought himself.

In the next instant she felt his breath, then his tongue, against her sex.

Her eyes popped open, and she lifted her head to see him. She couldn't close her legs, not that she really wanted to, because Clint's broad shoulders were in the way. "Oh, my."

"Hush." He showed no hesitation or uncertainty as he ate at her, his tongue stabbing deep, his face pressed into her.

Swept away on another rush of lust, Julie dropped back to the mattress and stared up at the ceiling in wonder. She'd read about this, but never experienced it. And my, had she been missing out. The pleasure of his mouth and tongue were almost too acute to bear.

She knotted her hands in the rumpled sheets and tried to stay still. Impossible. Her hips lifted, twisting against him, moving with the rhythm of his tongue. He shifted position, and she felt his fingers squeezing into her again, filling her up, gently moving, and it was too much.

His rough tongue teased and stroked her clitoris, then began suckling, pushing her higher and higher, and before Julie could get her bearings she was coming again, screaming out loud this time, all but mindless in her orgasm.

The second she quieted, Clint left her in a rush. "Don't move."

As if she could? She might not ever be able to move again. As it was, she couldn't get enough breath, and her legs and arms were tingling, little aftershocks of pleasure still snapping inside her.

Vaguely she heard a drawer open and some rustling, and Clint was there between her thighs, lifting her hips in his hands and pushing into her.

Julie's first thought was that he'd never fit. There was no pain, just an incredible amount of pressure. His muscles strained; her already shattered nerve endings twitched and convulsed around him.

He growled, a low, grinding sound of pleasure, then whispered, "Relax for me, baby," and he pressed harder.

Julie gripped his shoulders. "I'm trying."

"Good girl."

She felt the head of his penis penetrate, and caught and held her breath.

"Easy now . . ." And with one long, steady push, he began burying himself inside her.

She didn't mean to, but Julie automatically fought his control. She had been with men, but none as large as Clint—in more ways than one. Discomfort built, and she wasn't at all sure she could accommodate him. She flattened her hands on his chest, but it was like trying to hold back the tide.

Staring into her eyes, his expression taut and determined, Clint continued to lean into her. "All of me, Julie Rose. All of—" He went still, his jaw clenched, his eyes squeezed shut.

Sweltering heat built inside her, exaggerated by the heat emanating from Clint. Julie panted for breath. Beneath her palms, his skin burned. And he looked so distressed, almost in pain.

She couldn't bear it. She'd rather die than cause him pain. Not that sex with Clint would kill her. Just the opposite. He'd already shown her more physical pleasure than she'd ever known. She almost smiled at her absurd, errant thoughts.

Forcing herself to relax, Julie took two deep, shuddering breaths, then lifted her legs around him, opening herself to him. To let him know it was okay, she stroked Clint's chest. She wanted him. All of him. Every single inch.

Clint opened his eyes, his face strained as he studied her. "You're okay, Julie Rose?"

"I'm . . . wonderful."

His eyes narrowed. His jaw worked. And with one hard thrust and a guttural groan, he buried himself deep. Julie gasped, but didn't cry out.

"Stay with me," he urged before covering her mouth with his. Other than the consuming kiss, he kept himself still inside her, waiting until she uncoiled, until she softened around him.

When he felt the sting of her nails on his shoulders, he pulled out—and sank back in.

They both groaned.

He did it again, over and over, his patience unending. Julie felt the sweat glistening on her skin and on Clint's shoulders and chest. His biceps were huge as he braced himself a little above her, sparing her his weight, watching her, absorbing the sight of her. He was so attuned to her every move, each small sound she made, that Julie felt beautiful for the first time in her life.

Tears dampened her eyes as they strained together, and Clint dipped his head down, licking them from her cheek. "Come for me again."

Julie shook her head. "I can't."

"Yeah, you can," he insisted.

"No, Clint." A whimper bubbled up with just the thought. "It's too much." But even as she said it, she felt the response building. Like a sexual being, a woman focused only on the excessive needs of her body, she had no control at all.

Eyes burning and bright, Clint murmured, "I'll help," and he slipped one hand between them. Rough fingertips touched her clitoris, and she flinched away. "Easy, baby. Shhh." Using his fingers, he opened her more, adjusted the tilt of her body so that her clitoris was exposed, so that she couldn't escape the thrust and drag of his penis as he entered and left her body.

More tears gathered in her eyes as her swollen flesh burned.

"Just go with it, baby," he crooned, and he thrust harder, keeping his pelvis tight to hers, using one arm to draw her left leg up along his side, penetrating her more, leaving her no room to maneuver—and Julie exploded for the third time that night.

Clint's low rumble of pleasure barely penetrated her lacerated senses. As if in a dream, she felt the rough shuddering of his body as he came with her, the utter stillness that settled over him moments later, before she faded away to oblivion.

With utmost care, Clint separated his body

from hers and fell to his back. He labored for breath—and he smiled. God almighty, Julie Rose was a powder keg waiting to be ignited. She wasn't experienced enough to recognize her own body's reactions, not the way he was. When she'd begun tightening around him, signaling the rise of another climax, he'd almost lost it. Three times. Three orgasms, all from him.

One arm up above his head, the other resting across his middle, Clint allowed himself to focus on the possessive pleasure he felt. They were good together. Hell, they were great together.

After his heartbeat slowed and he could breathe normally again, he turned his head to look at her.

She looked like a woman who'd been ravaged—which he supposed fit. Her nipples, a pale pink, were now soft and velvety and looked very sweet. He rolled to his side, examining her.

Her slim, pale legs were still slightly sprawled, her chest still rising and falling in labored breaths. Dead to the world, out for the count, her limbs were lax in the way of sound sleep.

His heart filled his chest. Damn, but he liked her. And he loved her body. Slim, trim, and very soft. Pure woman. Her mousy brown hair was a mess, half over her cheek, one long tendril caught in her lips. Gently, Clint smoothed it away from her face.

A plain face—that made him so fucking hot he could have taken her again if she'd been awake. But she needed her rest, and he needed to curb his lust a bit if he didn't want to wear her out.

He lowered his hand to her breast, cupping around her, smiling at how delicate she was even here. She'd be an A cup, and it suited her to perfection.

Unable to resist, he leaned forward and drew her nipple into his mouth, softly suckling. She moaned, and her nipple tightened.

Satisfied, Clint raised up again. Damn, he felt content. He had a million things he should be doing, when all he really wanted to do was shut out the real world and sleep with Julie Rose.

He left the bed to dispose of the condom, and when he returned, he saw that she hadn't moved at all. Wearing another asinine smile, he pulled the sheet loose and tucked her in. If he kept seeing her naked, he'd ruin his own good intentions and take her again.

Naked, he went into his living room with the cell phone. He figured while he was up, he might as well call Robert's place again. Unfortunately, there wasn't much to hear: a few cancelled appointments, a brief phone discussion with Drew. Julie's uncle wanted to come over to see Robert, but Robert put him off. He told Drew that he didn't know anything yet. Robert's voice sounded funny, sort of garbled and filled with pain.

Was he worrying about Julie? Clint snorted. No, that one didn't worry about anyone—but himself.

Julie's uncle would have to be told something

soon. It wasn't fair to keep him in the dark. Then Robert got another call, this one from a woman he called "sweetheart." She wanted to see Robert, too, but just as he had put Drew off, he apologized to the woman and told her he'd see her soon, but not then, and not the next day. Probably not the entire week. The cheating bastard.

Well, he'd see Clint—tomorrow—because Clint wasn't asking for permission. He'd just show up, and he wouldn't be turned away.

When the recording ended, Clint reset it and went back to his bedroom. One look at Julie, sleeping like a peaceful angel after all the hell she'd been through, and he pulled back the sheet to join her. Hell, it was still early, but he couldn't resist cuddling her.

Other than sexual relief, he hadn't wanted anything from a woman in a long, long time.

With Julie, he wanted everything he could get, the sex for sure, but he also wanted to tease her, and laugh with her, and he damn sure wanted to keep her safe.

What he didn't want to do was return her. And right now, with her sighing so softly on his throat, he wasn't sure he would.

Chapter Ten

Two hours later, Clint woke hungry, for Julie and for food.

Still in slumber, she curled around him, her hair spread out over his chest, her cool palm over his left nipple, her thigh over his crotch. Jesus.

Clint lifted his head and stared down at himself. Yep, he had a boner. At thirty-eight, he could no longer claim to be a sexual dynamo. He'd left that distinction in his twenties, when sex had been a driving force in his life. These days he cared more about stability and financial security. He was working on both.

Sex, more often than not, was an afterthought that had to be dealt with when his body grew too taut to ignore. With Julie, he stayed taut.

Well, first things first. Since they'd missed

dinner, he was starving, but another hour wouldn't matter.

Turning Julie to her back, he pressed a kiss to her lax mouth. "Wake up, babe."

She mumbled something and swatted at him. Amused, Clint kissed her left nipple, once, twice . . . he drew her into his mouth and stroked with his tongue.

"Clint?"

He raised his head. "That better not have been a question."

She looked at him with sleepy eyes that quickly warmed. Putting a hand to his jaw, she whispered, "Hello."

"Hello yourself." He slid one hand between her thighs, just cupping her, nothing more. "Are you sore?"

She frowned, shifted, then nodded. "A little."

That stymied Clint, being he'd expected her to say something different.

She wiggled. "But not too sore, if that's what you're asking."

"It is." He put his forehead to hers. "Sorry, but you're irresistible."

"Uh huh."

Clint chuckled. "Now, why do you sound so skeptical?" He moved on top of her, and she naturally opened her legs for him. Framing her face in his big hands, he kissed her and, against her lips, said, "I haven't been this horny in years."

"Ummm. I've never been this . . . horny."

The prim, hesitant way she said the word had him laughing outright. He'd be willing to bet

Julie Rose had never used such language before now. "You're a daring wench, you know that?" He kissed her again, longer this time, and when he ended the kiss, her breath was rough and un-even. "Are you hungry?"

"Yes."

"Want to eat first?"

"No."

Damn. If he didn't stop grinning, he'd lose his badass reputation. "Okay, nookie first, then food, then a shower."

Apparently done talking, Julie bit his bottom lip and wrapped her long legs around his waist. Clint could take a hint. To give her time to warm up, he concentrated on just kissing her for a long time. First her mouth, which fascinated him. She tasted good, lush and hot and sweet. And when she curved her mouth into a smile, it trans-formed her face, making her truly beautiful.

Next he moved to her breasts, which fit his palms perfectly. He plumped them up, and when he sucked one nipple while plying the other with his fingertips, Julie went from warm to hot in a heartbeat. She had very sensitive nipples, and he had to hold her back so he could get a condom.

Sitting on the side of the bed, rolling on the rubber, Clint teased, "I've never been in danger of being raped before."

Julie came to her knees behind him, reached around, and tried to help. "I'm not sure you can rape the willing."

"Willing, huh?" He turned on her with a growl,

and laughing, Julie tried to scamper away. He caught her hips and flipped her to her stomach, holding her there when she would have turned back over.

"Clint?"

"You have such a cute ass."

She stuck her face into the mattress, a contradiction of brazenness and modesty. Clint stroked her bottom, down to her thighs, and finally between them.

Her voice muffled against the mattress, Julie said, "This isn't very proper."

"Neither is this," Clint told her, and using one arm, he raised her to her knees and moved behind her.

Julie started to stiffen her arms, but he put his palm to the small of her back, keeping her upper body lower than her behind. "No, I like you just like this. Offered up to me."

"Oh, God." She was back to being muffled.

"Remember, baby, you wanted to do exciting and new things, you want to live a little." Positioned behind her, his hands on her hips, Clint murmured, "Not too many things in this world are more exciting than seeing a woman like this."

She breathed hard. "All right." And with a lot of hesitation, "I'll try."

"It's deeper this way, Julie Rose."

She groaned.

"Tell me if I hurt you." And using his thumbs, he opened her and began easing in. She was already softened and slick, her tender flesh swollen, flushed dark pink. As he watched the head of his penis sink into her, she moaned raggedly, pushing Clint right off the brink. He gripped her hips tight in his big hands and sank into her, being very careful not to cause her discomfort.

It felt so damn good, he knew he wouldn't last. Balancing himself on one arm, he reached beneath her and flattened his hand on her belly. She went rigid in expectation, now knowing what he'd do.

"Open your knees a bit more, and arch your back."

Her shoulders tensed. "I don't think I can."

"Do it, Julie Rose."

She made a soft sound deep in her throat, then slowly spread her knees wider, lifted her bottom more, and Clint pressed his fingers to her, forcing her clitoris into direct contact with the friction of his heavy thrusts.

Julie cried out, pushing back against him, knotting her hands hard in the sheets as an anchor. She was so tight around him, squeezing him when he withdrew, accepting him with a sexy, shuddering moan when he reentered her. The sight of her pale bottom smacking against his thighs was the most erotic thing he'd ever seen.

He tipped his head back and gritted his teeth and came hard. Groaning, drowning in the racking pleasure, he still felt the moment Julie gained her own release.

He collapsed onto her, both of them flat, both of them gasping for air.

Clint started to move, but she whispered, "Please don't. Not yet."

He shifted so that his upper body weight was more to the side of her, kissed her shoulder, and said, "Better?"

She took a deep breath. "Yes."

"Whatever you want, Julie Rose."

"Thank you." And then, a few seconds later, "I like how you feel inside me, Clint. I like the closeness with you."

Clint's heart tumbled over in his chest. "Me, too," he whispered.

A few more minutes passed, and Julie gave a long sigh. "I think we need to shower before we eat."

Skimming his hand down her side, he said, "I dunno. I kinda like you all sweaty and sticky."

"Sticky from you."

He bit her shoulder. "And you."

"Yes."

Her fragrant skin drew him, and he took several more soft love bites before nuzzling her nape. He was inside her, wrapped around her, his head filled with her scent, his chest tight with emotions. It was almost . . . scary. And damn satisfying.

Too much, too soon. "C'mon, lazy. You ready to move yet?"

"I suppose if we must."

Clint kissed her ear. He couldn't stop kissing her. All over, all the time. "I'll be a gentleman, all right?" Before Julie could question him, he left the bed and hefted her up into his arms.

"Your head . . ."

"Is fine. Like the boys told you, it's hard enough to take a blow every now and then." Clint carried her into the bathroom and prepared the shower. They spent a nice leisurely half hour just soaking under the warm spray, washing each other. Playing.

Not since he was a kid had Clint played around. There hadn't been much room in his life for frivolity, not even with women. But Julie wasn't just a woman, and she made him feel like more than a mercenary—more than the man he'd always been.

At one point, Julie kissed his chest and said, "I love hearing you laugh."

Knowing he hadn't laughed much in the last few years reminded Clint of the things he wanted to explain to Julie.

He turned off the water and reached for the towel. Julie wanted to take it from him, but he insisted on drying her himself. "Let me have my fun, babe."

She shook her head at him. "You'd think I'd be used to dominating males by now, after—"

"Yeah, I know." Clint went to one knee to dry her legs, trying not to think too much about the future and where it might take him. "All your hulking male friends in Visitation, right?"

"Yes." Julie stared down at him. "Their wives complain, but jokingly. I don't think they really mind. Well, except for Alyx Winston. She's sort of chasing the deputy, Scott Royal. But Scott, like I said, is especially bossy, being he's in a position of authority. Maybe that's why Alyx hasn't caught him yet."

"Maybe Scott's outrunning her."

"Oh, no. He lets her catch him all the time."

Why that struck Clint as funny, he couldn't say. He wrapped the towel around Julie. "Is Alyx Winston related to Joe Winston?"

"She's his younger sister. She's a lot like Joe."

"Now, that must be interesting."

Julie shrugged. "I'm not sure Scott would agree. Alyx is pretty outspoken and outrageous— like Joe—but she's also very beautiful, too. She and Scott have a strange relationship. I'm not sure what's going on there, but then, I've had other things on my mind."

Clint looped his arms around her waist. "Yes, you have. But time and again, you bring these people up. You miss them?"

"Yes." Her brow puckered. "I suppose I keep mentioning them because, while I've had acquaintances all my life, I've never really had friends. Money can be very isolating. That's one reason I'm anxious to move to Visitation."

"To live off your teacher's salary?"

"Why not? A lot of people live without a trust fund. I don't need much in my life, just the basics." She wrinkled her nose. "As you might have already noticed, I'm hardly aware of fashion, so keeping up with the times isn't important to me."

Clint considered that. He should have used it as an opening to what he needed to discuss, but he wasn't quite ready yet. "Let's find you something to wear."

Back in his bedroom, he pulled on underwear and jeans, but when he started to pull on a black T-shirt, Julie took it from him.

"How about I wear this, and you go topless."

"Topless, huh? You telling me you like my chest?"

"I *love* your chest." She smoothed her hand over his pecs up to his shoulders. She sighed, then stepped back and pulled the T-shirt on over her head.

He wanted to ask her what she didn't like about him. She'd said plenty already on dominating men, enough to let him know her preferences. Problem was, he'd been a take-charge guy from his early teens. Never had he been the type to follow the pack.

Julie held out her arms. "What do you think?"

Her hair was still pinned up from the shower, looking sloppy and sexy and very feminine. His extra-large shirt hung on her slight frame, but her breasts and bottom did interesting things to the soft material.

"Good idea," Clint said. "You look better in my shirt than I do anyway. Now, let's find food."

Over egg salad sandwiches, pickles, and chips, Julie asked, "What will you do next?"

"About?"

She laughed. "Me. About this situation. I can't hide out forever, and I hate it that my uncle is worrying about me."

"I told you. I'm going to go see Robert."

"When?"

"Soon." *Probably tomorrow.* "Can I trust you to stay put and behave yourself?"

Julie stiffened. "I've about had enough of

that. You insist I trust you, yet you continue to rank me as an imbecile."

"I didn't mean—"

"If I *misbehave,* it could put us both at risk. Only an imbecile would do that."

Clint set aside his last bite of sandwich and went to her, hauling her out of her seat. "I trust you. I think you're a wonderful, very caring woman with enough brains for three people. That's not what worries me. But the fact is, you have on rose-colored glasses most of the time. You've lived a sheltered life and don't realize how many scum-bags inherit the earth, people who'd sell you out for little reason, and sometimes for no reason at all."

Julie hung in his grasp, her brown eyes far too observant. "Who sold you out, Clint?"

Well, hell. The woman was too observant for her own good. There'd be no avoiding it now. He picked up their plates and carried them to the sink, giving himself a chance to formulate his words. "I suppose you noticed that I'm not living in the best surroundings."

"What I noticed," Julie said, sidling up next to him to help with the few dishes, "is that you care about the people around you. Marlin and Emilio and Dwayne and Carmen. And they care about you. It's not where you live, but how you live that matters."

Would she always stun him with her outlook on life? "You know, you don't sound like a pampered society babe."

She nudged him with her hip. "That's because I'm not. My dad liked to spoil me, but he also made me aware of how fortunate we were. Several times a year we spent time helping those in need. He considered it part of my education. I think that's why I wanted to be a teacher. And being a teacher, I'm good at keeping track of my thoughts. So I'll ask again, who sold you out?"

Clint rinsed the last plate and put it in the drainer. "You want coffee?"

"I want an answer."

He grinned. Julie Rose was extremely cute in teacher mode. "Would you like coffee with your answer, because it's not a short story?"

Looking adorable in the big shirt and unkempt hair, Julie shooed him to the table. "All right. You sit and start talking, and I'll make the coffee."

Clint pulled out a chair and sat facing her. With no other alternative, he just blurted out the facts. "About three years ago, I narrowly missed doing jail time."

Julie didn't so much as flinch. "What happened?"

"I worked as a mercenary of sorts, saving up money so I could build a house and settle down somewhere. It paid well, and . . ."

She glanced at him, and her voice softened. "You like helping people."

Rubbing his ear, he admitted, "I do. But it got me in trouble, so for a long time, I gave it up." Then his voice softened, too. "Till you."

With the coffeemaker hissing, Julie joined him at the table. "Tell me what happened."

"It was pretty stupid, really. I was on my way home from a successful job. Feeling good, just driving easy. But as I passed this small community, I saw a woman come running out of her house. She had a bloody nose, a black eye . . ." His muscles clenched again in memory. "I can take a lot, but I can't bear to see a woman or a kid hurt."

Julie stayed silent, so he shifted his shoulders, trying to shake off his tension. "Some asshole came out the door after her. Typical hard guy—dirty jeans, wife-beater shirt—"

"There's a shirt for men who abuse their wives?"

Nothing helped him relax more than Julie's candid naiveté. "White ribbed undershirts are sometimes called that."

"I see."

"Anyway, I stopped."

"Of course you did."

Of course you did. Her faith in his moral code left him humbled. "The woman came running toward me, and the guy, if you can believe it, was still cursing and threatening her. He didn't seem to mind an audience at all, so I knew he was going to be trouble."

"And obviously he was."

Clint shrugged. That incident had turned into more trouble than he ever could have anticipated. "I got out of my car, and the woman ducked behind me, trying to use me for a shield.

All I knew was that she was hurt, and he wanted to hurt her more."

"You couldn't let that happen."

"No, I couldn't." Clint made a sound of mixed laughter and disgust. "The guy made a grab for her, and I decked him. It was pure reflex on my part. I didn't even think about it. But the pop to his chin was solid, and he went down fast. That shut him up for a bit, sort of stunned him, like he couldn't believe I hit him. And he was pissed."

"What did the woman do?"

"She went silent, too. No more sobbing, no more hysterics. She still had a death grip on my back, but it was so damn silent I could hear myself breathing. Then her husband told me to mind my own business, that it had nothing to do with me."

"Abuse has to do with everyone."

"Yeah, that's what I used to figure, too. Anyway, he pulled a knife and cut me." Clint's hand went to the long scar that ran from his ribs to his hipbone.

Julie covered her mouth.

He remembered her tracing that faint line, asking about it, and eventually touching her soft lips to him. "It wasn't a real deep cut, thankfully, but there was a ton of blood. The guy grinned, acted like he was going to cut me again, and I lost it. I beat the shit out of him."

Striking the table with her small fist, Julie said, "Good for you."

He laughed again, amused by her reaction, but

not by the memories. "Not so good. The broad ran in and called the police. She said I'd attacked her poor husband for no reason."

"But that's absurd."

"The cops had her story and their own eyes. And the guy was in bad shape." He shook his head. "So I got handcuffed." Clint met her gaze. "He spent damn near a week in the hospital, and it took me nearly that long to make the cops understand that I was defending her."

"And yourself."

"He claimed that was self-defense."

"Didn't they see her wounds?"

"Yeah, but with her swearing they were from an accident, that her husband was an angel . . ."

"Oh, Clint." Julie watched him with eyes full of understanding and sympathy. "She sounds like a very disturbed woman."

Staring down at the tabletop, Clint nodded. "I suppose." He rubbed his face. "I lost everything. What money I had was eaten up by lawyer fees and court costs. I might've ended up with jail time, too, if it hadn't been for her family."

"They backed you up?"

"Against their daughter's wishes. But her mom told me she couldn't take it anymore. So she and her husband and their other daughter all told one story after another about the domestic abuse they'd witnessed. Then a neighbor who'd seen the whole thing jumped on board. Before she knew the guy would be arrested, she'd been afraid to say anything. After that, it sort of fell into place. But I wasn't off the hook." Clint's hand curled into a fist. "I did hurt him, and there was no reason for it. I have better control than that. I could have taken him out with one punch, but instead . . ."

Julie put her small hand·over his fist. "You punished him."

"No one else had." His eyes closed. "If you could have seen that woman, what he did to her face, the bruises. She was his wife, but he used his fists on her."

Julie left her seat and crawled into his lap. "The more I know you, the more I like you."

At first Clint was rigid, lost in the awful memories of those days when he hadn't known what would happen, and hadn't even really known himself. Then her warmth seeped into him and the light scent of her skin wafted around him.

He hugged her tight, pressing his face into her neck and just holding on. Pretty soon, he felt Julie quicken, felt her soothing touches, meant to comfort, turn to exploration, felt her lips graze his fevered skin.

He had to smile again. She had the knack of chasing away any and all negative moods. She nuzzled his jaw, and he heard her accelerated breaths.

"Julie Rose?"

"Hmmm?"

Her voice was a little high, and her hands were now all over his chest. "I'm thirty-eight, baby. I need time to recoup."

"How much time?"

Clint stood with her in his arms. "Let's see. By

the time I have you screaming in pleasure, I should about be there."

He started down the hall, and Julie hid her face against him. "I'm shameless."

"Yeah, but I like it." And with a laugh he tossed her onto the bed. Following her down, he said, "I like it a lot."

Julie slipped out of bed early the next morning. She wanted to pamper Clint with breakfast. If any man deserved pampering, he certainly did. She had just picked up his dark T-shirt, but hadn't yet put it on, when she heard the sheets rustle.

"Hey?"

She turned with a frown. "I was so quiet. How did you hear me?"

With a shadowing of beard on his hard jaw and his silver-tipped dark hair mussed, he looked sleepy and sexy and all male. "Come back here."

The man reeked of temptation. Julie took a step back to resist his lure. "No. You go back to sleep. I'll wake you when breakfast is ready."

His lazy gaze moved over her nude body. "You want to make me breakfast?"

"I'm an adequate cook. Not with fine cuisine or anything, but I can handle breakfast."

His attention lingered on her breasts, and he spoke absently. "Don't leave the apartment."

"I won't."

"All right." His attention finally lifted to her

face, and he gave a crooked, very endearing smile. "Since you wore me out, I won't argue." He closed his eyes and settled back into his pillow.

Appreciating how at peace he looked when sleepy, Julie watched him a moment more, then crept out of the room. Her ankle felt fine today. Her body tingled, and her heart was full. She grinned in pleasure.

She, Julie Rose, had worn out a hunk like Clint Evans. She was unaccountably proud of herself—and very much in love.

Of course, she couldn't tell Clint she loved him. They hadn't known each other long, and he already thought her naïve and sheltered, not to mention his silly assumption that her attraction was based on his rescue. If Mojo or Red had been the first on the scene, she still would have been drawn to Clint. She couldn't say why, other than she noticed so many admirable layers to him.

He was all man, no two ways about that. His height, bulk, and confident ability really did remind her of Joe and Bryan and Scott, but Clint's language alone saved him from any serious resemblance to Bruce.

There was a lot more to Clint than his physical capabilities, though. He cared. About everyone. In that way, he reminded her of Shay, Bryan's wife. And thinking of Shay . . .

Julie got out a frying pan, the bacon and eggs and butter. Once she had bacon sizzling in the pan, she picked up the phone on the kitchen wall and dialed Shay's number. She didn't worry about the early hour because Shay was nonstop energy in a deceptively relaxed manner. She wasn't in the least surprised that Shay answered on the first ring, and that she was not only up, but getting ready to leave the house.

While Julie cooked, she and Shay chatted. She'd missed her friends, and although they had a lot to catch up on, it wasn't her kidnapping that concerned Julie right now. Besides, Shay had no idea she'd been taken from her home, so she saw nothing unexpected in Julie's call. And Clint had said not to mention it, so Julie wouldn't.

No, she wanted to talk about Clint's neighbor, Carmen.

Without giving away her location or her relationship to Clint—if what they had could even be called a relationship—Julie explained Carmen's circumstances.

Shay wasn't in the least judgmental, and she was a good listener with incredible insight. Satisfied by Shay's suggestions and her willingness to get involved, Julie was just hanging up when she felt eyes on her back. Turning, she found Clint lounging in the door frame.

He wore only jeans, and those weren't zipped or snapped. Heartbeat accelerating, Julie visually traced his upper body, from the dark hair on his broad chest to his firm abdomen and along that silky, teasing line of hair that led from his navel down into his open jeans. She sighed.

His feet were bare, his arms crossed over his chest, his expression forbidding.

Just to confuse him, Julie smiled, while giving Shay her goodbyes. "All right, Shay. Thank you, again. I'll check back with you in about a week." Julie nodded, laughed at Shay's enthusiasm, and said, "You, too. Bye now."

She put the receiver back in the cradle and turned to the stove. "I'll have everything on the table in just a minute. How do you like your eggs?"

"Cooked." Clint pushed away from the door, and even though Julie couldn't hear him, she knew he now stood right behind her. "Who were you talking with, Julie Rose?"

Having never cooked for a man before, Julie wasn't sure how many eggs Clint would want, but she'd made him three. They were fried perfectly, not a single yolk broken, and she put them on the plate with care. "That was my friend, Shay. She's married to Bryan, the man who used to be a bounty hunter but now owns a security business."

Clint's hands closed on her shoulders, gently kneading. "And why were you talking to her?"

Julie picked up the plates, ducked under Clint's arm, and headed to the table. "Shay's a philanthropist of sorts. You see, she's very wealthy—"

"Another rich lady?" Clint smirked. "The wonders of Visitation grow by the minute."

"No, not *another* rich lady. Shay's nothing like me. She's . . . free."

That made Clint frown.

Trying to find the right way to explain, Julie

twisted her hands together. "For her entire adult life, her money has always been her own, to do with as she pleases. And it pleases her to help others. She funds women's shelters, safe houses, and organizes a lot of charity events. Other than writing out a check or working at the soup kitchen, I've . . . well, I've never really tried to help an adult before, just children—my students—so I decided I could use Shay's advice, and her money, too, since my money is in a trust."

Clint's eyes narrowed. "If you think I'd take money—"

"You?" Julie blinked. "Oh, no. Clint, you're *more* than capable of taking care of yourself. Why, I wouldn't be surprised if you'd already amassed quite a reputable savings account again."

Bemusement wiped the annoyance from his face. "Actually, I have. I'm saving it up to make a fresh start. That's why I live here still, so I can save more money."

"I assumed it was something of that nature. You're far too intelligent and resourceful to stay down long. But Carmen is different."

"Carmen?" As if Julie had just taken the strength from his knees, he pulled out a chair and dropped into it.

She, too, sat and indicated his plate. "Please, eat while it's hot. I hope you like your bacon crispy."

He picked up a slice and bit into it. "Mmm. It's good. Now, what's this about Carmen?"

Julie was afraid he'd be mad at her, and while that wouldn't stop her from doing what she considered right, she didn't want to waste a single moment of her time with him in disagreement. After a deep breath, she tried another smile.

"Carmen is so vulnerable. She's an educated, gifted woman who knows what she's lost. That must be an unbearable reality to suffer. But Shay has some ideas for getting Carmen into a program—Shay knows of a lot of programs, even those for drug abuse—and she has some ideas on how Carmen can make a fresh start. Shay knows everyone. She has scores of connections. If anyone can help Carmen, it's Shay."

In two bites, Clint ate one entire egg, all the while watching Julie. "You're excited about this, aren't you?"

"Yes."

He nodded. "Breakfast is great. Thank you."

"You're welcome." Julie started to relax.

While pondering her ideas, Clint continued to eat. "Carmen might not agree, you know. I've tried before to talk her into getting help."

"I know. But Shay has a way of slipping the help in on people. If it can be done, Shay can do it."

Clint watched her again. "You're one hell of a woman, do you know that?"

Heat rushed into Julie's face. She wasn't sure she'd ever get used to compliments. "Thank you, but I haven't done anything except put Shay on the case."

"I'm just surprised you don't want to reform Marlin, Emilio, and Dwayne, too."

In for a penny . . . "Wellll . . . I did have some thoughts about them."

Clint laughed. He sat back in his chair, smiled at her, shook his head and laughed again. "Eat up, babe. Your breakfast is too good to go to waste."

Julie finished half her food before sneaking another glance at Clint. He'd all but cleared his plate, even used his toast to gather up any egg yolk he might have missed. She'd never been the domestic type, but it thrilled her that he'd enjoyed her efforts.

He caught her watching him and sat back in his seat. "A sexy woman and a good breakfast." He saluted her with the orange juice glass. "What a perfect way to start the day."

"You're not upset that I called Shay?"

He guzzled down his juice before reaching for the coffee. "You didn't tell her about the kidnapping."

"No, of course not."

"Then why should I care? And by the way, men get mad, women get upset."

He could be so exasperating. "You do seem hung up about these subtle differences between men and women."

He eyed her breasts. "I love the differences between me and you."

The phone rang before Julie could think of anything to say to that. Clint got up to answer it, saying, "Evans here," then, "Hey, Mojo," and with one quick glance at Julie, he turned his back and walked into the other room—where she couldn't hear.

Apparently he wanted to speak in private. He and Mojo were probably making decisions about when and how to return her to her old life.

Because she didn't want to go, Julie would do her best to change his mind.

Chapter Eleven

Clint dropped onto the threadbare couch, settled back and put his feet up on the coffee table. "Anything new?"

"Maybe. And I don't think you're going to like it."

So far, he hadn't liked anything to do with Julie's kidnapping. "Let's have it."

"Petie wasn't arrested with the others. He got away."

"Shit."

"That's not all." Mojo hesitated for only a second before adding, "Now he's missing."

Through the kitchen doorway, Clint could see Julie moving around. She'd finished her breakfast and was pouring herself more coffee. "What do you mean, he's missing? Red can't find him?"

"You know Red, he can find out anything about

anything. But thanks to the car registration, getting Petie's address was a piece of cake. Thing is, he's not there."

Red had connections that boggled the mind. The man seemed to know an insider everywhere. "So Petie's lying low."

"I don't think that's it. I went to his place and snooped around. Someone ransacked his apartment. It wasn't vandalism, it was a search. Drawers were dumped, and all the typical hiding places were gone through. Pain meds were still on the counter, and since I figure you broke his jaw, he'd have taken those with him if he just wanted to hide out."

Julie went to the sink and ran hot water to wash the dishes. Clint's gaze never left her. He noticed that she wasn't favoring her ankle this morning at all. "I'll go have a talk with Asa."

"Let me know when, so I can back you up. Red has some commitments with Daisy, but I've got the day free."

Glancing at the wall clock, Clint said, "I'll leave here in about an hour." Julie started to hum, again drawing his attention. She opened the cabinet beneath the sink and bent to retrieve the dish liquid. Thanks to her lack of panties, Clint got an eyeful. "Damn."

"What?"

He cleared his throat. "Nothing."

Mojo wasn't one for idle chitchat, so he didn't question Clint's distraction. "Allowing you time to get there, let's say ten—"

"Make it noon." Clint stood, his muscles already twitching in carnal anticipation.

"Noon?"

"Is that a problem?" He detoured into the bedroom, grabbed up a condom, and headed for the kitchen.

"No."

"Good. I'll see you then." Clint hung up the phone.

Julie turned with a smile. "Is everything all—"

He smothered her mouth with his own, not as gentle as he should have been, unable to temper the need.

Odd, given how many times he'd already had her, but hunger raged inside him. Julie was here, with him, in his kitchen, in his life. Damn it, already in his heart.

She pushed back. *"Wait."*

Trying to collect himself, Clint breathed hard. Jesus, he'd all but mauled her. She deserved some tenderness. She deserved special care. "Julie Rose, I—"

She turned off the water, dried her hands, jerked off his shirt, and pressed herself back to him. "Okay." Her eyes were already soft and dazed. "Now."

Clint had never considered himself a particularly lucky man—until Julie Rose came into his life.

Scooping an arm below her knees, the other around her back, Clint lifted her to sit on the edge of the table. He shoved his jeans down, tore open the condom packet, and rolled the rubber on with shaking fingers.

The second he moved toward her, Julie opened her arms—and her legs.

Much more of this and he'd probably die of a heart attack. A guy his age could only take so much stimulation.

He caught her shoulders and pressed her flat to the table. "Put your legs around my waist."

She did so immediately, breathing hard, squirming in an effort to rush him. Her heels dug into the small of his back and her slender thighs squeezed him.

"You want me, Julie Rose."

"Yes. Right now."

"You're not ready yet." He moved against her, stroking her vulva with the head of his cock, feeling her open to accommodate him, how wet she got with each glide across sensitive flesh. "But soon," he whispered in awe, "real soon." He bent and put his hot mouth around one nipple.

Her nails bit into his shoulders. "No teasing now, Clint. I mean it."

He believed her. "All right." He repositioned himself and sank into her. Julie cried out, a sound that went straight to his heart, twisting the emotion and need inside him.

She tipped her head back, her mouth open, her expression contorted in the way of undiluted pleasure, natural and real, like Julie herself. Clint pounded into her, harder, faster . . . He felt the heat rise and knew it was all over for him.

"Ah, fuck," he groaned, and began coming with no way to stop it.

Julie's eyes opened, and their gazes clashed. He got lost in her acceptance, felt more connected to her than to any other human being he'd ever known.

Unable to bear it, he kissed her, hard, rough, his tongue in her mouth, and before he finished his release, she tightened around him, her thighs quivering, her hands knotted in his hair. He swallowed her raw cries, cradled her to his chest, and let her ride out the storm.

Leaving her today would be hard.

Leaving her forever would be . . . impossible.

Clint had a lot of things to think about, so why was he still dwelling on Julie Rose? Damn it, he had to clear his head, not picture her sighing softly on the kitchen table, so spent that her independence hadn't been an issue, and she'd let him take care of her. Never before had he wanted to pamper a woman, but with Julie Rose, he took as much pleasure in bathing her, in cuddling her, as he did in making love to her. It was different, for sure, but still so damn enjoyable.

He had to stop thinking about the trusting way she let him use her body, as if she knew in her heart that he wanted only to bring her pleasure.

Urging her to take a nap, he'd carried her to his bed, tucked her in, and kissed her goodbye.

But now, he had to concentrate on business.

He glanced behind him as he went up the walk to Asa's place. Discreetly positioned, Mojo could keep an eye on things. If Clint didn't return in ten minutes, Mojo would come for him. Not that Clint expected any problems; he and Asa had an understanding now, and while Asa was a cold-blooded crook, he had his own code of ethics. Mojo was there because, understanding or not, Clint didn't take chances, especially not when Julie Rose depended on him.

Before he reached the front door, one of Asa's jackals confronted him. Clint remembered the fellow's name was Trent.

At his most polite, Clint said, "Tell Asa I want to see him."

"He's not seeing anyone today."

Eyes direct, body language clear, Clint took one step up the porch. "Be a good lad, Trent, and tell him anyway."

His pride ruffled, Trent tapped on the door and relayed the message to another. A minute passed, and Clint was given entrance. Trent glared at him as he went past, but Clint ignored him. He didn't waste time gloating or prodding a lackey.

Though noon had come and gone, Asa sat at his kitchen table, dressed in a black and red silk robe with the newspaper spread out before him. Fragrant coffee steamed from a mug at his elbow. A carafe and a plate of fruit pastries were close at hand.

Clint nodded his greeting. "Sorry to disrupt your morning."

Asa lounged back. "It's more afternoon than morning, but such is the life of a man in my position. Business is best late at night, and I enjoy the luxury of sleeping in. Coffee?"

"Thanks." As long as they kept things cordial, Clint might obtain some much needed info.

Asa motioned for a young woman to bring another cup to the table, then dismissed her. They were left alone.

Indicating Clint should help himself to the sugar and creamer, Asa said, "I'm pleased that you obliged my wishes."

Clint threw one spoonful of sugar into his coffee, took a drink to gather his thoughts, then met Asa's smug satisfaction. "How's that?"

"You killed Petie."

Clint paused. The fine hairs on the back of his neck stood on end. His senses screamed an alert. "Petie's dead?"

Asa's smile faded into a formidable frown. "You didn't kill him?"

"I punished the bastard, just as I said I would. I broke his jaw and gave him more bruises than he could count." Clint set the coffee aside. "But no, I didn't kill him."

Two seconds passed before Asa began laughing. Given his deep, rough voice, his laughter sounded more like the croup than any type of amusement. "A broken jaw, eh?" He laughed and laughed some more. "Fitting. Petie was a pain in the ass, a punk who ran his mouth far too often."

"Whatever he was, the question remains: Who the hell killed him?"

Lifting rounded but still bulky shoulders, Asa said, "That, I do not know. I assumed it was you, so I made no inquiries. A dangerous thing, assumptions. But he is dead. He was found late last night in a parking lot in the downtown area."

Asa named the bar and the location, a place Clint recognized as common ground for many crimes. Only thugs hung out there. "How'd he get it?"

"Three close shots." Asa touched his stomach, his chest, and then, making a gun of his fingers, shot himself in the head. "Whoever killed him made sure he was dead."

"Any suspects?"

Laughing again, Asa said, "I thought it was you. But if you mean the boys in blue, they're likely stumped, and given Petie's lifestyle and where he was found, they'll dismiss it as a random act of violence, a fitting end to the type of life he led."

"But it wasn't random?"

"I think not." Asa eyed Clint. "My expert opinion? He was killed so that whatever information he had would die with him. The plot thickens, doesn't it? What did Petie know, who hired him, et cetera, et cetera."

Jesus, the situation seemed to grow worse rather than better. Clint stared down at his coffee a moment, lost in thought.

Asa said, "Shall I assume if you broke Petie's jaw, you rescued the lady?"

"Yeah."

"She was . . ." Asa hesitated, and something very ugly darkened his face. "Unharmed?"

Knowing exactly what Asa meant, Clint tightened, always on the verge of anger when he thought of what Julie Rose had been put through. "She wasn't raped, but they threatened her with it."

"Then Petie is lucky he's dead." Asa's raw voice barely rose above a whisper. "I have no tolerance for rape, and if they threatened it, they would have done it. Eventually."

"Yeah." Clint shook off the awful thoughts. He had to keep his head now. Julie needed him to figure things out. "She'll be okay."

Asa curled his mouth into a cynical smile. "Because you'll make it so?" He lifted his coffee cup. "Sounds to me like you're getting personally involved."

Clint was about to comment on that when Asa suddenly looked toward the kitchen doorway. His expression was at first alarmed, then magically transformed into a gentle smile of welcome. "Marie. How long have you been waiting? Come in."

He stood and held out his arms. A strikingly beautiful woman with Asa's dark coloring came cautiously into the kitchen. Petite but lushly built, dressed in expensive, feminine clothes, she embraced her brother while stealing a wary glimpse of Clint.

Odd, Clint thought as he, too, pushed back his chair in respect. How could a man as cold and ruthless as Asa look so adoring and protective when holding his baby sister? And baby sister described her, because she didn't look to be more than twenty-one or twenty-two.

The woman seemed so skittish, Clint wondered how much she'd heard.

"Marie," Asa said with a flourish, "this is Clint, an acquaintance of mine." Beaming with pride, Asa added, "Clint, my sister."

Clint held out his hand. "Ma'am."

While Marie did have her brother's hair color and skin tone, her eyes were a startling light blue. They were eyes that would capture a man's attention—and Marie must have realized that, given how she quickly, almost fearfully, averted her gaze. She accepted Clint's hand in a brief, barely polite greeting.

"I'm sorry that I've interrupted your discussion. It sounded . . . important."

Asa responded with emphatic denial. "You can never interrupt, you know that." He kept his arm around the woman. "My sister is quite shy," he told Clint.

Clint remembered what he'd been told, that Asa's sister had been brutally raped, and that her mother had died trying to protect her. Sympathy welled inside him. With stylish clothes and attention to hair and make-up, Marie attempted to look as composed as any other woman. But the turbulent emotion in her face told a different story. Her brother might not see it—but Clint did.

Using the awkward moment to make his exit,

Clint said, "I'll leave so you two can chat. Asa, I appreciate the coffee and your time."

Asa nodded. "Now that you have me intrigued, you will keep me informed."

It was a demand, not a question, and Marie's gaze moved between the two of them. Clint shrugged. "Odds are, you might know before I do." He slid a business card across the table. It listed an untraceable phone number, no name, no address. "I check the number daily." Clint glanced at Marie, and found her staring at his card. "Ma'am."

Her head jerked up, her smile forced. "Goodbye."

Asa moved protectively to her side, and as Clint left, he heard Marie whisper, "Why was he here? You said something about a woman . . ."

Asa shushed her. "Don't fret over it, Marie. The woman is fine. Clint is taking care of her."

"But who is she? *Where* is she? What—"

And then Clint couldn't hear anymore. He frowned, thinking that Marie's voice sounded familiar, and was bothered by the depth of her interest. No woman should have suffered what she did. He hoped the men who hurt her had gotten retribution. Knowing Asa, they surely had.

The second Clint got in the truck with Mojo, he told him about Petie.

Mojo digested that information with typical introspection. "Now what?"

Until Mojo asked, Clint wasn't sure what his next move should be. Then he made a sudden decision based solely on gut instinct. "I'm going to go see Robert, Julie Rose's ex-fiancé. Know where he lives?"

Mojo nodded and put the truck in gear.

It wasn't a long drive, maybe a little over a half an hour. But all the way there, Clint's tension rose. He *knew* something was wrong, though he had no idea what. "Keep your eyes open. This feels messed up."

"Maybe you should skip it."

"Can't." Clint opened the truck door. "I have to find out what the hell's going on. Just keep watch. I should be back in ten."

Clint strode up the spotless walkway and rapped on the front door. No one answered. He leaned on the doorbell, and when that still didn't produce results, he slipped a small case out of his pocket. Extracting a long, thin metal pick, he jimmied the lock with the expertise of a professional burglar. The heavy, ornate door swung open on well-oiled hinges.

Given the deadbolt had been left unlocked, maybe Robert wasn't even home. But Clint still wanted to have a look around. Senses finely tuned to any noise or movement, he methodically went through each downstairs room until he heard a slight noise from the kitchen.

His knife was at the small of his back, his gun in an ankle holster. He could get either one in less than two seconds if necessary, but so far, he didn't feel the need to have them in hand.

Following the sound, Clint made his way down the hall, through the dining room—and there, at the kitchen table, his face so bloody and swollen it was barely recognizable, sat Robert. Clint stared in shock at the damage done to him.

Robert half slumped at the table with a steaming cup of tea in front of him and a bottle of pills at his elbow. The poor bastard. Someone had worked him over good.

Clint leaned into the doorway. "I want to know what's going on, Robert. And I want to know now."

Robert would have jumped in surprise if he'd had the energy. But he hurt everywhere, the pain sinking in each day, growing worse and worse instead of better. "Evans." His words sounded like mush, formed by his thickened lips and swollen jaw. "What are you doing here?"

Clint strode forward and pulled out a chair. "You're alone here?"

Robert half shrugged. "Other than you."

Seating himself, Clint nodded. "Good. How about I ask the questions, and you do your best to answer them, leaving out the bullshit and half truths for a change."

Hands shaking, Robert extracted a tiny pill and placed it gingerly in his mouth. The hot tea burned his split and bloodied lips, making him wince. He nodded, then lifted a hand toward the teapot. "Tea?"

Clint looked around before leaning his elbows on the table. Robert knew the kitchen was a mess, but he hadn't dared let anyone in, not even the cleaning lady.

He peered at Clint. "You locked the door again?"

That chilling gaze that Robert remembered so well settled on him. "A locked door won't keep you safe if someone wants to pound on you again."

"I know. But I don't want Drew or . . . anyone else to come in and catch me like this."

"Anyone else, meaning your girlfriend?"

Robert could tell that Clint expected him to lie. But lying had gotten him nowhere, and now he had to change tactics. "Yes. She'd be very upset to see me like this." The irony of it struck him, and he gave a gasping, pain-filled laugh. "Especially if she found out who did it."

Clint stared at him as if he could see his soul. And maybe he could. Robert wouldn't put it past him.

"Who did?"

Another sip of tea didn't bolster his courage at all, so Robert gave up. He had a feeling Evans would find out one way or another anyhow. "Asa Ragon."

A chill seemed to enter the room. "I just saw him."

That startled Robert. "Why? You said he didn't have Julie."

"He didn't. He also didn't have bloody knuckles, so try again."

Robert managed a smile that felt like a train wreck. "I misspoke. Asa *had* me beaten. He just watched."

"Why would he do that?"

"Money, why else?" But if Asa ever found out that Robert was involved with Marie . . . God, he'd probably blow his brains out.

It took Clint a moment, and then understanding showed on his face. "The building he
wanted to sell. He's making you pay him for what
he lost when the sale didn't go through?"

Robert saluted him. "At least I made a good
decision when I hired you."

In a lethal voice meant to instill fear, Clint
said, "That remains to be seen, Bobby. So, why
don't you go to the cops?"

"I can't." Not without losing Marie, and that he
wouldn't do.

Clint didn't push that just yet. Instead, he
shrugged as if Robert's decision didn't really
concern him. "Fine. You don't want to involve
the cops, that's your business. Then just pay Asa
and be done with it."

"I don't have the money."

Evans picked up a gold-edged spoon, a china
cup, then eyed the rest of the kitchen, which had
cost over a hundred thousand to redecorate.
"Right. Try again."

"I don't, damn you." Losing his temper hurt,
and Robert moderated his tone. It took him a
second to catch his breath, to tamp down the
agony that movement caused. "Most of my money
is in investments and stock . . ."

"So cash in."

He shook his head. "Drew is involved in almost all the same enterprises. He'd know if I extracted money, and then he'd ask why. He has a
lot of influence—ask Julie if you don't believe
me. He could have me cut out of almost every

deal. If Drew wished it, I would be broke within a month."

Without an ounce of sympathy, Clint said, "Julie walked away from his money. Why don't you?"

Temper frayed, Robert pushed his fists against the table and half stood, which was all he could manage without some help. "Julie's not in love, damn you!"

Oh, God, it hurt to breathe, hurt to move. Robert sank back into his chair with a shuddering groan—then groaned again when he saw the awful expression on Clint Evans's face.

Lips tight, eyes narrowed, Clint whispered, "Who do you love, Robert?"

It was all over, Robert knew it. The best he could do now was follow Clint's example and be a man, be honorable and brave and try to help Julie the best he could. She deserved at least that much from him. "Not Julie, if that's what you're thinking."

"I wasn't thinking that. Not for a single second." Suddenly his eyes widened, his expression filled with incredulity. "Oh, shit no. Even you couldn't be dumb ass enough to fall for Asa's sister."

Robert met his gaze without flinching. "Yes."

"Damn it. I knew her voice sounded familiar."

Robert didn't understand, and before he could question Clint, his tone grew softer, more menacing. "Did you have Julie kidnapped, Robert?"

"*No.*" Robert squeezed his eyes shut. "I swear to God, I didn't. I honestly thought Asa had taken her, as a threat against me because of the money he feels I owe him. That was bad enough, with my guilt almost eating me alive. But now . . . I don't know why anyone would want to hurt Julie."

As if he had all the time in the world, Clint stood. He came around the table and put an arm around Robert.

Panicked, Robert said, "What are you doing?"

"Helping you to the couch. I have a friend who can look you over, see if you need any medical attention. Something tells me you haven't been to the hospital."

"No, I don't want to see anyone—" Humiliation cut off his words as Clint more or less lifted him and took him to the den. *Bastard.*

Clint laughed. "Yeah, save that for someone who gives a shit about your opinion, Burns." He put Robert on a leather sofa. "We have a lot of talking to do, and you can't do it without a little medical attention first."

Panting in his pain, sweating with it, Robert leaned back on the couch. Clint left the room, but returned less than a minute later with an eerily silent, black-eyed man who looked like he hated the world and everyone in it.

Without a word of greeting, ignoring Robert's groans and gasps of agony, the dark man moved him so that he lay flat. He started an inspection that didn't take Robert's dignity into consideration. He wasn't actually rough, but he sure as hell wasn't gentle either.

"Some cracked ribs. Broken nose." The man stood. "Nothing too serious."

Robert hurt all over, and this devil said it wasn't too serious? "I am so reassured," Robert quipped.

Clint laughed. "Amusing, isn't he?"

The other man shrugged. "I can fix the nose."

"The hell you will!" His outburst cost Robert, and he reclined with a moan.

They continued as if Robert wasn't in the room. "Nothing can be done for the ribs. He needs to stay still and rest."

Clint leaned down and looked Robert in the eye. "C'mon, Bobby, don't be a baby. Your nose is crooked as a dog's hind leg. Do you want it to stay that way? Do you want it to look like mine?"

"God, no."

"Then buck up and try not to cause a fuss." Clint stepped out of the way, and the dark man loomed over him.

"Close your eyes."

Because Robert didn't know what else to do, he closed them. Warm, hard fingers clasped the bridge of his swollen, aching nose, and a second later, he heard a loud snap. He shouted with the awful pain—but then it was over.

"Keep some ice on it to make the swelling go down."

Robert just lay there, speechless. How the hell had he sunk so low?

Clint dragged a heavy, stuffed cherrywood chair over close to the couch. "Now. Let's talk."

"I don't know what to say."

"You can start by telling me more about Marie."

That alarmed Robert as nothing could have. "Why?"

Clint didn't cut corners. "Because it occurs to

me that she has more reason than anyone else to want Julie out of your life. And with her brother's connections, it'd be easy enough for her to have orchestrated a kidnapping."

Robert shook his head.

"Also, Petie, the man who had Julie, was executed at close range. If it is Marie, she's playing a very dangerous game with very dangerous people."

"No." Robert would never believe that of her. Sure, she was jealous of Julie, but she was also sweet and kind and gentle. She was nothing like her brother. "Marie is innocent in all this. She's—"

"Listen to me, Burns. Somehow all this fucking drama is connected to Julie's abduction, and I'm going to figure this out, even if it kills you."

That caused Robert to do a double take. If it killed *him?* But he'd known from the start that Evans was capable of killing. And at the moment, despite the calmness of his voice and his relaxed position in the chair, he looked almost anxious to do so.

"Look at it this way," Clint said. "If Marie is involved she could be in serious danger."

Robert gulped. With no choices left to him, he did as Clint Evans insisted: he talked.

Clint's mind cramped as he drove toward his apartment. For half an hour he'd tried to talk himself out of his worry, but damn it, Julie Rose did bring out the old lady in him. He'd fretted more since meeting her than he ever had in his entire life. He might as well get a cane and park his sorry ass in a rocker, because around her, he'd definitely lost his edge.

He tried to tell himself to stop worrying, that she was safe in his apartment. She'd promised to stay put, and as Julie liked to remind him, she was smart enough not to put herself at risk.

But damn it, he'd lived by his instincts too long to dismiss the fear completely. It had begun creeping up his spine the moment Asa told him Petie was dead. And when he saw the job done on Robert, and realized Robert was involved with Asa's sister, it'd taken all his control not to rush home.

He was only another ten minutes away, but still . . .

Cursing himself, Clint drew out his cell phone and dialed the apartment number. On the third ring, just when he'd been ready to panic, Julie picked up. "Hello?"

She sounded breathless and rushed, and relief washed over him in a debilitating wave. "Hey, babe."

"Clint? Hello! Where are you?"

"Just a few minutes away. What took you so long to answer?"

"Carmen's cutting my hair."

His heart stopped. His stomach hit his knees. Then he roared, *"She's what?"*

"Don't you yell at me, Clint Evans. It's my hair, and I'll do with it whatever I please."

All kinds of awful, mind-boggling disasters flooded his brain. He envisioned her soft brown tresses lopped off at her ears, or teased out the way some hookers wore it. Or . . . Damn it, he *liked* her hair the way it was. He liked the texture, the length, the color.

"She did my make-up, too. I look so different."

No, fuck no. Through his teeth, Clint rasped, "You tell Carmen I'm on my way, to stop whatever the hell she's doing."

In her prim teacher's voice, Julie said, "I'll do no such thing. Besides, she's almost done now. Goodbye."

And she hung up on him.

Pedal to the metal, Clint slipped through a yellow light, took a corner a little too fast, and swung his jeep into a parking space with panicked precision. Bounding up the stairs two at a time, he reached the hallway just as Carmen's door shut.

So she'd run off, had she? The coward.

He looked at his apartment door and his blood ran cold. He'd rather face a gang of knife-wielding hooligans than see Julie done up like a whore.

And he'd rather take a beating than hurt her feelings.

Drawing a fortifying breath, he put his key in the lock, opened the door, and stepped in.

In the kitchen doorway, outlined by sunlight

through the window above the sink, Julie stood uncertainly, waiting for his reaction.

Wow. And . . . wow again. Clint absently shoved the door shut behind him, unable to drag his gaze off her.

"Well?" Julie asked.

He shook his head. He got hard. He swallowed. "You look . . . great." And she did. *Bless Carmen.*

Her smile did it, pushing him right over the edge. "Didn't Carmen do an incredible job?"

Again, Clint nodded, words beyond him.

Julie laughed. Holding out the sheer gauze skirt that just skimmed her ankles, she turned. Her hair, now trimmed to just below her shoulders and lying in soft curls, swung around with her. The skirt was some pastel flowery pattern, paired with a pink tank top. She was barefoot, but wore an ankle bracelet, and her eyes somehow looked bigger, her lashes longer, though whatever make-up she wore was so subtle, Clint couldn't quite pick it out.

He started for her.

Julie ducked behind the couch. "Oh, no you don't. Not until you apologize to Carmen."

In a stern tone, Clint said, "Come here, Julie Rose."

As usual, his stern tone had no effect on her. She laughed again, her eyes twinkling, her cheeks either flushed or rosy with make-up. "You have to apologize, Clint. You might have hurt her feelings."

Clint circled the couch, keeping Julie in his sights. "Did she say that?"

"No, she thought it was funny that you got mad." Julie circled, too, staying just out of reach.

"Don't make me chase you, baby."

Wagging a finger at him, she laughed almost hysterically. "You have to behave."

Clint shook his head. "I'll behave. I'll even apologize. Later."

Julie kept backing up. "Now, Clint . . ."

Done waiting, desperate to hold her, to prove that she was okay and his, Clint went over the couch to get her. Julie screamed and turned to run.

And Clint's door banged open with so much force, it bounced off the wall.

Clint realized that he'd forgotten to lock it just as two big men filled the doorway. They both looked disreputable, but for different reasons. Clint took their measure in the blink of an eye. One was big all over, oozing menace, prepared to fight. The other wore tattered jeans and a snug black tee, with long, unkempt hair and the scraggliest beard Clint had seen in this century.

Damn it, he'd put Julie at risk with his carelessness. In a single leap, Clint placed himself in front of her, protecting her with his body. The two men faced off with him, the bearded one somewhat distracted, the other balanced in the way of a man familiar with hand-to-hand combat.

It was a standoff, but Clint wasn't about to wait for someone else to act first. He attacked.

And all hell broke loose.

Chapter Twelve

Clint took a swing at the bearded guy, but, without thought or effort, he somehow managed to duck. In no hurry, without a care, he moved to the side and raised a brow in inquiry.

Clint never missed, and the fact that he had now set him off. He turned to the other man, who backed up one step.

"Now, hold up just a—"

Clint didn't let him finish. This guy was the bigger of the two, and Clint sensed he was more of a threat. With practiced ease, Clint turned on him, grabbed his arm, and twisted it painfully behind his back. At the same time he crossed his other arm around the man's thick neck. After locking the hold in, Clint could choke him out or break his arm or his neck with little effort. Most men would have been groaning in agony, but this one just went still.

Julie jumped up and shouted, "Oh, my God!"

The man Clint held didn't groan. No, instead he said, "Damn, woman, what have you done with yourself?"

Seeing red, Clint started to twist the arm a little more, but Julie rushed forward.

Still holding perfectly still, the man said, "Honey, if you don't want him neutered, you better tell him to turn me loose."

Julie gasped, and said to the man, "Don't you dare hurt him."

Outrage knocked the wind out of Clint. "Don't hurt *me?*"

Her new hairdo mussed, her eyes dark with nervousness, Julie rounded on him. "Now, Clint, this is not a time to be macho."

Dumbfounded, Clint stared at her. She dared chastise him with two intruders present? His temper shot up another notch, on the verge of erupting. Teeth locked, he explained, "I'm the one in control, Julie Rose, in case you failed to notice that."

But then the man he held said, "Actually, if you'd care to take a peek, I could remove your balls at any second."

Scowling at that too-calm, almost amused tone, Clint indeed looked down. And he saw a shiny, sharp blade held in the big bruiser's left hand, now pressed just below his testicles.

Ho boy. Clint hadn't even seen him draw the knife. He squeezed the right arm an inch higher. "Drop it."

"As soon as you turn me loose, I'll do exactly

that." Then he said, "And, Jamie, I swear to God if you choose this particular moment to laugh, I'll brain you."

Jamie? Clint felt as if he'd been dropped into a circus. "Jamie Creed?"

"Oh, now you did it," said the man threatening his family jewels. "He'll think he's famous, and we'll never get him to quit being such a weirdo."

Fathomless eyes stared at Clint, sending a shiver down his spine. "Joe's not going to hurt you, and you're not going to hurt him."

A groan nearly escaped Clint. Everything started to sink in. It couldn't be, but still he asked, "Joe, as in Joe Winston?"

A robust laugh filled the air. "Julie, have you been telling tales out of school? Now give, honey. What have you said about me?"

Joe Winston was obviously a lunatic. Clint was prepared to break his arm or neck or both, but all he wanted to do was joke. Pissed, Clint released him with a shove hard enough to knock him to his knees.

He didn't even stumble. But he did flip his knife a few times and then tuck it away in a blur of motion. As if Clint had asked, he said, "It's a balisong, or butterfly knife. Comes in handy sometimes." He added in idle warning, "I'm *real* good with it."

"I can see that." Trying to regain his aplomb, Clint crossed his arms over his chest and stared at Julie. "You invited them here?"

She gasped so hard, she damn near knocked

herself over. "No, I did not! I told you I wouldn't
tell anyone." She marched up to him and pointed
a finger at his face. "You're never going to trust
me, are you?"

Joe dropped his big, hulking body down onto
the couch with a sigh. He crossed his arms behind his head, crossed his ankles on Clint's table.
"Actually, she called Shay, so this number was on
the caller ID. No one thought anything of it until
Jamie showed up in a tizz swearing the world
was ready to end. Then Bryan and I—Bryan is
Shay's husband and a real handy fellow with
tracking people down—did some checking and
traced the number back here."

"My number is unlisted."

"Yeah." Joe bobbed his eyebrows and grinned.
"But I know people. Bryan knows people. It was
easy enough to get the info."

Clint understood that, because he knew people, too. "I don't believe this."

In an exaggerated, soothing tone that irritated
more than anything else, Joe said, "Why don't
we close the door and all relax? Then we can figure out why the hell Jamie dragged me here,
claiming Julie was in serious peril, on the verge
of death, when it looks to me like she's just having a good old-fashioned flaming affair." He
winked at Julie. "And by the way, good for you,
hon, on the new look and the fling."

Clint wanted to hit him.

He wanted to hit the other one, too, even
though that fellow did no more than linger in
the room, looking around and sort of . . . ab-

sorbing things. Clint didn't like it that they were here, that they'd gotten the better of him, that they'd caught him unawares. He'd have to show them who was in control.

But first things first.

He shut and locked the door, then went to Julie Rose. She still appeared miffed, so he caught her chin and tipped her face up. "I trust you, babe. They just took me by surprise."

"Really?"

"Yeah."

Her frown smoothed away and she smiled. "Well, all right, then."

Damn, her smiles were great, taking her from plain to sexy in the blink of an eye. Clint bent and kissed her, quick and hard, and that made her flush. He smoothed her cheek with his thumb and smiled, too.

A little rattled, she gestured to Jamie. "Come on in and sit down, Jamie. Would anyone like coffee?"

Coffee? Clint couldn't believe her attitude. He snorted, then walked over to the one known as Jamie Creed, the one with supposed psychic powers. "So you think she's in danger?"

Jamie didn't blink. "I know she is."

Clint couldn't help it—he got drawn in. Jamie was so sure of himself, and there was a mystical air about him that rocked Clint's logical foundation. He believed in intuition and instinct. Perhaps Jamie just had a bigger dose than most.

He had no reason to trust Jamie, except that Julie Rose trusted him. Given the two men were her friends, and they were here now, Clint figured he might as well clue them in. "I'm afraid you're right."

"I know I am."

Smug bastard. "Like she said, come in and sit down. Since you're her friends, I don't have to kill either of you."

Joe laughed and tugged on a small diamond stud in his ear. "I was never in danger of being killed."

With an evil smile, Clint said, "It's hard to fight with a broken arm."

Joe shrugged. "I've fought with broken bones before. But losing your gonads . . . now, that'd slow a man down."

Clint took that on the chin. His shoulders bunched, his hands curled into fists. "Not if he thinks he's defending his woman."

Julie made a sound of affront. "Your woman? What kind of chauvinistic, caveman comment is that?" She shook her head, but then said in a smaller voice, "Really? Am I your woman?"

Jamie circled the room, stopping in front of them all. He gained their undivided attention just by moving. He turned to Julie. "You need to leave here."

Clint's muscles bunched even more. Jaw out, eyes burning, he growled, "She's not going anywhere."

"She has to."

"Not without me."

Dark, sort of spooky eyes took his measure. "No, not without you." Then Jamie dropped a bombshell. With no warning at all, he said, "I know you love her."

Clint drew back. *"What?"*

"What!" Julie all but shrieked at the same time. They looked at each other.

Joe Winston chuckled. "Get used to it, buddy. Jamie does this stuff all the time, telling things you don't want told, forcing you to bare your soul before you're ready. He's an aggravating ass, but he sort of grows on you after a while."

Julie whipped around, giving Clint her back and wringing her hands together. "Jamie," she hissed in an agonized whisper, "please behave."

Clint took a step toward her. He didn't want her upset, but he had no idea what to say. He wasn't good at apologizing, or spilling his guts, or getting all emotional and mushy. Hell, he was a soldier by nature, not a damn poet. "Julie . . ."

She held up an imperious hand, palm out, stopping whatever malarkey might have come out of his mouth. "No," she said. "It's okay. You don't have to say anything."

That pissed Clint off. "The hell I don't."

Jamie interrupted their budding argument. "We need to get her away from your place. Not this very second, but soon. You're the target now, not her, so being near you is dangerous to her."

That distracted everyone. Clint looked at Joe, who just shrugged, before glaring at Jamie. "What the hell are you talking about? Julie was the one kidnapped."

Joe's feet hit the floor with a solid thud. "You were kidnapped?"

Julie's chin went in the air. "Clint told me not to talk about it."

"For the love of . . ." Clint threw up his hands. "That was then. Not now."

Shrugging, Julie said, "Yes, I was kidnapped. Clint rescued me before I was hurt."

"Thank God." Joe looked at Clint with new respect.

"Then Robert—my ex-fiancé who hired Clint to get me back—asked Clint to keep me for a while."

Intrigued, Joe leaned forward, elbows on his knees. "He asked Clint to keep you?"

Julie nodded.

"And why's that?"

Clint gave up. "Maybe coffee is in order after all. Let's go in the kitchen and I'll tell you everything." He headed that way first, but noticed Julie Rose hanging back, giving Jamie hell in a whisper.

He shook his head.

Joe nudged him. "You haven't told her yet?"

Clint knew exactly what Joe meant. "I've only known her a few days." He got the coffee down out of the cabinet and set it on the counter. "And those few days have been spent trying to sift her friends from those people who only pretend to be her friends." Clint glanced at Joe. "Julie Rose seems to trust everyone, but I'm more cautious."

Joe nodded. "No hard feelings. I'd have been cautious, too."

Giving his acknowledgment of that, Clint

added, "Today, I think I finally got it figured out."

Joe leaned against the counter while Clint rinsed out the carafe. "You think you know who had her kidnapped?"

"Her ex-fiancé's new girlfriend."

Julie strolled into the kitchen, looking sassy and sweet in her new clothes and with her newly styled hair smoothed back into place. "Marie Ragon? Don't be ridiculous."

Joe tugged at his earring. "Used to be, I would have discounted a woman. Experience has taught me not to be so dumb."

As Clint filled the carafe, he wondered what run-ins with female villains the indomitable Joe Winston had suffered. "Babe, you caught her in bed with your fiancé. She wants you out of Robert's life. That gives her a motive."

"But I am out of his life. That is, we're only friends now."

"That's not the way he tells it. Marie, and everyone else, believe you're still engaged."

"Why would they think that?"

"Because that's what Robert tells them. He said he's afraid if your Uncle Drew found out you weren't together, he'd cut him off and ruin him financially."

"Oh." Julie pulled out a chair. "Yes, if Uncle Drew thought Robert had hurt me, he might retaliate that way. I told you that he feels responsible for me."

"Marie also has the means, given she's Asa's sister." And then to Joe, "Asa is this little slum

king who has a record a mile long. He likes to
think of himself as powerful." He turned to
Julie. "He had Robert beat up."

Worry brought Julie back out of her seat. "Is
Robert okay?"

"He'll live."

"Clint Evans, that is not an adequate evalua-
tion of his health."

Despite everything, Clint grinned. Julie Rose
was so amusing when she got fired up. "He'll be
okay, but it might take a few weeks."

"He found out about Robert and Marie, didn't
he?"

"No. If he had, Asa might've killed Robert.
He's damn protective of Marie." Clint turned
the coffee machine on and crossed his arms
over his chest. "Marie was raped once. Since then,
I gather Asa hovers over her like a guardian
angel."

"Oh, my God." Julie covered her mouth with
a hand. "That poor woman."

"Exactly. You can imagine how Asa would feel
to know Robert had made her a mistress. Robert
probably would not live out the day. But actually, the bone of contention between them now
is that Robert interfered in a business deal and
it cost Asa money."

"Money that Asa wants him to pay back?" Joe
asked.

"That's about it. Only Robert doesn't have
the money. All he has in free cash is the money
Julie's uncle gave him for her ransom."

Outraged, Julie dropped back into her seat again. "He wanted to use my ransom money to pay off Asa?"

"Afraid so. Robert figured he couldn't have Asa arrested because that might alienate Marie. He can't pay him off because your Uncle Drew would know and not like it. He's trapped."

Joe comprehended the entire scenario. "So he hired you instead of just paying? And in doing that, he probably saved her life."

"Likely. If the bastards had gotten their money, Julie Rose would have been dead before I could have reached her."

"So in a way," Julie mused, "I owe Robert my gratitude."

"Don't even think it." Clint sat at the table near her, and Jamie came in, still looking around as if he hadn't seen an actual apartment before. Did he live in a damn cave, then? Clint wondered.

Julie asked, "What did Asa do to Robert, exactly?"

Still watching Jamie, Clint shrugged. "He has a few cracked ribs, and his face looks like hamburger."

She winced. "Poor Robert."

"Don't you dare feel sorry for him, Julie Rose. He probably started all this by cheating on you with Marie. And he thought Asa had you from jump, sort of to get even, to force him to pay up. But he didn't level with me. He half hoped I'd take care of Asa for him, so Marie wouldn't be able to blame him. If he had any conscience at all, he'd have told me every damn detail up front, to better the odds in your favor."

Julie patted his hand. "I'm sure he took one look at you and knew you'd keep me safe."

Disbelieving her attitude, Clint turned to Joe, and Joe half smiled. "Women," Joe said. "You gotta love them."

There was that damn L word again. Clint fought a grimace. To change the subject, he barked at Jamie. "Why the hell do you keep pacing around? You're making me jumpy."

Jamie stared at the kitchen window with a frown. "It's not me making you nervous. It's your instincts." Jamie frowned, drew a deep breath, and said in an eerie hush, "Something's going to happen."

Unable to dredge up any doubt in the face of Jamie's absolute conviction, Clint pushed back his chair and stalked to the window. He looked out—and caught a flicker of sunlight on steel. *"Down."*

Joe Winston reacted, tackling Jamie and taking him to the floor while Clint turned and dove for Julie.

The kitchen window shattered, blown out by a bullet—that narrowly missed Clint's head.

Julie lay flat on the floor, dazed, with Clint crushing her, completely covering her with his muscular body. Someone had shot at him! She struggled to get up.

Joe cursed as he rolled off Jamie. "That was too damn close for comfort."

Pushing up to his elbows, Jamie turned his

head toward Clint. He seemed unfazed by the assault. "You're the target now, not Julie."

"Oh, no." Julie's throat felt tight. "But why?"

Clint helped Julie ease into a sitting position. "Are you okay?"

"Yes." She shook all over and couldn't stop touching Clint, but she wasn't hurt. Dear God, she'd almost lost him. "You were *shot* at."

"I'm okay." Livid, Clint turned to Joe. "It has to be Marie. And I've had enough."

Typically for Joe, he rubbed his hands together. "Let's go get her, then."

Julie grabbed Clint before he could stand. She knotted her hands in his shirt and tried to shake him. "You have to call the police!"

Jamie stood and brushed himself off. "I don't know."

Everyone turned to him. Joe groaned, Julie didn't know what to feel, but Clint just looked more furious.

"You don't know what?" he demanded.

Jamie stared at the shattered window and shook his head. "Who did this."

"It was Marie."

Shaking his head, Jamie said, "It might have been a man."

"Marie probably hired some of Asa's thugs." Clint pulled Julie closer, as if to prepare her, then admitted, "The guy who took Julie, Petie Martin, was found shot to death."

It felt like someone had shoved all the air out of her lungs. Julie couldn't breathe, couldn't think. Her world was coming down around her.

First, Joe and Jamie showed up with ominous predictions, and then Jamie said Clint loved her and . . . now this.

"If you're wrong," Jamie mused, "then Marie could be a target, too."

"That doesn't make any sense." Clint watched Joe sneak over to the sink and peer above the basin to see out the window. "It's clear?"

"Far as I can tell. But I wouldn't take any chances."

"Me, neither." Curled around Julie, Clint dragged her out of the kitchen and well away from any windows. Even now he wanted to protect her, when Jamie had just explained that he was the one in peril.

"Scott wanted to come with us," Joe told them once they were all situated in the sitting room. "But with no sheriff around, he had his hands full."

That surprised Julie. "Where's the sheriff?"

"He finally quit. He hadn't been of much use in years anyway. But now Scott has his hands full keeping things together and trying to find someone to fill the position."

Jamie looked at Clint, his gaze unflinching. "But that'll work out in the end."

Sometimes Jamie was so hard to understand. Julie wrapped her arms around her middle. "So Scott believed you, Jamie? When you told him I was in trouble."

Appearing disturbed, Jamie paced away. He rubbed the back of his neck, his head down. "Yes."

His face pinched. "Everyone seems to take me seriously these days."

Jamie didn't look happy about that, prompting Julie to go to him. Clint didn't want to let her go, but she patted his hand and he finally understood. She touched Jamie's back. "Are you okay?"

He didn't answer. "I don't like this."

"This?"

She'd never seen Jamie so troubled before. He was generally the most enigmatic, unreadable man she'd ever met. He simply didn't show emotion.

He slanted her a dark, almost angry look, then shrugged away her touch and strode to Clint. "We need to leave here right now."

"But we have to call the police," Julie protested. "Someone tried to shoot Clint."

"He can take care of that later. I don't like to mix with the police." Jamie didn't take his gaze off Clint. He stated again, "We have to get both of you out of here."

Joe propped his hands on his hips and addressed Clint. "I've known Jamie awhile now, long enough to know to heed what he says. If he says it's not safe to stay, then it's not."

Jamie frowned in thought and shook his head. "Actually, it's unsafe *not* to go."

"That doesn't make any sense, Jamie."

He rubbed his forehead. "It makes sense somehow."

Julie patted his shoulder, to let him know it was okay. "Whatever you say, Jamie." She hoped

Clint meant it when he said he trusted her, but this would be a huge test of his faith in her. "I'm ready if you are."

Aggrieved, Clint studied her for a long moment before nodding. "Yeah, all right. What the hell? But where are we going?"

Jamie headed for the door. "To see Robert." He looked over his shoulder at Clint and held out his hand. "I'll drive your vehicle. You go in Joe's truck."

Joe laughed. "Nice try, Jamie, but you don't have a driver's license." Jamie started to speak, and Joe held up a hand. "I understand what you're saying. Whoever shot out the window might still be out there, which means Clint and Julie won't be safe in a recognizable vehicle."

Julie glared at Jamie. "Then it wouldn't be safe for you either."

"No, it wouldn't," Joe said.

Clint smoothed her hair back from her face. "I don't think anyone would recognize her like this. Her hair's different, her clothes are different from what she usually wears. Let me grab a hat and sunglasses, and maybe no one will notice us. We can all go in Joe's truck."

"We won't all fit." Calm as death, Jamie again held out his hand for Clint's keys.

"Forget it," Clint growled at him. "Julie doesn't want you hurt, so you damn well won't get hurt. Understand?"

"It'll be a squeeze," Joe interrupted. "But with Julie on your lap we'll manage."

Within five minutes, they were ready to head out the door. Clint asked Joe, "Are you armed?"

"Got my knife."

Reaching to the small of his back, Clint produced the lethal blade that Julie remembered from the night he'd rescued her, when he'd used it to cut her ropes. "Me, too. I also have a Beretta 9mm—"

Jamie said, "You won't need it. It'd be better to leave it behind." He turned to the door. "Let's go."

To Julie, it seemed that Jamie was in an awful rush. Annoyed, but keeping his temper in check, Clint pulled on a baseball cap and dark sunglasses. To help in their disguise, they walked out with Joe's arm around Julie, Jamie in front, Clint following up the rear. Both Joe and Clint were watchful, reminding Julie again of how alike they were.

Once they were on the road, it didn't get much better. Joe drove, but his gaze constantly scanned the area, just as Clint's did. Jamie leaned sullenly against the passenger door, unconcerned with his surroundings, lost in thought.

It all seemed very scary and suspenseful to Julie. She didn't have what it took to be a mercenary or a bounty hunter or a law official. Being a teacher provided all the danger and excitement she could handle.

Clint absently rubbed her back, and occasionally he pressed a kiss to her temple. Did he care about her? Jamie claimed he loved her, but they hadn't known each other long. Long enough for her to be certain of her feelings, but men were different. Big, badass, kick-butt men were especially wary of love and all the trappings.

She tipped her head back to look up at Clint. His hand came to her cheek, cradling her face, and he frowned at her. "You okay?"

"My legs are a little cramped, and I'm worried. Otherwise, I'm fine."

Clint hugged her tighter. "No worrying, babe. I'm not about to let anyone hurt you."

Without taking his gaze from the scenery, Jamie said, "She's worried about you, not herself."

Clint raised a brow, doubting that, and Julie wondered why men insisted on thinking themselves invulnerable. Clint was hard enough to feel like steel, but he was still made of flesh and bone, and someone had tried to shoot him.

She rubbed her cheek into his palm, saying, "It's true. I wouldn't be able to bear it if anything happened to you, Clint."

His thumb teased the side of her mouth. "Then I won't let anything happen to me either."

"Will you two lovebirds knock it off?" Joe shifted his shoulders and grumbled low. "I'm trying to concentrate here."

Clint grinned. "I can see why you said he's an outrageous chump."

Julie protested. "Outrageous, yes, but I never called Joe a chump."

"You should have."

"Is this where I turn?" Joe asked in exasperation.

"Yeah, hang a left."

When they arrived at Robert's house, Drew's car was in the driveway. "Company?" Clint questioned.

"It's my Uncle Drew." Julie squeezed Clint's hand. "He's not at his best when he's worried, and I'm sure he's been frantic for me. Just know that he means well, okay?"

Clint shrugged. "He's not going to hurt my feelings, Julie Rose, if that's what you're fretting about."

"I was more concerned with you hurting his. He's been through enough."

Clint didn't respond to that.

Without pause, Jamie opened the passenger door and stepped out. Joe hurried out, too. "Hold up, Jamie."

But he didn't. Jamie sauntered up the walk and, without knocking, opened the front door and went in. Surprised that it wasn't locked, Joe, Julie, and Clint filed in behind him.

Following Jamie, they made their way through the entrance hall and toward the kitchen. Julie called out, "Uncle Drew?" As they went, she peered into the other rooms, but they were all empty.

There was a heavy silence, then, "Julie!" Drew erupted from the kitchen, looking breathless and rumpled. He wore a huge smile. There was visible relief on his aristocratic face—and a gun held loosely in his hand.

His gaze moved quickly from Julie to the others, stopping on Clint. The smile faded. His elated surprise changed to a stony expression of disbelief. "You."

Stunned by his appearance, his manner, and the sight of that lethal weapon, Julie went blank. How did he recognize Clint? And why in the world did he have a gun?

Clint cursed and tried to drag her behind him, but Julie resisted. "Uncle Drew?"

As his burning eyes focused on her, his face contorted. "What is this? Why are you bringing *him* here?"

Julie stared at that gun. "How do you know Clint?"

He blinked hard, and Julie could see him struggling to bring himself together, to form a believable lie. In a more moderated tone, he said, "Why, dear, he's the man Robert sent to rescue you. Robert has told me all about him."

Using his left hand, Drew smoothed back his gunmetal gray hair and straightened his shoulders inside his expensive suit coat. It didn't help his overall appearance one bit.

He looked Julie over from head to toe. "You're all right?"

Sensing that they'd walked into a trap, Julie tried to stall for time. "I'm fine." But before she could stop him, Clint moved to stand in front of her, and Joe moved to stand beside him. Julie couldn't even see Drew around the wall of muscled male shoulders blocking her view.

Drew laughed, a far from pleasant sound. "All this time I was worrying, praying . . ."

"Planning?" Clint asked, and he sounded so angry that Julie shivered.

The laughter died. "Apparently I didn't plan well enough. Come in, then, and join the party."

Julie tried to see over Clint's hard shoulder, but Clint began pushing her back toward the entrance door. She dug in, resisting his efforts. Did he really believe she would run off and leave him alone to deal with her uncle?

Joe seemed to consider it a great idea, and he, too, tried to nudge her away without drawing Drew's attention.

Jamie was the only one not set on trying to protect her. He took the three steps forward that put him next to Drew and peered into the kitchen. He turned to Clint. "This must be Robert and Marie."

"Oh, my God." Julie shoved her way around the men. "Uncle Drew, what in the world is going on here? What have you done?"

"Come in, my dear. Take a seat and I'll explain everything, I promise."

Clint clamped a hand around her upper arm, drawing her to a halt. "She's not going anywhere."

Aiming the gun at Clint, Drew said, "If she doesn't want a bullet in your heart, she will, for once in her life, do as she's told."

With horrifying clarity, it all fell into place. Julie felt dizzy with the awfulness of it. "It was you, Uncle Drew, wasn't it? You're the one who shot at Clint."

"Don't be ridiculous. I merely hired a street ruffian to do it for me." And with a sneer, he said, "Apparently he wasn't as competent as he boasted."

Unable to bear seeing a gun aimed at Clint, Julie went into the kitchen. Robert sat at the table, his head in his hands, and next to him was the woman she'd found in his bed. That seemed like a lifetime ago, and while Julie had been angry at her then, now she felt only pity. Dark mascara tracks marred Marie's beautiful face, and her bottom lip quivered. The poor girl was frightened out of her wits—with good reason.

The men followed Julie, and Drew stepped back cautiously as they entered, using the gun to urge them along. "I never intended for anyone to be hurt."

"No," Clint said, "you just intended for your niece to be kidnapped."

"It was a fine plan," Drew stated. "I turned off her alarms, I hired men suitable for the job, I covered every detail. Everything would have been perfect. If only Robert and Julie had reacted as they should have."

"What is it I was supposed to do?" Julie asked.

"Take a seat," Drew told her again, with a distinct lack of emotion, "and I'll tell you."

Chapter Thirteen

Joe said, "How the hell do I blunder into things like this? Seems like every time I turn around, someone wants to shoot me."

Jamie said, "You won't get shot."

"Gee, thanks, Jamie. I'm so reassured."

"I know."

They were both nuts. But Clint understood that they weren't just telling jokes. Jamie, strangely enough, was dead serious. He really thought he knew what would happen in a situation so volatile that Clint couldn't think beyond keeping Julie safe. Joe was slick enough to talk nonsense, just to keep Drew distracted, and that helped—but not enough.

Seeing Julie's face, her emotional devastation at such a betrayal, Clint wanted to strangle Drew with his bare hands. But he held himself still, letting Joe do his thing so that the damn lethal pistol stayed off the women.

Drew stood back against a wall, the gun held out stiffly, aimed at no one in particular. It surprised Clint that Drew was such a slight man, elegant even with dark circles lining his eyes and a pasty complexion. It seemed as if the turn of events had thrown him. He wasn't a man accustomed to improvising. And it was clear that Clint and Joe made him nervous.

Yeah, Clint thought, *you weren't expecting real men on the scene, were you, you ass?*

Robert finally raised his head. "I'm so damn sorry, Julie."

She had just started to sit at the table, but when she saw Robert's face, Julie cried out. "Dear God. *Robert.*" She rushed to his side and knelt by his chair.

Drew's wild gaze followed her. "Oh, yes, *now* you care about him, when it's too late." His sarcasm made him sound maniacal and unbalanced. "Where were you when he needed you most, Julie?"

Showing no caution at all, Julie snapped, "I was kidnapped, thanks to you."

"No, my dear. I found you earlier today. You weren't still in their clutches. You were off behaving like a common slut, trolling with that gutter trash." He tipped his head toward Clint, making it clear who he meant.

Hurrying to the sink, Julie doused a cloth in cold water. "Gutter trash, Uncle? Clint is honorable, which is more than I can say for you."

"You dare compare him to me?"

Drew went livid, but Joe pulled out a chair, laughing a bit too loud, again taking Drew's attention. "So how'd you find her, old man?"

Gathering himself in a pompous show, Drew sniffed. "Robert had some idealistic intentions of becoming a real man, or so he said. He confessed everything to me, how he'd intended to steal my money—"

"Julie's money," Robert corrected, then groaned.

"—and he told me that he'd hired Mr. Evans, that Julie was safe. I went along, showing sympathy with his plight, relief that you were supposedly safe, though truth be told, you were probably better off with the kidnappers. At least they didn't feign some romantic attachment in an effort to get at your trust fund."

"I don't give a fuck about her trust fund," Clint growled, earning a disdainful look from Drew.

"Of course you don't." His smile was caustic and cold. "It was easy enough to put a watch on Robert's home, and after Mr. Evans showed up here earlier today, I had him followed."

Joe said, "You must be slipping, Clint."

Clint shook his head. "I knew something was wrong, but damn it, I thought it was with Julie, not with me."

"What a ridiculous assumption. I wanted you out of the picture, Mr. Evans, so that Julie and Robert could be reunited."

Julie's mouth fell open. "You'd have killed an innocent man just to see me married?"

Drew frowned. "He's not innocent. And, of course, now Marie will have to go, too. It's what your father would have wanted."

"My father wanted me to be happy!"

"And marrying Robert will make you happy. You'll see."

Joe turned to Jamie. "He's going to shoot us all?"

Jamie said, "He's considering it."

"Of course I'm not," Drew snapped. "Julie is my niece. Her father entrusted me with her care. I would never hurt her."

Marie covered her mouth and moaned, rocking back and forth.

Being the amazing woman she was, Julie handed Robert the icy rag and then put her arm around Marie. "Shhh," she whispered. "It'll be okay, Marie. You'll see."

Drew's face contorted into a mask of disgust. "You want to help that little whore? She's the one who ruined *everything* by throwing herself at Robert!"

"She's not a whore," Robert raged, and Julie quickly placed herself in front of him.

Hands on her hips, her chin elevated, she faced the devil. "If you truly don't want me hurt, if you really want my happiness, you'll let them all go."

"Julie." Drew's face softened and he dared to smile. "They would report me to the authorities. No, my dear, now that you've ruined everything, they have to go."

Christ, Clint thought with frustration, Julie

pushed too hard, trying to protect everyone. Drew said that he didn't intend to hurt her, but it was never wise to antagonize the insane—and he believed Drew to be nuttier than a fruitcake.

Clint considered the situation. He had to do something, but what? With Julie bounding around the room, trying to shield everyone at once, his options were limited. He needed her to move behind him or behind Joe. Or hell, behind Jamie. Just *behind* someone, so she'd be safe from stray bullets.

Then he could attack.

If he got shot, well, he'd survived worse. He doubted Drew was such a good marksman that he'd manage a fatal blow while fending off an assault. At the moment, Drew's hands were shaky, his eyes bloodshot, and he was far too emotional to show any precision.

"Don't do it," Jamie said, staring at Clint. "You don't need to."

Well damn, there went his element of surprise.

Livid, Drew swung the gun around at Clint. "Do what? Damn you, what are you planning?" Drew looked far from genteel with a sneer on his face.

"Actually, I was planning to kill you."

Julie leapt across the room, meaning to put herself in front of Clint, but Clint took swift advantage of her nearness. He caught her and pushed her toward Joe.

Joe, knowing exactly what Clint wanted, came out of his chair in an instant, grabbing her and shoving her behind him. When she fought him, he said, "Let's see some of that common sense you're known for, Julie."

Drew faced off with Clint. "You shouldn't have gotten involved."

"I'd be dead if he hadn't." Very slowly, every movement filled with pain, Robert pushed to his feet. He clutched his ribs with one arm and leaned on the chair back with the other. To Drew, he said, "Because Clint kept her, I was able to give half the ransom money to Asa. That's probably the only reason I got a beating instead of a bullet."

Marie gasped. "My brother?"

Nodding, Robert said, "I thought he had Julie. I thought she was taken because of me, because Asa feels I owe him money." Robert turned his battered face toward Marie. "I'm sorry, sweetheart. I couldn't bear for you to know. I didn't want you to see me as a failure."

Marie shook her head. "I don't understand."

"I ruined one of Asa's business deals and he wants me to pay him for the loss." He shifted uncomfortably. "But I didn't have the money to do that."

Big tears streamed down Marie's face. "I would have talked to him, Robert. Asa would do anything for me."

"Maybe. But then both he and you might have thought I used you just to get out of a debt." He drew a shuddering breath. "Nothing could be farther from the truth."

Marie closed her eyes. "I wish you had trusted

me." More tears spilled down her cheeks. "Because I trust you. Completely. Don't you see, Robert? I didn't think I'd ever be able to love anyone until I met you."

For a single heartbeat, it was silent in the room; then Drew went ballistic. "Stop it! My God, your displays of melodrama are enough to make me ill."

Jamie pointed a finger at Drew. "You're going to die, you know that, don't you?"

Confusion written on his florid face, Drew blinked hard as if he'd forgotten Jamie was there. "Who *are* you?"

Eyes deep and fathomless, Jamie said, "I'm no one."

Julie said at the same time, "He's my friend."

Jamie's eyes narrowed at that, but he held silent.

"And that one?" Drew indicated Joe with a wave of the gun, nearly stopping Clint's heart because Julie was right beside him.

"Also my friend." Julie struggled against Joe's grip, but he kept her held securely behind him. Her voice rose to an angry shout. "I have friends, Uncle Drew. Male friends, female friends. I care about them, and I'm not going to let you hurt them."

"I gave you everything," he rasped.

"No. Not everything. The one thing I wanted most, I got on my own with no help from you, and no help from my trust fund."

More confused by the second, Drew lowered the gun. "What?"

Jamie half smiled. "I'll give you a hint. He's in this room."

Drew looked at Robert.

Julie knotted her hands in her hair and gave a low shriek of frustration. "No, you ass!" And she pointed an imperious finger at Clint. *"Him."*

Odd, how even with danger thick in the air, Clint felt his heart swelling. Jamie was right, he did love her, and no way in hell was he going to let some loony relative hurt her or the people she cared about.

Despite Jamie's predictions, Clint would take charge of the room. Starting now.

He moved one step toward Drew. "Why have her kidnapped, you son-of-a-bitch? What did you hope to prove by endangering her that way?"

Baffled by Julie's reply and Clint's question, Drew stared blankly around the room, encompassing everyone. "Don't you see? With Julie in peril, Robert would be concerned. He was given the ransom note and the money to rescue her. He should have realized how much he loved her. The men I hired told him that she'd be killed if he didn't pay."

Julie breathed hard, clasping her hands together. "They also threatened to rape me."

"I know." Unapologetic, Drew continued to try to explain, as if what he'd done made perfect sense. "I wanted you to be afraid, so that when Robert rescued you, you'd be grateful to him. I wanted you two to realize that you need each other so that you'd get over your little disagreement and reunite."

Very slowly, Marie pushed to her feet.

Clint wanted Drew's attention on him, not on anyone else. He moved one step nearer. "They hurt her, Drew, did you know that? Was that part of your warped plan, too?"

"No, that's not possible. I promised them good money to follow my—"

"They did," Clint insisted, inching forward another step. "When I reached her, they had her half stripped and were mauling her. She was tied with ropes, covered in bruises. They hadn't fed her or given her water." Another step nearer. "She fainted in my arms, damn you."

Drew's face lost all color. "I told them to keep her safe. They promised she wouldn't be harmed."

Drew was still out of reach, but soon, soon Clint would be close enough to grab the bastard. "They ogled her. They touched her. *They hurt her.*"

Sweat dampened Drew's forehead. Spittle gathered at the corners of his mouth. He gave a half-hysterical laugh. "Well, I'm certainly glad I shot Petie. I knew he hadn't followed orders, but I didn't realize—" Beseeching, he turned to Julie. "Darling, I'm so sorry. After I shot him, I searched his apartment to try to find out what he'd done with you. But he was dead, and the others were in jail, and I couldn't find even a single clue."

Julie shook her head. "I can't believe you did this to me."

"It was a good plan," he insisted. "I even had a flunky inform Asa Ragon as to where you were. I thought Asa would go after you himself, given how he feels about women, and then Robert could have confronted him, too . . ." He beseeched Robert with a look. "Yes, I knew you had a little contretemps with Marie's brother. If you'd come to me, we could have taken care of him."

Marie knocked over her chair. "You . . . *you monster.*" Her loud, shrill voice froze everyone to the spot. She moved toward Drew with jerky steps, uncaring of the danger, totally out of control.

Taking a step back, Drew yelled, "I didn't hurt your damn brother!" He lifted the gun to defend himself. "Stop. Get back!"

"You put your own niece through hell." Marie wasn't crying now. Her pale eyes were icy cold, filled with hatred. "You let her think she'd be violated by those animals. You allowed them to manhandle her, to scare her. *You're her uncle.* You should have been protecting her. What you did was evil, vile—"

"Get back, I said!"

Robert gasped for breath. "Drew, for God's sake, lower the damn gun!"

Clint cursed.

In a panic, Drew started to squeeze the trigger.

Things happened so fast, it all seemed a blur. Clint leapt for Drew, knowing he'd never reach him in time.

The gun went off with a quiet pop, thanks to the silencer. And Robert, who lunged in front of Marie, grunted in pain as the force of the bullet sent him into the table, upsetting all the chairs.

Clint's shoulder impacted with Drew's middle, knocking the wind out of him in a loud whoosh. The gun dropped from his limp hand, skittering across the floor to the other side of the room. Together, the two men fetched up hard against the wall, then dropped to the marble floor. Clint didn't notice the pain in his knees as he drew back his fist and slugged Drew in the jaw.

Drew's head snapped to the side, and he slumped, no longer trying to fend Clint off.

Clint drew back again, and Joe grabbed his arm. "He's out, man. Stop."

Clint easily pulled free, fueled by adrenaline and fury. Drew had put Julie at awful risk with his sick plans. She could have been killed, first by the kidnappers, and then by Drew himself. Clint growled, his arm cocked back—and Julie Rose threw herself against his chest.

He felt the hot sting of her tears on his throat, the desperation of her hands on his shoulders. He heard her small sob.

By small degrees, Clint's head began to clear. His thudding heart slowed. He gasped a few times, then wrapped Julie close, squeezing her until she protested with a squeak.

"Clint?"

Her voice shook, and he tucked his face into her neck, unable to let go. "It's all right now, Julie Rose."

"But Robert's hurt. You have to do something."

Joe said calmly, "I've got it, Julie. You can stay with him."

Clint heard Joe on the phone, calling 911 and efficiently detailing the scenario. Cops and paramedics alike would soon storm the quiet, classy neighborhood.

Julie's hands sifted through Clint's hair. "Are you all right?"

He nodded, took several deep breaths, then glanced at Drew. Blood ran from the older man's nose, trailed around his gaping mouth and covered his chin.

Clint knew he was going to be ill. He pushed away from Julie and stormed down the hall in search of a bathroom. She followed him.

"Here," Julie said, and threw open the door to the first-floor powder room. Clint landed hard on his knees in front of the commode, and Julie, bless her heart, closed the door behind him, giving him privacy.

Minutes later when he came out, she was there waiting for him, mouthwash and a cool, damp washcloth in her hands. She smiled tremulously. "Better?"

"Jesus." No man should have to suffer such a debilitating, embarrassing weakness. He tipped the mouthwash up and gargled, then stepped back into the bathroom to spit. His stomach still roiled, worse than ever before because, now that it was over, Clint realized the fear had been worse than ever before.

Never in his life had he been in the position

of protecting someone he loved. Innocent by-
standers, sure. People he'd been hired to save,
no problem. But someone so near and dear to
his heart? It sucked.

His stomach hated it and his mind recoiled at
the thought of what the others might think.

As if she'd read his mind, Julie hugged his
back and said, "Joe's paying you no attention at
all. Both Robert and Drew are barely conscious,
and Marie is concerned only with Robert."

Sticking his head in the sink, Clint gulped icy
water and splashed his face. Finally feeling human
again, he faced her. His eyes were gritty and his
muscles were mush. With a trembling hand—
trembling—he touched her cheek. "You're okay,
baby?"

"I'm fine. It's Robert who's hurt. Well, and
Uncle Drew, but—"

Clint snarled, "I could have killed him for
what he did to you, Julie Rose."

"I know." Julie smiled and patted his chest in
an absurd effort to soothe him. "But you didn't.
You're methodical when you fight, Clint, not
out of control, and you're far too honorable to
kill a man unless it's the only way to save another life. You abide by the law, protecting women
and children and other men. You have a con-
science and a big heart, and you're so gentle."

Clint stared in blank disbelief. He could be
ruthless, and not always by choice. More often
than not his instincts just took over. No, he hadn't
killed anyone except in wartime, and other than

the man who made a habit of abusing his wife, he
hadn't ever lost control. But he did despise the
damage he did, even when necessary. "I'm not
an easy man to be with."

She laughed. "That I definitely know."

The laugh did it. Clint hauled her back into
his arms, squeezing her some more. Unwilling
to turn her loose, he lifted her up and carried
her back to the kitchen. Julie nuzzled his throat
and held on and returned his hug.

Drew's eyes were open, filled with pain and
wariness and confusion, but he hadn't yet moved.
Clint dismissed him and went to check on Robert.
The bullet had caught him in his upper arm, not
his chest. Already, Joe had the bleeding nearly
stopped. "He'll be okay?"

Joe glanced up, then away. "Yeah. If that beating didn't kill him, a knick with a .38 won't."

"Where's the gun?"

Joe reached back and pulled it out of the
waistband of his jeans to hand to Clint. Then he
eyed him cautiously. "I trust you won't use that?"

Clint half smiled, knowing Joe wouldn't have
given him the gun if he'd had any real concerns.

"Normally I'd be all for it, you understand,
and God knows the bastard deserves it, but with
the cops already on the way . . ."

"I'm not going to shoot him."

Nodding toward Marie, who had Robert's
head in her lap, Joe said, "I don't think she can
make the same promise."

Her hands still stroking Robert's forehead,

Marie whispered, "It's true. He's an evil man who deserves death." Her voice was hoarse, broken by emotion. "No woman should ever suffer rape, or even the fear of rape."

Joe gave her a long look. "I agree. Now, hold his hand, Marie. I hear the ambulance sirens. He's going to be fine." Joe went to the front door to let everyone in.

After a shuddering breath, Marie looked up at Julie. "I am so very sorry. A lot of this is my fault—"

"Don't be ridiculous." Sliding out of Clint's arms, Julie straightened her clothes and went to Marie. "You can't blame yourself for my uncle's actions."

"But—"

Julie wouldn't have it. "No, Marie. All you did was fall in love with an engaged man, but what Robert and I had wouldn't have lasted anyway."

"You're sure of that?"

Julie glanced at Clint. "Very sure." She offered Marie a smile. "I hope you two can work things out."

With an obvious effort, Robert got his eyes to open. "I'm not letting her go, Julie."

"Of course not."

"I've been a selfish pig, a coward, but I swear to you, I never wanted you hurt."

Julie nodded. "I know that, Robert. Love does strange things to people."

"I'll need to call my brother," Marie said. An uncharacteristic determination added maturity to her face. "He'll accept Robert, or lose me. Period."

Footsteps thundered down the polished wooden hallway, and seconds later the kitchen was overrun with officials. Paramedics worked over Robert and Drew, and cops pulled out notepads to start the long series of questions.

Knowing they'd be occupied for hours, Clint righted two chairs, urged Julie into one, and pulled the other close so that he could hold her hand. While waiting for their turn to be interrogated, Clint tried to figure out what to do with the future.

One thing was certain, he wouldn't let Julie go. If she insisted on living in Visitation, then he'd damn well live there, too. Whatever it took to make Julie Rose happy.

The cops were securing the scene when Joe leaned down near Clint's ear. "Jamie's gone missing. It'd probably be best not to mention him at all."

Bemused that he hadn't realized that on his own, Clint searched the room, and sure enough, Jamie Creed was nowhere in sight. "What the hell?"

Julie blew out a long sigh. "He does that. He's always so very . . . alone. Even when he's with people."

Clint nodded acknowledgment of that. "He said he was nobody."

Joe shrugged. "He'd like to believe it, I think. But mixing Jamie with the cops would never work. They'd probably lock him up as a nut, and

Jamie would be telling them their future the whole time."

The three of them smiled—and silently made a pact not to mention Jamie Creed and his odd contribution to the safe outcome of the day.

Halfway down the block, ready to turn the corner and disappear from sight, Jamie Creed glanced back to see the emergency vehicles in their grand display of lights and sirens. He turned away. With the sun in his eyes and a good three miles to the highway, he kept walking—and he didn't look back.

No one needed him now.

He tucked his hands into his jeans pockets and ducked his head, grateful that Julie hadn't been hurt, that Joe and Clint were unharmed, and that Robert and Marie would both be fine.

He squinted down at his feet, seeing the frayed edges of his jeans, the worn leather on his boots. He counted his steps so that his mind didn't linger on the people who wanted to befriend him. They didn't understand that any type of real relationship was impossible. If he got close to anyone, it would destroy him, obliterating who and what he was.

Better that he should help people who needed him than indulge friendships that would never work out in the end.

He kept walking, and soon a trucker gave him a lift. It might take a while to get back to North Carolina, but that didn't matter either.

There was no one waiting for him. And that's how he wanted it.

That's how it had to be.

"Come and eat," Mojo said.

"I'm not hungry right now."

Red propped his hands on his hips. "That's bunk. You're just moping."

Daisy punched his shoulder. "Can't a woman enjoy a moment of private thought without you two harassing her?"

Julie smiled. She liked Red's wife a lot. She hadn't met Mojo's girlfriend yet, but maybe that would happen soon.

"Go on," she told them. "Enjoy your weekend off. You've both earned it."

Mojo snorted at that. "All we did was help you move."

Julie shook her head. They'd saved her and befriended her. And yes, they'd helped her move all her belongings to Visitation. "You've been wonderful. But look, Bryan and Bruce are starting a game of horseshoes. Surely you don't want to miss that."

Red rolled his eyes, then took his wife's hand. "Let's go, honey. We'll stomp them."

Julie shielded her eyes from the early July sunshine as she watched them walk away. They fit right in with the laid-back, easy nature of Visitation, and they'd been welcomed as if they were native born. She wished they didn't live so far away, but they promised to visit. Mojo even talked about buying a boat.

Julie turned away from the crowd. Nearly everyone in Visitation had turned out for the Fourth of July celebration. Some were swimming, some boating, some hugged the opposite shore and fished.

Fresh humid air wafted around her and birds chirped from all the nearby trees. It was a beautiful summer day, and she was both more content and more desolate than she'd ever been in her life.

Finally, at the ripe age of twenty-nine, she was free. Totally independent. Completely on her own.

It wasn't nearly as satisfying as she'd always imagined.

With her thoughts on her Uncle Drew, she strolled over to a large, leafy tree to find some shade. Drew would remain locked up until his competency hearing, at which time it'd be determined if he was rational enough to face criminal charges or life in a mental hospital. He would never again interfere in her life.

A small part of her couldn't help but be sad that she'd lost her closest relative. But a larger part was still angry and hurt at so much deception and manipulation. Regardless of what the courts decided, she knew she'd never want to see him again. He'd threatened not only her life, but the man she loved. That was unforgivable.

To keep herself from dwelling on the negative, Julie had thrown herself into getting her life organized. Using the ransom money that Robert still held, she'd made certain that Mojo and Red got paid. Clint had flatly refused any compensation and had, in fact, been incensed that she'd suggest it.

With that taken care of, she'd secured a permanent teaching position in Visitation, then located a small, affordable house that was both close to the school and within driving distance of the lake. She had her privacy, a job she loved, and a new house to occupy her time. Her life was *exactly* as she had envisioned it—before meeting Clint.

Since meeting him, her priorities had changed in a drastic way.

Julie sighed and tucked her hair behind her ear. Three long, endless weeks had passed since that debacle at Robert's home. Though he'd carry that bullet wound forever as a reminder of his misdeeds, Robert had almost fully recovered. He had changed quite a bit, become more of a man thanks to Clint's influence and the events that had affected his life. Julie held no grudge against him.

Neither did Marie. Believing love could conquer the obstacles they'd be sure to encounter, they planned to marry in just a few weeks.

It seemed everyone was happy. Everyone but Julie. And it was her own selfishness that kept her from total bliss.

She wanted everything.

She wanted Clint.

After she moved to Visitation, he continued his work as a repo agent, often taking jobs in or around North Carolina to be close to her. They dated, talked for long hours, and made love at every opportunity.

But did Clint love her?

Julie heard some raucous laughing and looked up in time to see Scott Royal, the deputy, toss Alyx Winston into the lake. Alyx was fully dressed, not in a swimsuit.

Laughing like a loon, Alyx climbed out, chased Scott, and finally caught him near the picnic tables. She threw herself into his arms, soaking the front of his uniform.

The two of them often provided the entertainment at various parties. And there had been plenty of parties lately. Shay Kelly was on a roll, sponsoring one event after another with proceeds going to the underprivileged—in Clint's neighborhood. Thinking of the young men she'd met there, Julie intended to take part, too.

"Penny for your thoughts."

Startled, Julie shook off her melancholy and fashioned a smile of welcome. "Hello, Carmen." Even with Julie now living in Visitation, their friendship had grown. They'd taken turns visiting and spoke often on the phone.

Carmen shook her finger at Julie. "Why are you over here hiding all by yourself?"

Is that what everyone thought? That she was hiding? "I'm not."

"Baloney." Carmen took note of Julie's clothes, nodding approval at the feminine white sundress and casual sandals. "You learned, didn't you? You look gorgeous."

Julie blushed. "Forget my clothes. Do you have news for me?"

Carmen preened before saying, "Actually, I do. There's some mandatory substance abuse counseling, then reeducation."

Crossing her fingers, Julie asked, "And then?"

"In six months, as long as I stay clean—and I will—I can reapply for a contingency license." Carmen grinned. "If that goes through, my full privileges will be reinstated."

"Carmen, that's wonderful!"

Julie hadn't heard Clint's approach, but she felt his muscled arms slip around her from behind. "It's not going to be easy."

"I know." Carmen smiled at them both. "The thing is, I'm tired of being tired all the time. I'm tired of screwing up my life."

Clint reached past Julie and cupped Carmen's cheek. "You're a strong woman. You can do it." He wrapped his arms around Julie again, pressed a kiss to her temple. "And we're here if you need us."

"Shay said the same thing." Carmen's smile trembled, looking poignant and a little too emotional as her warm gaze searched Julie's face. "She also told me you're the one who got the ball rolling."

"I only made a phone call."

"No." Carmen reached out for Julie's hand. "You showed faith in me. It was so . . . unexpected. I dunno. You got me thinking, and caring again. Thank you."

Clint gave Julie a squeeze. "She's a teacher," he said with pride. "What else would you expect from her?"

Shaking off the excess sentiment, Carmen said, "I'd expect her to go after what she wants."

"Yeah?" Clint asked. "And what's that?"

Carmen rolled her eyes. "If you don't know, then you're a lost cause." She gave them both a wave and sauntered off to join the others near the bounty of picnic food.

His big hands on her shoulders, Clint turned Julie to face him. "What was that all about?"

Knowing Carmen was right, Julie made a decision. "It was about taking control of my life."

"I thought you already did that. You relocated, changed jobs . . ."

"Now I want more."

Clint gave her a funny look, but Julie just shook her head, took his hand, and started dragging him toward the woods on the far side of the property. There were trails there for bird watchers, but few people ever used them. It'd be a perfect spot for their private conversation.

"Where are we going, Julie Rose?"

He continued to call her by both names, and Julie had long since given up on her complaints. Until now. She'd had enough. She wanted him for good. Forever. In sickness and in health.

"Drew will have his competency hearing soon."

Clint's mood always soured when her uncle got mentioned. "Whatever. I don't give a damn what they do with him as long as he's kept far away from you."

"The thing is," Julie said, hedging around the real topic, "my trust is frozen. It was to be released to me when I married, and not before."

Clint said nothing to that.

"I have a lot of money, Clint."

They had just reached the tree line and Clint turned abruptly, grabbing her shoulders and lifting her to her tiptoes. Nose to nose with her, he growled, "I thought I was clear on this. I don't give a damn about your money."

"I know."

That stymied him. "Then why are you bringing it up?"

She bit her lip, afraid of driving him away, but more afraid of living in limbo. "Because I don't quite know how to verbalize what it is that I really want to say. I thought the money would be a way to ease into it."

A look of worry etched his features. He set her back on her feet to run a hand through his hair. "Damn it, I hate fretting. I *never* fretted before you. You're making me old before my time."

"What are you fretting about?"

"You." Mindful of the other people milling around the lake, he caught her hand and dragged her into the tall evergreens. He glared down at her, then barked, "Deputy Royal thinks I should take the position of sheriff."

Julie's mouth fell open. Not once had she considered him saying precisely that. "Sheriff?"

His chin jutted out. "You've been pretty plain on how you feel about law officials."

She had no idea what he was talking about. "I have?"

"More than once, you've bitched about Scott being controlling."

Lifting her shoulders, Julie said, "You're controlling."

"I know, and you probably figure I'd be more so as a sheriff, but damn it, baby, it'd be a good job. I wouldn't have to travel back and forth all the time. I wouldn't have to be away from you." His eyes narrowed. "I could stay here. In Visitation." And then to make certain she understood, he added, "With you."

A near hysterical laugh bubbled up. Julie suppressed it by pinching her lips together. "I see. And why does that make you fret, exactly?"

Still appearing antagonistic, Clint took a step closer to her. "You had all these grand plans for your future." His hand slashed the air. "All that bunk about cutting loose and living it up, doing things you'd never done before."

Julie softened. "I've done a lot of them. With you."

"Sexually." He cupped her face. "But I want you to be happy. I don't want to cheat you out of anything."

"I am happy." She smiled from ear to ear. "And I think you'd make an excellent sheriff. You're more than qualified, and more than capable.

Scott's desperate to find someone for the position." Her heart felt full to bursting. "And then, as you said, you could stay here with me."

Clint kissed her hard and fast. "Is that what you want, Julie Rose?"

"What I really want . . ." A lump formed in her throat.

"What?" He kissed her again. "Tell me."

"I want you to call me Julie Evans, instead of Julie Rose."

Clint rocked back on his heels. He looked stunned. Speechless. Then slowly, a grin began to spread. "Is that a marriage proposal?"

Feeling like a fool, Julie lifted her chin and said, "Yes, it is. And I expect an answer."

Clint chuckled. "I'd be honored." He tunneled his fingers into her hair, holding her face turned up to his. "Now tell me you love me."

"I love you."

He nodded. "Finally, I can stop fretting."

Epilogue

With several people watching her every move, Julie paced the floor of Bruce's home, anxiously waiting for Clint to return. Alyx Winston and Deputy Scott Royal, Bruce and Cyn, were all gathered in the kitchen, waiting with her.

She'd sent Clint on a very difficult mission, and because he loved her, he'd agreed to give it a try.

It was Jamie's fault, Julie decided. He'd made himself scarce, staying up on his mountain and not coming down no matter how Julie wished it. Everyone wanted to see him again. The women all felt indebted to him. The men had learned to respect him. But no one had seen him since that awful day at Robert's house—when Jamie had claimed to be *no one*.

So Julie had sent Clint to find him. And once Clint managed that, he was to invite Jamie to their wedding. Julie had given him strict instructions to not take no for an answer.

But Clint had left hours ago, and since then a summer thunderstorm had exploded with fury. Lightning slashed across the black sky and crashing thunder shook the ground.

Bruce pulled out a chair. "Sit down, Julie. You'll wear a hole in my floor."

Alyx sipped a cup of cocoa. "Jamie will come again when he's ready."

"No." Julie shook her head. "Something's wrong. I feel it."

Cyn frowned. "Now you're starting to sound like Jamie."

"You feel it, too," Julie accused. "I can see it in your face." Everyone knew that Cyn and Jamie had a special bond. More than anyone else, Jamie had connected with Cyn.

Groaning, Cyn propped her elbows on the table and dropped her face into her hands. "I do. Blast the man, why does he have to be so stubborn."

Bruce, being a preacher and therefore practiced in patience, put his hand on his wife's shoulder. "Jamie has his reasons. We just don't know what they are."

Scott tapped his fingers on the tabletop. "Maybe I should go look for Clint. That damn mountain can be treacherous."

"I'll go, too," Alyx offered, which earned her a reproachful look from Scott.

"No way."

"But I can help."

"Believe it or not, Alyx, I can manage without your assistance."

Cyn made a sound of exasperation. "Don't you two start."

Suddenly the door crashed open. Soaked to the skin, with mud up to his knees, Clint rushed in. He was followed by blustering rain and howling wind, and he had to put his shoulder to the door to force it shut.

Eyes enhanced by spiked wet lashes, he turned to Julie. "You won't believe this." His gaze moved around the room, touching on Bruce and Cyn, Alyx and Scott, before returning to Julie. "I found Jamie."

Her heart in her throat, Julie slowly pushed to her feet. "And? Is he okay?"

"He's got a woman."

Everyone blinked in shock.

Wincing, Clint ran a hand through his drenched hair, and clarified, "That is, he had a woman. In his arms."

Cyn stared at him. Bruce frowned in incomprehension.

"He was carrying her?" Scott asked.

"Yeah."

"I don't understand," Julie said.

"Neither do I." Clint lifted his shoulders, as lost as they looked. "One minute he was there, holding a woman who looked to be dead to the world."

"Dead!"

Clint made a face. "Passed out. Maybe fainted or something. I barely saw him, so I couldn't be sure. I tried to get a better look, but I lost him. He went around a corner and just disappeared. I tried calling out to him, but the damn rain made it impossible and I kept slipping in the mud and finally—when I couldn't find his cabin, I just gave up and came back."

Julie turned to Cyn. "Was Jamie seeing anyone?"

"Not that I'm aware of."

Alyx said, "No, he wasn't."

Bruce cleared his throat. "Maybe she's a . . . friend?"

Clint worked his jaw, hesitated, and finally gave up. "Probably not a friend."

"No?"

He shook his head. "The thing is . . . she was, well, naked."

Julie half laughed—then realized Clint wasn't joking. "But that's absurd. She'd freeze in this storm."

Bruce paced to the door and back. "This doesn't sound right. Jamie might be in trouble. I think we should go see him."

"I already told you, I couldn't find his cabin."

Alyx heaved a sigh. "All right, already." She flipped back her long dark hair in a show of exasperation, then pushed back her chair. Arms wide in a show of benevolence, she said, "I'll show you where it is."

Slowly, Scott turned his head to glare at her. "How do *you* know where it is?"

Alyx picked at a fingernail, pretending a nonchalance that wouldn't fool an idiot. "I've been there."

Scott shook his head. "No."

" 'Fraid so." She shook her head. "But Jamie didn't want me to tell anyone. I promised him. Only now, if you really think he might be in trouble—"

Teeth clenched, Scott demanded, "When?"

Alyx bit her lip. "More than once."

Bruce didn't give Scott a chance to blow up. "All right, then. We'll pay Jamie a visit. If he needs our help, we'll give it. And if not, we'll leave the man in peace."

"We should probably get hold of the others first," Cyn suggested. "Joe and Bryan and Luna and Shay. They all care for Jamie, too."

Scott pushed back his chair. "This is starting to sound like an old-fashioned posse."

Bruce held up his hands. "As soon as the rain lets up, we'll go. Agreed?"

Everyone nodded, and a unanimous "Agreed" rang out, filling the small kitchen with good intentions.

Julie smiled to herself as she fetched a towel for Clint. It seemed Jamie had friends after all.

Whether he wanted them or not.

Spend some more time in Visitation!
Try Lori's other books in the series . . .

Say No to Joe?

You met Joe Winston in Lori Foster's *Wild*. Now, the Winston brothers' seductive, bad-boy cousin is back and up against a woman who's immune to his considerable charms . . . or so it seems . . .

Irresistible Force—Meet Immovable Object

Joe Winston has a routine with women: he exists; they swoon; roll credits. With his smoldering looks, macho style, and irrepressible charm, Joe can have any woman—except the one he really wants. Secretly, Luna Clark may lust after Joe, but she's made it clear that she's too smart to fall for him. He can just keep holding his breath, thank you very much. But now, Luna's inherited two kids who need more than she alone can give in a small town that seems hellbent on driving them away. She needs someone to help out . . . someone who can't be intimidated . . . someone just like Joe. Becoming an instant family wasn't exactly what Joe had in mind, but hey, it's a start, and you can't blame a guy for trying every angle . . .

After all, where there's a Joe, there's a way . . . straight into a woman's heart . . .

The Secret Life of Bryan

Jaded bounty hunter Bryan Kelly is head-over-hormones in lust with a woman . . . and what she does to his senses is criminal . . .

Double Trouble

Bryan Kelly has a few rules. Rule #1: Women are for fun, not commitment. Rule #2: He'll do anything for his twin brother, even switch places with him to find out who's sabotaging his charity. But playing a really good guy isn't easy around a luscious Shay Sommers. Which brings him to Rule #3: If you can't avoid temptation, succumb with abandon . . .

Society-pages icon Shay Sommers has made her name in charity work. And she'll go to any length to help these girls from the inside out. It certainly won't be hard to act the street siren with the gorgeous man who runs the place, even if he does seem less like a shepherd and much more like a wolf . . . one with a hungry look that's making Shay feel she might be his next dinner . . .

When Bruce Met Cyn

You first met Bruce Kelly in Lori Foster's steamy novel *The Secret Life of Bryan*. Now, Bruce comes into his own—and a whole lot of trouble—when he falls for a woman who is nothing like he is, but she's everything he wants . . .

When Opposites Attract . . .

Bruce Kelly has spent most of his life helping people who are down on their luck, guiding them toward making better lives. Compassionate and kind, Bruce understands that everyone makes mistakes, even if he's never actually done anything but color inside the lines. Nobody's perfect, but Bruce is about to meet a woman who's perfect for him. He's determined to show her that he can be trusted. And if that means proving it by being the absolute gentleman at all times, then so be it. No matter how many cold showers it takes . . .

. . . Just Get Out Of The Way

Cyn Potter is a survivor, with a sassy, gallows wit and a fierce independent streak to show for it. She's used to men wanting only one thing, and this girl is no longer taking applications from big bad wolves in sheep's clothing, thank you very much, drive through please and keep on going. But Bruce Kelly is actually different. Totally hands off. Sometimes she can see a hint of fire when he looks at her, but the guy treats her with the respect she's always wanted. Maybe too much respect, because truthfully? The guy is fine. Worth taking down a few defenses for . . . and a few other things. And maybe somebody needs to help Bruce start over and discover just how perfect being imperfect can be . . .

Jamie

For four books—from *Say No to Joe?* through *Just a Hint—Clint*—she's given her readers only glimpses of the mysterious mountain man every woman wants to know better. Now, *New York Times* bestselling author Lori Foster is ready to give readers what they crave . . . and this time it isn't just a taste . . . it's the whole man himself . . . just . . .

Jamie

Carrying a naked woman up a mountain in a driving storm—now there's a way for a man to start the day. But for Jamie, the unconscious redhead in his arms is an intruder, one who could bring him harm. He has his reasons for hiding out in this mountain cabin; for keeping his emotions hidden; for never, ever getting too close to anyone. And he's not about to stop now . . .

Before she passed out in his bed, she said her name was Faith—an appropriate name since he has to take her at her word. Who is she? Why is she here? Who sent her? And what is she doing to him? Jamie's used to feelings of wariness, isolation, of being on guard. What he's not used to is this dangerous, nearly uncontrollable new emotion raging through him . . .

Jamie wants Faith, as a man wants a woman . . . and it may already be too late to turn back . . .